OVERDUE: 10¢ per day

DATE DUE

P9-BHW-697

SE 15 '0 NOV 09 2013

IV 14 06

16226

M
DUN

Dunlap, Susan.
Rogue wave

16226

DUNLAP, SUSAN

ROGUE WAVE

DISCARD

MENDOCINO COMMUNITY LIBRARY
TEL. # 707-937-5773
P.O. BOX 585
MENDOCINO, CA 95460

DEMCO

VILLARD BOOKS NEW YORK 1991

ハ o 1 · 10/3/
ハ z z 96

ROGUE WAVE

SUSAN DUNLAP

Copyright © 1991 by Susan Dunlap
All rights reserved under
International and Pan-American Copyright Conventions.
Published in the United States by Villard Books,
a division of Random House, Inc., New York,
and simultaneously in Canada by Random House
of Canada Limited, Toronto.

Villard Books is a registered trademark of Random House, Inc.

Library of Congress Cataloging-in-Publication Data

Dunlap, Susan.
    Rogue wave / Susan Dunlap
        p.   cm.
    ISBN 0-394-58524-0
    I. Title.
PS3554.U46972R64   1991
813′.54—dc20   90-50659

Manufactured in the United States of America
9 8 7 6 5 4 3 2
First edition

FOR GINNY RICH

A book like this requires a lot of research and the help of busy, generous people. I would like to thank N. Tom Siebe, Chief Deputy Coroner of Sonoma County, for his expertise and patience, and San Francisco Coroner Dr. Boyd Stephens for his superb suggestions. (All my characters at the morgue herein are totally fictional.)

Thanks to Dr. Charles Yingling, professor of psychology and neuropsychological surgery, for his insights and graciousness.

To Ronald Lynn, oceanographer at Scripps Institute, for his technical help.

And to Captain Bob Gallia of *El Dorado I* in Berkeley, Linda Harrington, "Admiral" of bird rescue in Seward, Alaska, gymnast Natasha Hall, and Mike Lynch at Golden Gate Gymnastics.

And to Jennie Arndt for her unusual perception.

Her knuckles stood out white against the tan of her clenched hands. She could no longer feel where her skin stopped and the boat's wheel began. Her arms were nearly numb from the prolonged pressure, and her shoulders were so tense that she couldn't turn her head.

Robin Matucci stared through the spray-mottled window at the black water. The Pacific off the Golden Gate wasn't supposed to be so rough, not in October. She had miscalculated. She'd needed a storm, but not one like this. A black wall of water flung itself forward, and *Early Bird* jolted. She had to keep her feet firmly planted, one pressed against the bulkhead, knees braced.

The bow hit a wave and lifted sharply. The cabin door broke loose from its hook and banged. She clung to the wheel as much as steered with it. Risking a quick look behind her, she saw the body of Carlos Delaney, her deckhand, banging back and forth in the open stern. Delaney was drunk.

He'd been dry since he'd signed on, right up until they'd passed under the Golden Gate Bridge yesterday afternoon. But one taste of bourbon and that was the end of it. Half a bottle gone in record time, and the ocean getting rougher by the minute. When the blow came that felled him, he couldn't get out of the way. An inch lower, and it would have burst his carotid artery. Now his dark hair fanned over his goggles, and his thin lips were parted in a parody of the wry smile that had made her ignore her suspicions until it was too late. He lay like a stunned sockeye, waiting to be washed overboard.

What she would have given to have *Early Bird* headed toward shore! But in a storm like this she couldn't pull the wheel hard over and turn around, couldn't expose the starboard side to a wave, even momentarily, couldn't risk the boat broaching, skidding out of control, helpless against the next wave that would smash down on the starboard quarter and toss *Early Bird* over like a child's plastic tub toy.

But the sun had been out when they left the wharf! She almost laughed at that excuse—who was she going to tell, St. Peter?

Early Bird would go down. And no one would be surprised.

Robin grabbed the wheel tighter and stared through the windshield. The gigantic wave coming—*flying*—at her was so high the mast light reflected off it halfway up. She couldn't see the foam at its crest. It hit with a sickening smack. *Early Bird* lurched straight up, as if a rope had yanked up the bow. The wind battered her face, numbed her ears; still she could hear the scrape and thump of Delaney slamming into the bulkhead. Then the boat stopped, dead. The wind was silent.

Early Bird had crested the wave.

Momentarily, *Early Bird* hung in midair, and the only sound was the ominous whir of props spinning out of water. Then the boat slammed into the trough and walls of water rose round her. Her breath caught. It took her a moment to recognize that unfamiliar sensation: fear. She was never afraid, never let herself be.

Delaney moaned. The boat hurtled into the next trough, sending him flying. Water crashed into the windshield; the side window shattered. Glass spat across the cabin. Water lashed her face.

Through blurred and stinging eyes she stared up at the foam at the top of the wave as it began to curl down, aiming its full force at them with a viciousness she'd never seen in these waters.

There was no time left. She had to deal with Delaney. He was less than a yard from the cabin doorway. But the wave was too close now. Her hands froze on the wheel.

Early Bird flew straight up. Delaney slammed against the fighting chair in the cockpit. The boat shot down so steeply that she was sure it would pitchpole end over end. Water crashed over the bow and banged back and forth inside the boat. Hanging onto the wheel, she watched as Delaney bounced against the stern. His mouth was open. He was screaming! No. Of course he wasn't. Delaney was past screaming. That shriek was the wind. The boat slid backward; water swept over the stern. She watched Delaney go with it—over the stern into the ocean.

Her whole body shook. She pushed Delaney out of her mind. She couldn't afford to think of him, or of how slim were her own chances of surviving. The engine strained; with the props out of water, it would burn out.

Another wave exploded through the broken window; water poured over the stern and for a panicky moment she thought it would bring Delaney's body with it.

Location! She'd lost track. Was she too near the rocky mounds of the Farallon Islands? They could destroy her! She pictured the murderous sea smashing Delaney's corpse against the Farallon rocks. Unbeckoned came the horrifying vision of Delaney, as the Coast Guard picked up his mangled, bruised, dead, dead, body.

She steered automatically, despite her terror. And when the flames shot up from the engine room, she made no move to stop them. Before dawn off the coast south of San Francisco *Early Bird* sank.

2

Kiernan O'Shaughnessy sat staring over her office desk at the misty yellow finger of sun stroking the Pacific breakers. Dusk came early this time of year. Still, there was no place more beautiful than La Jolla, with its gray-green water lumbering toward shore, rubber-suited surfers gliding atop the waves, and adolescents on their boogie boards, balancing, balancing, grabbing for air, and finally flailing down into the surf. Beyond it all, the horizon dropped off in clouds of crimson like the fiery breath of ancient dragons.

"Dinner in ten minutes!" Brad Tchernak called.

The smell of garlic butter floated in from his half of the duplex. She pictured him, all six feet, four inches and 240 pounds of ex-football muscle, standing at the counter breading a trio of giant clams flown in fresh from Oregon. When she stood next to him, the top of her short dark curly hair came to his armpit. It was one of the drawbacks of being not quite five foot one.

Less than ten minutes. She pulled open a file drawer and extricated the Yault file.

The door between the flats swung into hers. Ezra, her Labrador–Irish wolfhound cross, padded in, surveyed the desk, shook his wiry brown head in disgust and sank to the floor. Kiernan laughed. "Liked this room better as a kitchen, eh, Ez?" She reached down and rubbed behind his ears. "You are a very spoiled dog. One kitchen in Tchernak's flat isn't enough? I've never had food here. Only coffee. And even you, you big beggar, draw the line at that."

Ezra looked accusingly at the printer, where the stove had once been. Following the dog's glance, Kiernan eyed the file cabinets that had replaced kitchen cabinets, the computer that sat on a shelf above the smallest refrigerator money could buy. From the first moment she'd conceived of this remodeling job, this commitment to the decadent life, it had delighted her. As she had told friends, it was the working woman's equivalent of Chinese emperors growing their fingernails ridiculously long because they knew there would be servants as close as a thumbnail, or in her case, the front half of a duplex.

She would always have a housekeeper, but not necessarily Tchernak. The job wouldn't hold him forever. She tried to shake off the thought. Maybe once the election was over and Tchernak had more time . . . But if the attention he'd been getting as a local spokesman for the campaign to impede offshore oil drilling was an indicator, his days of preparing baked sturgeon stuffed with Italian fontina could be numbered.

Kiernan gave the big dog's head a final rub. "Ezra, in spite of what you think, my flat does *not* need a kitchen. It needs an office with an ocean view."

Ezra groaned.

"Eight minutes," Tchernak called from his kitchen.

The phone rang.

"Don't answer that," Tchernak warned. "Remember our agreement."

It rang again.

"I'll be through in seven minutes."

"Like last week, huh?"

"Tchernak, you forget your place. You are a house*keeper*, not a house*mother*." She picked up the receiver. "O'Shaughnessy."

"Kiernan O'Shaughnessy?" a hesitant male voice asked.

"Yes."

"And you're a detective now?"

"Private Investigator. Who is this?"

"You're the same Kiernan O'Shaughnessy who was a doctor

at the coroner's office in San Francisco twelve years ago?" The voice seemed familiar, but she couldn't tell if the connection was muffling what she might have recognized, or creating a mechanical sameness that gave the illusion of familiarity. The man's nervousness was unmistakable. "Who *is* this?"

"Skip Olsen. From San Francisco."

"Uh huh?"

"I was with the police back then, when you were at the coroner's. *Harold* Olsen. We had a few stiffs in common."

Olsen. Now she was beginning to remember. Harold "Skip" Olsen, a beat cop. He'd been about thirty then. Shortish, sandy-haired, excitable. The morgue had made him nervous. And he'd always referred to the corpses, *her* corpses, as stiffs. She'd never seen Skip Olsen without feeling he shouldn't have been a cop. He was too unsure of himself. She remembered his pale blue eyes, and the way they followed people's movements. There'd been a puckered look to his face, as if he was sure that even though he wore a uniform no one would take him seriously. But Kiernan had; she'd been wary of that insecurity, the type that led men to overcompensate. His was not an acquaintance she wanted to renew.

But even from the little he'd said, something didn't fit. The "Harold Olsen." *Sergeant* Olsen, or *Lieutenant* Olsen, is what Skip would have hidden behind. "Are you still with the police department?"

She could hear a quick intake of breath before he said, "No."

"No? How come?"

"Lamed out." Another nervous breath. "I was sorry to hear about your, uh, leaving the coroner's office up north."

He hadn't said "your being fired from the coroner's office." That small show of subtlety surprised her. But it did not move her to explain the circumstances: that her mistake had been a natural one; that all but one pathologist in northern California had been willing to support her. Instead she said, "You're calling me on business?"

There was another short pause. This one, she suspected, was the vacuum left by unfulfilled curiosity. Then he said, "I've got this drowning that might not be a drowning. I need you to check out the body."

"Wait a minute. *You've* got this case? You're not with the department anymore. Have you gone private?"

"I'm licensed. Not that big a deal for a guy who was a police sergeant."

"But?" she prompted, responding to his tone.

"I do background checks, things like that that don't call for much legwork. Like I said, I got lamed out—took a shot in the hip. They put my pelvis back together, but my days of fast getaways are gone." He gave an uncomfortable laugh. "But this isn't just a new case. It's connected to a hit-and-run I handled three years ago on beat."

On beat?

"The client is Maureen Brant. Here's the story. A party fishing boat—you know, the type that takes groups out to fish for a day or so—went down south of San Francisco. That was ten days ago. Two people were aboard, Robin Matucci, the owner and captain, and her deckhand, Carlos Delaney. Delaney's body, or what's left of it, was washed up on the Farallons. Matucci's never turned up."

"Not surprising," Kiernan said, warming to the subject in spite of her hesitation about Olsen. "I did the postmortems on a few Golden Gate jumpers when I was at Bryant Street. One was washed all the way out to the Farallons."

"Not much left, I'll bet. Farallons are the only spot around where the ocean floor isn't too deep for marine life. You got the whole food chain out there: plankton, little fish, salmon, albacore, sea lions and the sharks. And plenty of happy crabs on the bottom all the time. You drop something or some*body* in the water near there, don't expect to see them again. Or, if you do, they end up looking like lace tablecloths."

Kiernan recalled that false bravado of Olsen's; remembered him looking down at a drowned pimp on the slab and snidely

pronouncing, "Not so well hung any more, huh?" The pathologist at the next table had begun clipping rib cartilage. Olsen had
turned whiter than the autopsy table and run for the sink.

"Four minutes," Tchernak called, clearly irritated.

"Three years ago," Olsen hurried on, "Maureen Brant's
husband, Garrett, was found unconscious on the side of the
Great Highway out by the ocean. We figured he was walking by
the dunes when the car struck him."

Garrett Brant. The name sounded familiar.

"You remember the Great Highway?"

"I lived in the city for seven years. The Great Highway isn't
a place you forget," she said tersely. Skip Olsen had always
made her a bit terse—her and everybody else, too. But she did
remember the Great Highway, better than he'd have thought.
Oddly deserted for a metropolitan beach, the dunes beyond it
provided delicious if icy seclusion for lovers. Kiernan had discovered them in the spring of her first year of internship. For a
pair of interns trying to escape the long, harried shifts at San
Francisco General, the fog-covered dunes were a soft, secluded
womb for a sleeping bag, a foolishly romantic spot in which to
wrap each other close in a passion that blocked out thoughts of
hospital rounds, IVs, and death; a place to drink wine from
specimen containers while the May sun sank into the muddy
gray Pacific. In winter, angry gusts off the ocean tossed tons of
sand up and over the macadam, creating impassable dunes
where the road had been.

"Whoever left your client's husband unconscious chose one
of the places best suited to death by hypothermia."

"Three minutes, Kiernan!" Tchernak glared through the
connecting doorway to his kitchen.

"Okay." To Olsen, she said, "I've got to make this fast.
What's the link between the drowning ten days ago and this
three-year-old hit-and-run?"

"I caught the call on Brant back then. I could see he was
in bad shape the second I looked at him. It took exactly five-

and-a-half minutes for the medics to roll up, so I had plenty of time to observe him. I noticed two things: one was a trail of blood from his nose. The other was a couple of hairs stuck in the blood. Reddish hairs. And Brant's a blond."

"The blood was from traumatic hemorrhage?"

"Good guess, but no," Olsen said, a touch of satisfaction in his voice. "It was a one-in-a-million stroke of bad luck. The windshield had shattered and sent slivers of glass flying at Brant. There was glass everywhere. But—and here's the one in a million—one sliver went up his nose."

Kiernan shivered. "And lodged in his brain?"

"Right. Of course. There was no way I could know that at the time."

"Two minutes!"

Nodding at Tchernak, Kiernan said to Olsen, "But you realized that the red hairs had to have fallen in the blood after the accident."

"I bagged them, got the department to run a DNA check, and convinced a friendly tech to check it against every new San Francisco sample they ran. Three years and I came up empty."

"Until now."

"Right. Until the remains of that boat washed up on the beach. There'd been a fire. There wasn't much more left of the boat than there was of Delaney, but the remains included part of the wheelhouse. The lab needed to identify Delaney. So they ran the hairs. They didn't find a match for his, but they found the captain's, Robin Matucci's. And hers matched the hair stuck in Garrett Brant's blood."

"A DNA match in less than a week? Come on, Olsen. The tests for that are run sequentially; you can't complete them so quickly."

Olsen made an odd grunting sound. "Okay, Doc, semantic difference. What they ran was a PCR test."

"Not just a semantic difference. The polymerase chain reaction is only ninety-three percent accurate—at best."

"Yeah, but add to that that a witness saw a red convertible near the scene of the hit-and-run, and Robin Matucci drives a red sports car."

"Did she have it three years ago?"

"She did. And she's one of only fourteen women in all of San Francisco who've got both red hair and red convertibles. Maybe you've been gone too long to recall that San Francisco is fog land. Only people with money to blow buy convertibles so they can freeze."

Tchernak rounded the doorway, platter in hands. Ezra jumped up and bounded to the table.

"Have a seat," Tchernak grumbled "since you're the only one who's interested."

Refusing to acknowledge the jibe, Kiernan said, "The red convertible could have been borrowed. Still, okay, so the woman who captained this boat is a suspect in the attack on Brant three years ago."

"Yes and no."

"What?"

"The statute of limitations for felonious vehicular assault is three years and one day. The accident was just over three years ago. The statute's run out. And I'm off the force, so, for all intents and purposes the Brant case is closed. But for Garrett Brant's wife, it's more open than ever, and she wants to hire you."

"To do what? If Robin Matucci went over the side of the boat and didn't wash up on the Farallons, there's a lot less left of her than there was of Delaney."

"Officially, Matucci is only missing. And Mrs. Brant *believes* that. She wants you to find her."

Tchernak popped the wine cork.

The smell of garlic and olive oil mixed with the musty scent of dog that was attractive only to a dog-owner. Why was Olsen so obsessed with this case? She shook off the question and said, "I don't like wild-goose chases. I don't have the patience for them. My fee is considerable and I'm not willing to charge a client to hold her hand. And I definitely won't take her money for nothing."

"It's not 'nothing' to her. It's a long shot, sure, but one she's desperate to bet on. And you are the only person who can get her any odds at all."

Tchernak was pouring the wine.

"Why me?"

"Because she needs a detective who can eyeball Delaney's body and spot something that doesn't fit with drowning."

"Just what is it she wants me to find?"

"Proof that Delaney's death was no accident, that he was murdered."

"Whew! Two people go out on a small boat in the Pacific and one body is recovered and your client assumes that there was murder. That's quite a leap."

"We're talking about a woman who left Garrett Brant for dead on the Great Highway."

"Well, *bon appétit*, Ez." Tchernak lifted his glass.

Turning her back to the table, Kiernan said, "Still, Olsen . . . Does your client have any facts that support her supposition? Did the coroner's report find anything questionable?"

"The final report isn't in yet, but the word I got is 'drowning.' Still, he could have missed something. That's what Maureen needs you to find."

Kiernan sighed. "This sounds more and more like a waste of time, Olsen. I know the coroner's department in San Francisco. They're not slipshod. And they're not about to let strangers wander in to eyeball bodies. You need to be a representative of the family, or at least of the lawyer. They wouldn't let you or me waltz in and critique their work."

"That's where you're wrong. The acting coroner will let you in."

Behind her, metal clanked loudly against china. Ezra slurped, the sure sound of an illicit handout.

"Skip, it's been years since I was a resident with the San Francisco coroner."

"He'll let you in."

She asked the question she could tell he was angling for. "Why?"

"Because the acting coroner of San Francisco is Marc Rosten."

Her shoulders tensed and she could feel her face flushing. "That was a long time ago," she said, surprised by the anger in her voice. "And I don't like dealing with people who try to manipulate my private life. Find yourself another investigator."

Behind her the clank of silverware hitting china stopped.

"Wait! I'm sorry, Doc. I guess that was out of line. But the thing is this case is real important to me. You understand what those red hairs stuck in Brant's blood mean? After whoever hit him, that person got out of the car and stood over him. Then left him there in the cold to die. I got real hooked on this, and it's obsessing Maureen Brant, too. She's willing to spend the last cent she's got on it, and I just want her to have the best she can get. Look, at least talk to her."

Kiernan could hear the desperation in Olsen's voice. She remembered she'd heard some kind of rumor about him a couple of years after she'd left San Francisco. He'd been demoted. Had there been a scandal? She couldn't recall. But that would explain why he ended up back on beat before he retired. She glanced over at Tchernak, who was jabbing his fork into a clam's midsection. "Voodoo doll?" she mouthed, and had a fleeting sensation of sharp pains in her own stomach. To Olsen she said, "Garrett Brant's name sounds familiar."

"He's an artist. He had a couple of shows set up in California before the accident. They went ahead with them. He paints what they call 'interpretive landscapes.' One of the shows was in La Jolla. Maybe you saw an ad for it—the two pictures they used in the ad were called 'Winter Bear' and 'Alaskan Mud Flats.'"

Kiernan shivered. "I saw Brant's show down here. 'Alaskan Mud Flats' isn't a picture you forget. At first it seemed like just another pretty sunset painting, but I found I couldn't stop looking at it; no one could. It held you. There was something ominous in it. I don't know enough about art to figure out why, technically. I read the card beside the canvas—about the people who'd died walking across those mud flats. The mud looked perfectly solid. One woman took a shortcut across them and that solid-looking mud sucked her down thigh-deep and hardened around her legs like cement. She couldn't move. Her husband tried everything he could to get her out. Nothing helped. And then the tide came in—up over her chest, her neck, her nostrils. She drowned."

Kiernan felt the same clutch of gut-fear she'd had three years ago. Such intensity of feeling was quite an endorsement for Garrett Brant, she thought.

As if reading her mind, Olsen said, "The critics felt Brant could have become the most perceptive landscape painter of our time. The guy needs your help."

She shook her head, half-smiling. Olsen was probably sincere, but there was something of the dangerous mud flat in him, too. However honest he was, the slurping sound of deceit pulled at his words. But that wasn't Brant's fault. And it wouldn't take long to talk to the Brants. She had to admit she was curious about the man who said so much on so many levels in a picture of mud and sun and water. And the idea of forcing Marc Rosten to give her something was not without appeal. "Okay," she said. "I'll talk to them. Tell them to come here tomorrow."

"Can't do it. Garrett Brant can't travel, and Maureen won't leave him. You'll have to go there."

Kiernan sighed. "Okay. Where are they?"

"I don't know exactly. Somewhere around Big Sur. Go to a grocery called Barrow's, on Route 1, just past the sign for the town of Big Sur. She'll leave you directions. I'll call and tell them you'll be there tomorrow around noon."

"In the meantime, fax me whatever you've got on the Brants, Matucci, and Delaney. And Olsen, include the info about yourself, why you were demoted. I don't take cases unless I know who I'm dealing with."

3

Dr. Marc Rosten, *acting* coroner of the city and county of San Francisco, washed the soap-and-Clorox mixture off his hands. He hadn't noticed the din in the autopsy theater when he'd been working, but now the babble of pathologists dictating their findings, the sloshing of fluids, the metallic clanking of instruments hitting the porcelain tables, and the whir of a saw cutting through the frontal bone of a skull seemed deafening.

He looked back at the corpse on the gurney. He'd done the autopsy last week. It had been a relief to leave it to someone else to close—or at least to sew up as much as any autopsy assistant could manage to do. Five days in the ocean—not a pretty way to go. Despite the air-circulation system installed to pull up bacteria that might harbor contagion, the autopsy room still reeked with the sharp odor of body fluids, of bleach and burning bones, and of dead flesh gone rotten.

It had been twelve years, but he could still recall his own first day here. He wouldn't have wanted a corpse like Delaney's then. But twelve years had changed a lot of things. The bloat didn't bother him the way it would have, nor the head that the crabs had eaten down to the bones. You couldn't be squeamish in this line of work. And it wasn't the exposure cases that got to him, it was the ones who looked as if they might get up off the table and go home for dinner. The ones a doctor might have saved—that *he* might have saved if he'd stayed with internal medicine rather than opting for forensic pathology.

But he'd been such a damned coward. He'd made a mistake, and he'd flagellated himself year after year for it. But there was no sense in going over it again and again. After all, he'd picked up the pieces, stuck to forensic pathology, and here he was: acting coroner. Not bad for a guy who'd regretted his choice the moment he'd applied for the residency.

He was a good administrator. That had surprised him. It had surprised everyone. Marc Rosten, the guy who couldn't keep his mouth shut, who couldn't slow down enough to plan, who trusted his smarts and played his hunches, who spent the last quarter of his internship in bed with a knockout brunette when the other guys could barely muster enough energy to get *out* of bed after a thirty-six-hour shift. . . . Who would have pegged him for an administrator? And if he proved himself as acting coroner this month, he'd be getting offers from all over the country. He'd be in a position to negotiate, to sign on with the people who were committed and willing to come up with the money to make their departments tops. He wouldn't have to spend his time fighting to stay within budget in some small county, making do with outmoded equipment, missing subtle indicators of death because there wasn't enough staff or equipment, thanks to a board of supervisors who knew they wouldn't get votes by allocating money to the dead. This time next year he'd be running his own first-class coroner's department.

If he kept things going smoothly here. He'd already had a call about this drowning. But there was nothing unusual about it. Nothing but the eyes, and however abnormal they might be, they hadn't killed the poor bugger. No, it was asphyxia due to drowning that had done this guy in. The blood chloride levels in the chambers of the heart weren't the same, so Delaney hadn't been dead when he entered the water; he had indeed drowned.

He took a final look at the body and rolled the gurney back into the freezer. Besides, this ex-cop who'd called about Delaney was off the force for a reason. And it wasn't because of a better offer. He'd called the department to check on the guy. He hadn't gotten the whole story, but he'd heard enough to know that Olsen was not going to be a problem, not if Olsen was relying on cops to help him out. Olsen didn't matter. The postmortem was fine. Everything was under control. And would be for another two weeks.

Rosten stepped into the changing room, stripped off the scrub pants and stood thinking. If he'd done this well here, what could he have done as a diagnostician? He could have helped these people before they ever reached the slab. He did save lives; he knew that. The data he collected from the corpses, the conclusions he drew, the recommendations he made to Public Health, they all fended off future epidemics, aided future treatments. But he didn't save *these* lives. He had made one wrong decision and for the rest of his life, no matter how intelligent, how dedicated he was, he would always be too late.

4

"There's no good hour to drive through Los Angeles; the last one was before 1975," Kiernan muttered, standing by the new cherry-red Jeep Cherokee wagon in the driveway.

Tchernak squeegeed the residue of sea-brine off the windshield. "No one told you to leave La Jolla at four in the morning. You could fly to Monterey, rent a car, save yourself hours."

"And leave you the Jeep, huh? That would take the sting out of my absence?" She opened the door. Ezra aimed himself at the driver's seat. Flinging an arm around his furry neck, she yanked him out and slammed the door. "Down, Ezra! I appreciate your concern for my comfort, Tchernak, but I have to remind you that investigators train themselves to spot the underlying truth."

Tchernak grinned. "You told me you bought the Cherokee for Ezra. He's already bigger than the Triumph. It's only fair to leave it here with him." Backlit by the streetlight, Brad Tchernak's face looked craggier, his grin more wicked; with his four-A.M. uncombed spikes of hair catching the light, he resembled a grizzly coming out of hibernation.

"You and Ezra can make do for a day or two."

"We could come with you," he said hopefully.

His offer was not new, and not one she wanted to encourage. Wondering what Tchernak was up to and worrying about Ezra were the last things she needed when she was on a case. "What about the Initiative Campaign? Aren't you scheduled to speak at some rally today?"

"Do I catch a note of jealousy?"

She laughed. "Employer's pique."

"You can make light of it now," he said, suddenly serious. "But if Prop. Thirty-Seven fails, don't be surprised when your ocean view is splattered with oil-drilling platforms. *Seventy* new platforms off the California coast, that's the prediction. According to the Central Coast Regional Studies Program, the probability of a large spill off our coast as a result of drilling is ninety-nine percent. It's going to happen! And everyone: the coast guard, the scientists, even the oilmen themselves agree that there is no way to clean up a big spill."

She held up a hand. "Tchernak, you're preaching to the converted. I know the state can't prevent drilling beyond the three-mile limit. I know that Prop. Thirty-Seven instructs them to create every impediment legally possible to that drilling: no new roads, no zoning changes, no sewer hookups for the onshore support. How's that for four in the morning!" She reached up and patted his muscular shoulder. "Besides, I ordered background searches from BakDat."

"Don't exactly trust Olsen in San Francisco, do you?"

"Not hardly. If this case doesn't pan out I'll have to eat the cost, but that's better than going in cold."

Slightly mollified at the prospect of computer play, Tchernak gave up. "Okay, but show a little restraint this time. Don't go into homes where you're not invited."

She climbed into the Jeep and backed out before he could go on about the seductive lure of housebreaking. It was a topic she was sorry she'd ever mentioned to him.

She headed up the empty street and caught the freeway north. Her underlying agenda, basically the same as Tchernak's (use of the newest vehicle), was rewarded. The Jeep handled firmly, responded quickly, and the fun of sitting up high looking down at the other cars hadn't paled yet.

When she reached Santa Barbara, Kiernan opened the basket Tchernak had packed—a thermos of coffee, a blueberry corn muffin and a still-warm container of braised tofu, tomato, and killer-chili pepper scramble. As she ate, she looked across the white, palm-guarded expanse of the Santa Barbara beach at the lapping blue water of the Pacific and out on the oil-drilling platforms beyond. She would really miss Tchernak if he left, she thought.

As Tchernak had smugly pointed out, the coast road was much better suited to the Triumph. The narrow road wound in and out sharply, hugging the mountains. On the ocean side there was no railing, just a drop of fifty, a hundred, two hundred feet. By late morning the sun had cleaned the sky. It sparkled off the macadam, the rock, the leaves of oak and eucalyptus, and the azure blue water of the Pacific. On the few straightaways, cars like her Triumph pulled around the Jeep. And though she knew it was ridiculous, she felt humiliated, like a sheep nipped by a border collie. She had to fight the urge to step on the gas and see just how well the Jeep could corner. "Two-hundred-foot drop!" she reminded herself.

South of the town of Big Sur she pulled into the parking lot beside Barrow's Grocery and called Tchernak. Using the car phone still gave her a thrill of pleasure. Tchernak picked up the receiver on the sixth ring. "Brad Tchernak here."

"You're surviving, then?"

"I am. But Ez took out his anguish on your phone cord."

"Shit!"

Tchernak laughed. "I've already gotten another one. That's what you have servants for. And now the news from BakDat. Maureen Brant, thirty-one, has a driver's license, but they can't get the address yet."

"Motor vehicles won't release addresses any more. Go on."

"Most recent work history was with the Department of Social Services in San Francisco. Ended three years ago. No activity on the social security number since."

"What about Garrett Brant?"

"John Garrett Brant, thirty-one, last driver's license was five years ago, in California. But his last Social Security card activity was in Alaska. Two years of sporadic entries from the Flamingo Bar, Janit-temp, and Ready Cab. And then one big entry from Arts of the Land Foundation."

"What about Robin Matucci?"

"Ah. Now this is interesting. Robin Matucci, twenty-eight, coast guard licensed navigator, Social Security activity in San Francisco for two and a half years—she paid as an employer with *Early Bird*. And she owns a house in the Marina district of San Francisco."

Kiernan whistled. "The fishing must have been very good indeed. Even after the earthquake, houses in the Marina still go for half a million. Anything else?"

"Nothing at all on Delaney."

"Haven't they run him?" The fax came when ready; there would have been no explanation on what was still missing.

Tchernak laughed. "I knew you'd ask. I called. They ran him, but there's nothing."

"Nothing?"

"Not a thing. They thought it was odd, too."

"Damned odd. His Social Security payments from the last month or so would be too recent for them to pick up," she mused. "But what was he doing before that?"

"Don't deckhands work for tips?"

"Do they?" Kiernan asked, aware of a hollow sensation in her chest: apprehension. Justified apprehension, when she was facing a case that could pivot on something she knew nothing about. "I'll call you between two and two-thirty, okay?" She hung up and headed inside the grocery, a small building, with dry weathered planks, and the musty smell of a place that sits under fog too much of the time.

"Can I help you?" A plump woman with gray-streaked brown hair sat in an old overstuffed armchair behind the counter.

"I'm Kiernan O'Shaughnessy. I need directions to Garrett Brant's place."

For an instant the woman looked puzzled, then she said, "Oh, you mean Maureen's. I forgot her husband's name. Nice woman, Maureen."

"You don't know Garrett?" Kiernan asked, as the woman reached under the counter and extricated an envelope.

"Never seen him. Most times I forget Maureen has a husband. Or I would if she didn't buy so much food. He's not social, that's what Maureen says. She says that if she's pressed. Otherwise, she don't say nothing at all about him."

Reclusive artist? That didn't seem out of character for the man who painted "Alaskan Mud Flats." Kiernan took the envelope, bought a Coke, stopped in the restroom, and headed back to the Jeep. It was then that she noticed the envelope was sealed.

"Looks like Maureen Brant isn't any too social either," she muttered as she tore it open. Not so odd in a woman who was anxious to spend her last penny on revenge.

She started the engine and turned south, then east at the second turnoff, a narrow, windy road with the type of broken pavement that reminded her she was in earthquake country. The macadam ended a mile inland, but the dirt road continued four more miles, twisting like an old telephone cord. Jeep country! The piny aroma of the redwoods lent a coolness to the warm

October noon. Kiernan slowed the Jeep and looked up, a hundred yards into the sky, to the tops of these trees that might have been fullgrown years before Columbus learned to sail. The priests at St. Brendan's, the church of her childhood in Baltimore, had urged the catechism class to be in awe of God. She'd scorned the idea as much as she had the priests and the Church, but the sense of oneness with unmoving time had struck her the first time she'd seen a redwood.

This would be reason enough to explain why Garrett Brant never ventured out to the highway.

The Brants' cabin, Maureen's instructions said, would be behind a cluster of redwoods on a bluff off to the left.

When she saw it, she stopped dead.

Cabin was hardly the word for it. It was a two-story house clearly by Bernard Maybeck, the architect who'd designed the most striking buildings in the San Francisco area at the turn of the century. She hadn't realized Maybeck had accepted commissions this far south of the city.

As Kiernan climbed the dirt-and-plank steps from the road to the bluff, she wondered what wealthy recluse had commissioned Maybeck to build this small chalet miles from a paved road. Back when it was built it would have been much more inaccessible than it was now. And the "cabin" had a swimming pool, cracked and empty, a depository for leaves.

The whole place had the look of neglect. The woman who opened the door could have been a personification of it. Maureen Brant's dark-blond hair was streaked with gray, grown out of what must once have been a fashionable layered cut. Her skin was pale and puffy from alcohol, or middle age, or both. Her shoulders drooped, and her pale flowered shirt and yellow shorts seemed faded, but her eyes—hazel, flecked with brown—were intense and angry.

When Maureen Brant spoke, none of that anger was evident in her voice. "Come in. My husband's in his studio out back. We can talk in the living room." She led the way into a dark, paneled room with an enormous tiled fireplace, pre-Deco radiator covers intended more for beauty than transmission of heat, and faded, green-and-pink-flowered overstuffed sofas. Magazines had been straightened into piles on a rug that showed intermittent lines of vacuuming. The vacuum cleaner stood against one wall, still plugged in.

Maureen Brant sat down on the nearest couch, perching so close to the edge that the sofa cushion tilted precariously. Kiernan could picture her collecting the magazines, nervously tapping the edges into a pile, then, distracted by a piece of lint or the feathered leaf of a redwood on the rug, rushing out for the vacuum and taking symbolic swipes at the long-uncleaned carpet. Now she sat unmoving but for a thumb that rubbed back and forth across the reddened skin of her first finger.

Kiernan sat next to her. She was about to ask for a glass of water when Maureen blurted, "Robin Matucci killed her deckhand. It's been less than two weeks. You can find evidence. And you can find her."

"Slow down. You don't know any of those things. Maybe they both just drowned."

"I know she killed my husband."

"Killed? Did you say he was—"

"Yes, he's out there, painting from photographs he took before the accident." Her thumb rubbed across the finger, pressing the raw skin white, drawing it taut as a scar. "He's not dead, not in the medical sense. For me he's dead. His work is dead. Our life is dead."

Kiernan nodded. The woman's voice echoed with the shaky cadence of despair.

"At first I thought Garrett would get better. It was a freak accident, the sliver of glass up his nose. It sounds like part of a standup comedy routine, doesn't it? Who would think a little bit of windshield could wipe out his short-term memory? Drain the life from his work. Destroy our lives." The thumb rubbed faster, harder.

Kiernan put her hand firmly on top of Maureen's and held the thumb still. She pictured Olsen cackling, recalling her insistence that she couldn't abide cases that amounted to holding client's hands. Shaking off the thought, she said, "Just tell me what happened."

More calmly, Maureen said, "It was almost a year after the accident before I realized he'd progressed as much as he was likely to. Do you know about his condition?"

"No."

"There was a perforation of the mediodorsal nucleus of the thalamus in the brain. At first Garrett was very disoriented, but gradually he improved. I used to be a social worker, so I probably understood more than the average person. I should have known better, but still I assumed he'd recover. I couldn't accept that he'd never be himself again. After I accepted he wasn't going to change, that nothing was going to change, nothing could change, I realized what a devastating thing someone had done to me. I felt I was holding in an arsenal of hate. I needed to know who did this dreadful thing, who to hate. I was sure that when the police found the culprit and slammed him in jail, I could relax."

Done to *me*. "And—" Kiernan encouraged.

"And then the statute of limitations ran out. Legally it's not murder, you know, just hit and run. The statute is only three years and one day. It's past, over. If the culprit walked into the Hall of Justice in San Francisco now, there would be nothing any of us could do. I couldn't believe it. I barely dragged myself out of bed for days. Even Garrett noticed. It was only his needing me that made me get up at all. And even that . . . What difference does it make? I kept asking myself. The statute of limitations has run out." For the first time, she looked directly at Kiernan, fury blazing in her eyes. Slowly, she said, "There is no statute of limitations for me."

For *me*. "And now you know that his assailant was Robin Matucci?"

"When the police told me someone had died at the same

time she disappeared, I was elated. Sounds awful, doesn't it?"
She hurried on. "I've lived alone too long now to bother with
artifice. The man was a stranger to me. Carlos Delaney, those
syllables don't conjure up anything in my mind. Except a
chance. She killed him, just like she killed Garrett."

"You don't know that."

"I do!"

"You believe you do. It's not the same."

Maureen shrugged, then smiled suddenly. "No need to tell
me I'm bitter and obsessed. I'm not oblivious, too."

Kiernan returned the smile and released her hand.

"I've thought about the person who hit my husband every
day and every night for three years. Anyone who would leave
Garrett lying in the cold sand to die is exactly the sort who would
push a man overboard."

Kiernan shifted on the cushion. A breeze fluttered her
collar; the room wasn't cool, but the smell of redwood and
eucalyptus made it seem so. "Let us assume that Robin Matucci
did kill her deckhand. A murder at sea would be extremely
difficult to prove. But if you're intent on doing so, your best bet
would be a detective who specializes in boating accidents. Private investigators have very specific specialities. I work on cases
that require medical expertise."

"That's why I want you. There's not much left of the boat.
There was an engine fire, but that's not unusual, the coast guard
said. There wasn't an explosion, though, nothing that could have
killed anyone. The answers aren't going to be in the boat, they'll
be in Delaney's body. The coroner classified Delaney as a simple drowning. I want you to examine his body, to find something
that proves she killed him, so the police will have a reason to
find and prosecute her."

Kiernan shook her head. "There is no way I could make
that promise, surely you know that. The coroner's department
has examined the body. If there was a bullet wound, a knife
wound, or anything that clearly indicated murder, they would
have found it."

"But they weren't *looking* for murder. A subtle method
could have escaped them, right?"

Reluctantly, Kiernan nodded. "All things are possible. But
this is a man who drowned in the Pacific. If he's got bruises,
they could just as easily have been caused by his fall overboard
as from Matucci bludgeoning him. You'd need something very
obvious to substantiate murder. The best I could realistically
hope to find would be something that didn't quite fit, like the
hair stuck in your husband's blood, something that doesn't
scream murder, but merely says things aren't quite as they
should be."

Maureen Brant sank back against the sofa and smiled.

Kiernan held up a hand. "Suppose I did find such evidence, where would that leave you? Exactly where you are, sure
Robin Matucci is a murderer, and with nothing you can do about
it. The woman is dead, or at least missing."

"But I'd know."

Kiernan shrugged. "The thing is, Mrs. Brant, because of
my medical background my fees are considerable. It doesn't
seem to me that you'd be getting your money's worth, when
half-a-dozen other detectives could—"

She sprang forward. "No!" It was more of a squeak than a
word. "I don't want someone else. Look, Garrett won a prize
from the Arts of the Land Foundation. The last installment just
came in. It would keep us for five years if we lived frugally. And
we do. I can't work. I can't leave Garrett. We can live on the
insurance and his Social Security."

"But surely, a few luxuries now and then—"

"No!" Taking a breath, she said slowly, "It wouldn't matter
how much money I had, there is nothing I can buy. No matter
how much easier it would make it for me, I cannot bring new
things into the house. Garrett can't stand it if I do. But that
doesn't matter. Because there is only one thing that will make a
difference, and that is revenge. Find me a discrepancy in
Delaney's body." The overlay of grief in Maureen's voice was
gone, leaving only a shrill tone of desperation.

Kiernan could feel her own shoulders tensing against the electric atmosphere. "I need a glass of water," Kiernan said, starting toward an archway. "Is the kitchen through there?"

Despite the heat of the day, the kitchen was cold. The walls were paneled in the same mahogany as the living room, and the amber tile was old and grease-coated. A plastic water bottle stood on the sink. Kiernan shivered. What kind of life did Maureen Brant have, when even buying drinking water required half an hour's trip? Kiernan drank less than enough to quench her thirst and walked back to the sofa. "I'm not the detective for this job."

"Wait. Don't decide now. You have to meet Garrett before you turn us down. Do you know about him?"

"Not much more than the facts of the accident."

"Garrett's works are landscapes," Maureen said, tension and desperation in her voice. "But what he really evokes is the life of the community. There are no words for what he does. He couldn't have explained it if I'd asked him. He worked entirely from impression, feeling. It was as if he distilled every aspect of people's lives down to a single drop and then drenched the scene he chose to portray in that drop." She laughed shrilly. "It's so ironic. His gift was the ability to translate emotion into substance. That's more or less what the area around the third ventricle of the brain does, the area of Garrett's brain that she destroyed." Maureen swallowed hard. "Sorry. I try not to think about the fact that he can never understand that subtlety again. His work was so moving. I've seen people in tears just looking at a painting of his. Now I wonder what he sees when he looks at his own work."

Kiernan hesitated, feeling the same chill she had when she'd first seen "Alaskan Mud Flats." A mere gust of the chill that must have been an unabating gale for Maureen Brant. How could a man with the ability to create that visceral foreboding from a picture of mud and water be denied new landscapes, new emotions to bring to life?

Emotion was not a box she liked to open. For her the draw of investigation was the puzzle, and the chance to make things right. But she asked, "What was Garrett like to live with before?" She held up a finger. "Think a moment. Time can improve on the truth."

Maureen laughed. "No, I'm not going to tell you it was all good. He was gone months at a time, away painting. The two years before the accident he was in Alaska and only came down here six times. But that was okay. I was working. When you do social work you're in the middle of people's problems all day, and being alone at night is not a bad thing." She looked down at the floor. A ray of sunlight hit the dust and she dragged her foot across the ellipse. "But it was Garrett you asked about, not me. What I'm telling you about him is how he was for a week at a time, which is all I saw of him those years." Her eyelids half-closed as if she were looking inward at a remembered picture. "He was spontaneous, which meant there was always something or someone scattered in his wake. He could mesh with anyone and it made me jealous. Sometimes he could give the illusion of connecting, and he hurt people's feelings when they found out it wasn't quite genuine. He never once balanced a checkbook, paid the bills on time, or changed the oil in the car. But when he was with me he was with me totally. And when we made love the marrow of our bones were one."

Kiernan sat stunned by the intensity of Maureen's words, and by her own pang of jealousy for an intimacy she doubted she could ever let herself feel.

She forced her attention back to Maureen and was just about to speak when Maureen jumped up, opened a closet door and struggled to bring out three large canvases. Turning the first around, she said, "This was Garrett's last painting before the accident. He painted it here. He had a photo of the scene, but he didn't paint it from that. He would have been humiliated at such a suggestion in those days. Like painting by numbers, is what he'd have said. Look at the painting, see how alive it is?

It's not a copy of a piece of scenery, it's an expression of how it came together in his mind. The canvas was still drying the day he drove to San Francisco."

It was the same painting Kiernan had seen in San Diego: "Alaskan Mud Flats." Now, the mounds of brown seemed thicker, brighter, safer—milk chocolate wafers on a bed of dark chocolate pudding. But at the same time it seemed more ominous. Was danger conveyed in this harsh burnt yellow of the fading sun? Or was it in the faint blue-black lines lurking in the fluffy mounds of mud? She recalled the collective gasp from the crowd at the La Jolla gallery, when they had rounded a corner and come on the painting for the first time. But here, alone with it in the gloomy wooden house, the effect was not just menacing. It was unavoidable.

"Ironic, isn't it? Garrett paints this canvas that shouts 'Alaska is a siren that will kill you!' But Alaska doesn't kill him. He has to come back to San Francisco for that."

When Kiernan didn't reply, Maureen turned the other two canvases around. "He did these after the accident. The first was painted from memory. The second he did last week, from the photo." The elements were the same: the browns of the mud, the blue-blacks of the suck holes, the gold of the setting sun. But the paintings evoked nothing.

"Now I'd like you to meet Garrett."

5

Kiernan followed Maureen through a small, bare kitchen that held none of the gadgets Tchernak was so fond of—no microwave, no Cuisinart, no coffee grinder or rice cooker; no array of tempered steel knives worthy of a circus act.

Thirty yards behind the house stood what might once have been a barn, built in the Maybeck style. Dark wood, open beams.

Maureen put a hand on Kiernan's arm. "Don't tell Garrett why you're here." Before Kiernan could respond, Maureen called out her husband's name.

In the moment before the studio door opened Kiernan tried to picture Garrett Brant. Would his artist's eye sear beneath her skin, his smile disarm her? He'd be Maureen's age, about forty. No—BakDat listed her as thirty-one. She just *looked* so much older, Kiernan realized with a shudder. Had the past three years worn Garrett down this much, too?

The man who opened the door showed no sign of prolonged stress. He could have been any healthy thirty-year-old. There was no hint of gray in his thick blond hair, and his tanned face was barely lined. He was thin, a runner's type of thin, with a T-shirt sporting a picture from an old movie poster so faded Kiernan couldn't read the title, and cutoffs that showed sinewy thighs and thick calf muscles. His expression was bemused. He caught Kiernan's eye, stepped forward and extended a hand. "Hello, I'm Garrett Brant. How nice of you to come all the way out here to see us."

"This is Kiernan O'Shaughnessy, Gar," Maureen said.

"Kiernan! What a wonderful name, all stony stream and ferns and pines." Clasping her hand with both of his, he asked, "Now where is it we know each other from?"

Kiernan found herself momentarily taken aback by his poised approach. "We haven't met before."

His smile barely faltered. Keeping hold of her hand, he turned toward the picture window. "Come in. Let me show you my view. I have a pleasant view of the redwoods. I've loved these redwoods ever since I was a child visiting here. I've been in Alaska for two years, so it's nice to see so much California green, even though it looks as if it is going to be a dry summer."

Kiernan almost said, "It's October," but caught herself. Instead she looked at Garrett's view. Thick-bolled redwoods stood on either side of a fern-filled clearing. Their branches filtered the sunlight, dulling the sharp edges of the gray-green leaves, muting the rich forest colors so that the scene resembled a faded color-tinted photograph from the forties. Despite the nearness of the redwoods, there was a fair amount of light in the studio. Garrett's easel stood near the back window.

"May I?" Kiernan asked, before turning to face the work in progress.

Garrett nodded, running his fingers across her hand before he released it.

A preliminary sketch had been lightly indicated on the canvas. Kiernan smothered a gasp. The picture was of the mud flats. The same subject she'd seen inside. Three years had passed, and this was the same picture. The familiar photo was pinned on the wall next to the canvas.

"Tell Kiernan about the painting, Gar." Maureen's voice held a tautness that didn't match her words. Kiernan felt a stab of guilt; in the few moments she'd been in the studio she'd forgotten Maureen, so engulfing was Garrett's attention. Was this his ability to mesh with anyone that Maureen had talked about? And was Maureen reacting too, because it was being directed at another woman? Glancing at her, Kiernan noticed the rigidity of her shoulders, saw that her thumb was working away at the raw spot.

"I took that photo in Alaska before I left last month."

"You left there last month?" Kiernan asked.

"Uh-huh. It's a shame to leave Alaska in May. That's when you first start to see the grass. There's that odd scrunchy feeling when the frozen earth softens to mud. It's like walking on Styrofoam."

Kiernan laughed. Garrett looked at her, vaguely surprised, then smiled too, as if he were humoring a child.

"The painting, Garrett," Maureen insisted. "What are you aiming for in it?"

"What makes my work so individual, Kiernan," he said, still smiling at her, "is its sense of place. I present the people through their environment." His words, Kiernan recollected, were taken directly from the gallery brochure. But he had the air of an excited small boy telling a secret to a special friend. It was a very effective—and very flattering—presentation, especially since he must have given it many times. And yet there was something not quite right about it.

Kiernan held her breath for a moment. Although the studio windows were open, the air felt used and stale. She'd expected the place would smell of paint or turpentine, but all she could detect was a vague aroma of coffee. She made a decision. "What about the three paintings in the house?" she asked.

"Three?" Garrett shook his head. "You should have your eyes checked. You're seeing triple." He grinned at her, but the grin had a watery quality about it. "I did one, but it's not quite right."

Kiernan hesitated. Behind her, she could hear Maureen give a little gasp. "No, honey, there are three in there."

"Maureen," he said, shaking his head, "are you ladies playing some kind of joke on me?"

"Come back to the house and see, Garrett."

"There's only one painting, Maureen. You know that." His grin was firmly locked in place, but his jaw was tense.

"Humor me." Maureen led the way across the dry October grass. The tightness had spread from her shoulders to her back; she walked stiffly, as if the discs in her spine had turned to stone.

When Kiernan stepped inside, the chill and darkness startled her. It was one of those houses that would never be warm no matter how big a fire they built in the baronial fireplace. Maureen and Garrett were standing behind the sofa, leaning against the back. Neither was looking at the paintings, but Maureen's face seemed wary and hopeless. Garrett glanced around the room with the calm, indifferent expression of someone who has been away for months and is reacquainting himself with his surroundings.

The earliest of the paintings was propped up by a table, the other two against a wall. "There, Garrett," Maureen said. "There are your paintings."

"Paintings?" he asked, as if this were the first time he'd heard of them.

Maureen's lips quivered. She pointed to the canvases.

Garrett glanced at the wall, then focused on the picture by the table. "This isn't quite right," he said. "I'll do it over."

Maureen stepped closer. Her eyes, which had seemed so angry earlier, were tear-filled. "You've already done two more, Garrett. They're right here."

"No, no." He reached for her arm as if to comfort her in her delusion, but she moved away quickly, the veins in her neck rigid. "Look at them, Garrett!" Her voice was louder, shriller. "They *are* yours, aren't they?"

"Well, they look like mine." His face twisted in bewilderment. He moved closer to the canvases, squatted down in front of first one, then the other, peering at the brushstrokes.

"You did paint these, didn't you?" Maureen insisted.

"It's my style, certainly." He stood up. His expression changed from confusion to fear. "Someone sure copied the way I paint, or at least tried to. But these are flat, lifeless. The guy who did them must've been an accountant or something." It took

Kiernan a moment to realize that the hollow, nervous sound he made was meant to be a laugh.

"No one copied you, Garrett. No one's been here but us, right?"

"No one we *invited*, hon." He glanced fearfully from his wife to Kiernan. "Forgers don't knock at the front door. Anyone could creep round to my studio during the night." His hands were shaking.

Maureen's face was bloodless. "*Crept* in? Painted those canvases and left them in the house?"

"They're not worth taking away," Garrett said, almost inaudibly.

"Garrett, you know you painted all of these . . ."

"No!" he cried. "Only one. I've only painted one. You know that." He cringed away from Maureen. Horrified, Kiernan found herself taking a step backward.

"Those things don't belong there!" he shouted. "Those walls must be bare. Nothing can be on them." He grabbed one of the canvases and flung it to the floor. The frame cracked. He tore and ripped at the canvas itself, and when it didn't give, flung the whole thing into the empty fireplace.

Maureen swallowed hard. For several moments she stood unmoving, then walked stiffly over to Garrett, who was staring out of the window, his body at attention. She put a hand on his shoulder. "Aren't the redwoods magnificent?"

Kiernan moved beside the couple in time to see the fear wash out of his face, leaving it momentarily blank. There was no trace of his earlier anxiety, she noted. He turned abruptly away from the window, looked at Kiernan and grinned. "Hello. I'm Garrett Brant. How nice of you to come all the way out here to see us."

Kiernan gasped. Mechanically, she extended a hand.

Garrett glanced quickly, questioningly, at Maureen and when she said nothing turned back to Kiernan, still smiling. "Now where is it I know you from?"

Kiernan swallowed hard. "Do you remember my name?"

His smile quivered but held. He took her hand in both of his. "Why don't you tell me again. You know how painters are, all picture, no memory space for words. You're . . . ?"

"Kiernan O'Shaughnessy."

"Kiernan! What a wonderful name, all green glades and fast-moving water. Kiernan, it was good of you to come. Maureen's not as fond of seclusion as I am. She's a city girl. She wouldn't have chosen the woods for a vacation." He smiled. "But we're only here for two weeks, right, Maureen?"

Maureen gritted her teeth, then nodded. In the moment before she spoke, Kiernan watched her remold her face, squeezing out the emotion, glazing it with pleasantness. "You've got work to do, Gar. Don't let us keep you."

"Okay. You ladies have fun, now." He caught Kiernan's eye and smiled. "See you later, uh—. Don't you dare leave without saying good-bye."

Maureen walked him into the yard. Looking at them, Kiernan found it hard to imagine they could ever have been lovers, ever have been anything but mother and son.

6

Garrett Brant looked at the redwoods beyond his studio window. He smiled happily. *The trees . . . just like they were when I was a boy here. Almost as if time had stopped.* He moved closer to the window. *There's the scar in the bark, where my swing hit it—*

He heard the door creak behind him and whipped around. The wall of photographs caught his attention. *Odd that the edges should curl so soon. I just put them up when Maureen and I got here.* His gaze shifted to the snapshots of the mud flats of Cook Inlet. He shivered despite the heat, remembering the stories of those deceptively solid stretches of land which, when the tide was out, were covered with algae—green, chartreuse, golden-brown. Thanksgiving colors. He shivered again. He no longer *thought* of the woman the mud had sucked down, he *felt* her terror, recognized the moment when she knew she would die, *knew* the moment when the salt water covered her face and drowned her. He turned to the canvas on the easel. *Had he captured all those nuances? There must be three levels in the painting: safety, danger, death.* He let his eyes half close; saw Sally, his neighbor in Anchorage. Sally looking at the first sketch he'd done of the flats, swearing she'd never walk there again. He felt again the warm flush of helping, maybe saving. When the canvas was done, *if* he caught the peril, maybe it would warn people. "Alaskan Mud Flats" would get lots of attention if he won the Arts Foundation grant.

The studio door creaked again. He turned toward it and waited an instant before taking a blue and green jacket off the hook and placing a hand on the knob. *Why am I leaving? I must have decided to take a break. If I can't remember even that, then I really* must *need a rest.* He smiled, recalling himself standing in the studio, hearing the buzz of the intercom and Maureen telling him to come into the main house; there was a telegram for him. He could *see* her pale face, flushed now with excitement, could see her waving the envelope at him. "The committee, Garrett . . ." she'd said, but he couldn't hear anything else, just knew that her voice seemed different somehow. *Odd to lose that memory so soon. Must be the pressure. This San Francisco business to take care of. Waiting to hear about the grant.*

The grant. He felt again the simultaneous tensing of his shoulders and the rush of relief. *Made the cut. They don't telegraph losers. Five finalists. Only four days to go, to know for sure. No more carting slides to galleries, no more gallery owners clos-*

ing shop before they get around to paying me my share of a sale. No more being too tired to paint because I've spent all night— night after night—vacuuming tasteless beige office after tasteless beige office. But his face didn't reflect that frustration, as if it had settled so deeply, so intimately in his body that it had no need of superficial exhibition. He could still sense those corporate types, feel them grumbling about wastebaskets, dirt on the carpet, as they strolled past him out to the California Tavern. He smiled suddenly. His hands tightened in anticipation. *Next week the grant. Then, there would be a future.*

7

Maureen walked slowly back into the dining room. She looked drained. "Kiernan, all those months in the hospital and the rehab center, I thought he'd get better. But he won't, ever. For him, it's all the way it was three years ago. It's like life's a movie and for Garrett it stopped in that one frame. He'll be forever twenty-eight. In the middle of his Alaska paintings. He won the Arts of the Land Foundation Award for them. He would have been so pleased. He does know he was one of the finalists, but the notice of the actual award came too late. Sometimes I tell him about winning it." She swallowed. "I show him the letter. He's surprised, pleased."

"That must be some small comfort for him. To be able to relive a wonderful moment afresh?" Kiernan said.

Maureen closed her eyes. "For Garrett, yes. But I see the difference. Before the accident he would have been excited. Now he's pleased. That's one of the side effects of his type of brain injury. Emotion fades. Maybe it's the result of no longer having a future. Or maybe it's the constant uncertainty. Garrett has no facts to hang onto, what happened five minutes ago is gone for him. He has no idea what season it is, you saw that. But he understands enough to know he *should* know, so he's always searching around for clues, or for something that will allow him to rationalize what he's only been guessing at."

"Like living in a constant earthquake?"

"The only solid ground Garrett's got is in his distant memory. His injury resulted in a very special kind of amnesia. Damage to the mediodorsal nucleus of the thalamus is linked with a frontal syndrome . . ."

Maureen was repeating herself, Kiernan thought as she interrupted. ". . . And the frontal lobes deal with the sense of purpose." She could see why Garrett Brant's paintings showed less life with each effort. With no commitment to hold him, he would become easily distracted; his conviction in the uniqueness of his vision would fade as the range between high and low disappeared.

"His hands start to shake by evening. Once in a while we shoot at tin cans. It's something to do." She shrugged apologetically. "He's got an old Ruger revolver. But now he has to use both hands to hold it steady."

"You said his capacity for emotion has faded. But he certainly reacted to these paintings, when he saw them in here."

Maureen's eyes filled. "Oh God, that hurts. I know better than to try to reason him into the present. The neurologists tried a lot at first—we all did. I couldn't believe he was gone. He's not a person anymore, he's a holograph. He has flashes—sometimes they'll last as long as a minute or two—when he seems like the old Garrett. Sometimes in bed he looks at me the way he used to, as if we two are the only people in the world; I can hold his attention longer then. And there are some things you just don't forget." She swallowed hard. "I don't know why I'm telling you all this. But it's been so long since I've really talked to anyone. In bed—that's where it's worst. Mechanically Garrett's great.

Still knows all the right moves. But they don't mean anything to him."

"Take your time," Kiernan said gently, watching Maureen awkwardly rubbing her wet cheeks. She hoped her voice did not betray her horror of misery such as Maureen's: misery for which she knew no relief. She was clumsy with this kind of grief. For her, pain was something to be denied. She'd learned from her sister, Moira, how to run from pain so fast that it could never catch up with her—until Moira died. She'd let her guard down only once after that, with Marc Rosten—and afterward she'd never allowed herself to dwell on that mistake. At this moment she wanted more than anything to get away from Maureen Brant, run full out to the Jeep, and floor the gas pedal. Instead, she took a deep breath, put a hand on Maureen's arm, and led her to the sofa. Her own fingers felt cold, but Maureen's skin was icy. "Garrett didn't sound unsure of himself when he met me, Maureen."

"You didn't know him as he was before. He has no idea who you are, of course. And he won't remember ever having met you—you can walk into that studio a hundred times today, two hundred times, and he'd greet you the same way each time: 'Now where is it we know each other from?' "

She jumped up and began pacing. "I hate it here in this gloomy house, but it's the only place we can live, the place we were—the day before Garrett lost his memory. I couldn't stand to have him in Anchorage or San Francisco, disoriented the whole time, wondering how he got where he was, why there's oil on the beaches he used to visit south of Anchorage, why the buildings he remembers in San Francisco before the earthquake aren't there any longer." The mechanical pacing, back and forth, up and down, continued. "When I go to the store, I have to lock Garrett in so he doesn't decide to go for a walk. If he got lost, he'd never find his way home again. I leave him a note: 'Door may be stuck. Relax. I'm going for locksmith.' Same note whenever I go out. He probably reads it anew fifty times when

I'm gone." She looked down at Kiernan, the anger in her eyes cutting through the mist of despair. "If Robin Matucci had killed him, I would have forgiven her. Garrett, the man I knew and loved, is dead. A fading photograph of himself. For me, the moment of his death comes a thousand times a day. And it will as long as we both live.

"Will you take this case?"

Kiernan's own hands were clenched into fists. She could feel Maureen's need, the power of her thwarted passion. She wished she were the kind of person who could wrap her arms around Maureen and let her sob. But she knew that to help meant to think clearly, to provide the logic Maureen had lost.

"All right. I'll go to San Francisco, look at the deckhand's body, and if there's anything about it that doesn't fit in with a simple drowning, then I'll investigate."

Maureen crumpled onto the sofa. "Thank you. I don't know what I would have done if you'd—"

"Don't be too relieved. There are a couple more stipulations. One is a contract."

"Fine."

"And the other is that you answer my questions with complete honesty."

"Of course. Why shouldn't I?"

Kiernan shook her head. "No one wants to trust a stranger with their secrets. We all withhold bits and pieces of things. I'm asking you to try to be more honest with me than you've been with yourself." Kiernan had given this little lecture before and seen clients nod in agreement. But she never really expected that kind of openness from them, never believed in its possibility. A compromise between honesty and self-protection were all she could really count on. "First, what do you know about Robin Matucci?"

Maureen rested her elbows on her knees. "Besides her hitting Garrett, you mean? Only that she's captain of a charter boat called *Early Bird*. It's docked at Fisherman's Wharf."

"How did you hear about Delaney?"

She leaned forward. "Skip Olsen called. He was the cop who handled Garrett's accident. He's been a brick."

"Have you been in touch with anyone else?"

Maureen shook her head.

Was there a moment's hesitation before that denial?

"Are you sure? Think."

"Nobody except Garrett's doctors and the rehab people. We had friends in San Francisco, but Garrett didn't want to see them when he came down from Alaska. Which was odd, because normally he'd have been off to some gallery before he'd even unpacked." She shrugged. "But this time he seemed nervous from the minute he arrived. He insisted I tell no one he was back. He said it was so we could spend some time alone together without all his friends descending on us."

"What do *you* think the real reason was?"

"I just don't know. Maybe he was avoiding someone."

"Who?"

"I don't know. He'd been in Alaska for four months. Possibly someone from the bar where he was bartending. Or some guy on the AlaskOil maintenance crew."

"Were any of his fellow workers from either of those places in San Francisco?"

"I did ask him that. He said no."

The cooling breeze chilled the sweat on Kiernan's shoulders and made her aware of how tense she'd become. "I know this is hard for you, Maureen, but every insight you can give me will make it that much more likely I can help. Please think calmly about what I'm going to ask. Garrett said he wanted to spend time with you. But he went to the city alone. Why?"

"He said he had a meeting."

"What kind?"

"With a representative of a gallery."

"Why didn't he take you?"

"The representative was a woman. Garrett believed, and he was right, that there's always a sexual element in any negotiations between men and women, and that this woman would do better by him if he dealt with her alone."

"Could he have been having an affair with her?"

The color vanished from Maureen's face. "No!"

Kiernan waited a moment. Maureen Brant's denial wasn't a statement but a protest. "But you've considered it, haven't you?"

Slowly the color returned, but irregularly, blotching her face. "Of course. I doubt there's any possibility I haven't thought about. If he hadn't insisted on going to San Francisco, alone, our lives wouldn't be over. What was so important? I have no more idea than I did three years ago."

"Who was the woman?"

"I don't know."

"Didn't you ask?"

"Of course I did—before he left, when he was in the hospital, when he came back here. I asked him this morning before you arrived. He wouldn't tell me before. He won't tell me now. Maybe he doesn't even remember her name. A lot of things have faded for him. It's like his mind is disappearing from the edges in."

"He still thinks like he did three years ago, right? So if he felt that he had reason to keep this woman's name from you then, he would still have that mind-set now?"

"I don't know his rationale. The point is he's not going to reveal her name."

"Maybe he'll tell me."

Maureen stiffened. "It's possible. But there was some reason he was keeping that secret, so to get him to reveal it you'd have to know the right questions, the right tack to take. A straight-out query wouldn't do it."

"What do you know about the gallery or the area it was in, or anything about it?"

"Nothing. Garrett was careful not to reveal anything."

Kiernan let her gaze rest on Maureen Brant for a long moment. What had that drained face expressed three years ago?

"How long was Garrett in Alaska without you?"

"Almost two years."

"Why didn't you go with him?"

"There was no way I could have survived in that cold. Besides, I had a career of my own—I couldn't just leave whenever it suited me. Anyway, Garrett would call me every couple of days—or, more accurately, nights. One of his self-appointed perks was making free calls from some of the empty offices—his way of getting even for such a drudge of a job: he was on a maintenance crew there. And the last time he called me he was really excited about coming here. I thought it was because he missed me. But I'll never know, will I?"

Kiernan took a deep breath and watched the branches of the redwoods sway in the growing breeze. Slowly she said, "I'm going to go and make a couple of calls from my Jeep. While I'm gone, I want you to consider very carefully about hiring me to find Robin Matucci. Finding her will mean discovering why Garrett went to San Francisco. Are you quite sure you want to know?"

Maureen started to speak, but Kiernan held up her hand. "No, don't answer yet. I'll be back in ten minutes."

8

Kiernan leaned against the Jeep, hoping that the deep cool and the fragrant aroma of the redwoods would scour away the grief and fear and demand that filled the Brant house. The presence of the millennia-old trees had always been able to calm her before, but today they might as well not have existed. She was still edgy when she climbed into the Jeep and grabbed the phone, ready to speak to Marc Rosten after twelve years. Should she be calm or angry? She laughed at herself. What difference would it make? She recalled only too well the year after Marc's departure, when *any* thought of him turned to fury. But she hadn't phoned him then.

She drove the Jeep back to where the road crested a hill and punched the number for the coroner's office. Marc Rosten wasn't in. She didn't leave a message. No point in giving him extra time to think. He'd had twelve years in which to explain himself. And he'd used the element of surprise last. Now it would be her turn.

She called Tchernak. "This is Brad Tchernak," his recording began. "What can I do for you? Leave your mess—"

"Hello?" Tchernak was panting.

"Hi. Been out running?"

"Ezra hates it when you're gone. He's been moping all day. I thought a long run would take his mind off you, or at least tire him out enough so he'd leave me alone. When will you be back?"

"I don't know. I have to go to San Francisco and see if there's anything that merits my taking the case. If there isn't, I'll be home the next day. Right now, I need you to find the insurers for Robin Matucci's boat."

"Are you planning to hook up with them?"

"Just covering bases. Insurance, you might say." She grinned. Her facial muscles felt strained, and she realized how tense she had become during her visit with the Brants. "I've got an acquaintance in the San Francisco coroner's office. I should be able to get into the morgue on the Q.T., but if I have to go to court with anything, I'm going to need a legitimate excuse, like a connection with the insurer, in order to see the body again."

"If your friend let you in once, why wouldn't he let you in again?"

It didn't do to tell Tchernak too much; Kiernan had learned that the hard way. "Rosten and I were interns together. We didn't part on good terms. Odds are fifty-fifty he might not let me in at all."

"Kiernan, it's been ten, twelve years since then. No normal person holds a grudge that long."

"Pathologists are rarely classified as normal."

"Even so," he said, "what could you have done that was so terrible he'd still have you on his blacklist all this time? Wait a minute. You threw him over, right? And then it dawned on him that he was missing something. No wonder he's still pissed."

She laughed. "Tchernak, if you had to sweep up all the blarney you throw out, you'd be behind the vacuum twenty hours a day."

"About this guy Rosten?" Tchernak insisted.

Kiernan sighed. "Truth is, I don't know what happened with Marc Rosten. I only know he was angry when we finished our internship. Angry enough to pull strings at the last moment and get a residency in the East. It was four years before he came back to San Francisco. I didn't see him then or later. But after I was fired from my own county coroner's office, I heard, third hand, that he was the only forensic pathologist in the Bay Area unwilling to sign a statement supporting me."

"*What?*"

She could picture Tchernak's tanned face knotting into a scowl. Before he could verbally slam Rosten into the turf, she said, "I'm sure you're right. Twelve years is a long time. He's probably forgotten whatever it was that set him off. Besides, I have to make this call. And Marc Rosten really does owe me one. Talk to you later."

She drove back to the house and walked past the abandoned pool to the Brants' open door. Maureen was staring at her husband's paintings of the Alaskan mud flats. At the sound of Kiernan's footsteps, she spun around stiffly. Her hand was streaked with blood. She had rubbed at the raw spot till the skin was gone.

"You haven't changed your mind, have you?" she asked in a tight voice.

Kiernan shook her head. "I'll go up to San Francisco and see if I can get into the morgue. I'll check with Olsen."

"Will you call me after you see the deckhand's body?"

"It'll be too late by then."

"Call me tomorrow, in the morning. We don't have a phone here, but I'll be at the grocery at eight."

"Make it ten. In the meantime, I'll need some background information on you and Garrett. The questions are on the form: full names, where you grew up—"

"But why on us? I want you to investigate—"

Kiernan rested a hand on the mantle. "This investigation is about Garrett. Any facts I have on him make it that much easier for me to judge what someone else tells me about him, which means I can also judge the validity of everything else they're saying."

"But *I'm* not the focus. Why do you want—"

"Look, at this point I've got virtually nothing to go on. I've no idea which bit of information is going to be important and which isn't, so I need everything I can get."

"Still, I—"

Kiernan stood up. "My way or not at all! This is a very iffy business. Just to get the ball rolling I'll have to call in a favor someone won't want to give. A favor erasing a big debt. And I'm not willing to waste that favor on a case full of holes, one on which I have to ask myself why my own client is hesitant to give me the name of the town she grew up in."

"No, wait. I'm sorry. I'll give you what you need."

Kiernan sat on the arm of the sofa, watching Maureen complete the form, read the contract and sign it. Had she caved in too quickly? Kiernan couldn't be sure. Never leave a question untended: that was one of the first rules of investigating; questions could be postponed, or withheld to ponder, but never merely passed over. When Maureen looked up, she said, "What else are you not telling me?"

Maureen's eyes closed and the muscles of her face tightened. The sunlight had moved eastward, leaving Maureen in the shade. Goosebumps formed on her bare legs. She opened her eyes. "I don't think this is connected. Or maybe I do and don't want to believe it. But I'm sure someone has been here, in the house."

"A burglar?" Kiernan asked skeptically. Five miles off the main road was a long way to come to rip off a television or stereo.

"He didn't take anything."

"How do you know he was here, then?"

"Things were out of place, just a bit." She looked up. "Garrett noticed. He's fanatical about things being in place now. Keeping things exactly where they belong, where he can find them, gives him stability. If either of us leaves something in a different place, he has no clue where it might be."

Kiernan slid down to sit on the sofa. "When was this break-in?"

"There may have been more than one. Gar complained about things being moved, but I didn't pay attention. It wasn't until yesterday that I saw a change I knew neither of us could have made. But maybe I was just looking more carefully."

"Maybe you were thinking about Robin Matucci."

"Maybe."

Kiernan turned to face Maureen directly. "Why didn't you tell me this before? It could be important."

"I realize that. I'm sorry. The whole thing's just so overwhelming. After the last three years to finally have the chance of getting that woman . . ."

Kiernan stared at her. "Maureen, is there anything else I should know?"

"No. You've got it all."

"You're sure? Think."

"I'm sure," she said, irritably.

"Okay. I'll be in touch."

"Tomorrow. Ten o'clock," Maureen insisted.

Kiernan headed the Jeep west, into the wind and the bright afternoon sun. Was Maureen's story of the break-ins true? Was that story what she'd been hiding? That was the question to hold and ponder.

Why had she agreed to take this case? Certainly not for the money, which at best she would feel guilty about accepting. Was it for the excuse to face down Marc Rosten? She mentally shook her head, knowing at the same moment that she was lying. Making Rosten break the rules for her was part of it. But not all. Was it the thought of passionate Garrett Brant, now become the ultimate unreachable lover? Or was it the absolute horror of Maureen Brant's future: life imprisonment with a man she could scarcely recognize?

9

Kiernan was in Monterey when she got through to Marc Rosten. "Rosten here." The voice was gruff, but a note of excitement tempered it. Kiernan could picture Marc Rosten poised anxiously for a call, a lab report, the answer to something he couldn't wait to know. But it was the Marc Rosten of twelve years ago she envisioned: a small, wiry man with black curly hair and watchful brown eyes that seemed always on the lookout, as if what he knew was never quite enough—as if the next elusive fact would be the one that would provide him certainty.

"Marc, Kiernan O'Shaughnessy."

"Kiernan? . . . Oh . . . Kiernan. . . . This is a surprise. What can I do for you?" There were pauses between each phrase.

His tone changed from the sharps of curiosity to the flats of wariness. No social niceties, she noted. But that had never been a part of their relationship.

"I need a favor."

"A favor?"

"I need to see one of your cadavers."

"Oh, are you back with the coroner's office?"

Was that a note of condescension? Obviously she wouldn't be back with the coroner if she'd needed his support. Taking a moment to make sure her own voice didn't betray her anger, she said, "No, I'm private, investigating a hit-and-run. Your cadaver is only incidental to it. I could get an okay from his family or his lawyer, but that would waste a lot of time. The trail goes cold fast in cases like this one."

Over the phone she could hear another phone ring, a door slam. "Surely," he said, "you recall the rule here: the morgue is not a zoo; we don't give tours."

"And surely, Marc, you don't expect me to believe that holds true for the acting coroner," she said, her fury seeping out of control. *Out of control*: that summed up her months with Marc Rosten.

"Kiernan, I'm in charge here. It's up to me to uphold the rules. I—"

"You owe me! You know that. Let me see Carlos Delaney's body and we're square. This is an easy out for you."

He didn't reply. She could picture him nervously moving a report from one pile to another, as if keeping things in motion would prevent them from settling long enough to threaten him. She pictured his bushy eyebrows drawn tight in angry consideration, his full lips pressed together. She could tell him she knew about his refusal to support her when she was fired, but she hated to waste her last card. Instead, she said, "I'll be there at eight tonight, at the parking lot door."

10

Marc Rosten slammed down the phone. "Damn her!" He realized his jaw was tight with anger, his free hand jammed into a fist. And his groin hard. That last discovery made him even more furious. "Damn her to hell!"

He glared down at the stack of "While You Were Out"s his secretary had put on his desk before she went home. Connelly at Northern Station about the Jessup report—third call. Connelly was one of those cops who never got the idea that bacteria couldn't be rushed. For Connelly, lab reports should take as long as it took to type them up. Well, Connelly could damn well wait. He crumpled the message and threw it into the garbage. Merke, the architect, re: the specs for remodeling the tox lab. An Anita Kole from the Northern California Association of Pharmacology, re: his lecture. Postmortem reports from the last two days to initial. Call from the tox lab. Call from Heins, the forensic dentist. Call from . . . Kiernan O'Shaughnessy. Dammit, he was not going to have thoughts of her interfering with his work. Not again. It had taken him nearly a decade to erase them.

It was too quiet in the Medical Examiner's office. The pictures of the ME's wife and kids were gone, but the place still had his potted plants, his desk set, and his chair—made for a man eight inches taller than Rosten. Every time he sat in it Rosten felt like a kid who has sneaked into his daddy's chair. He was used to the office he shared with three other pathologists, where the phone was always ringing, there was plenty of talk, and clerks would stop to chat when they brought in reports. There was always something going on.

He picked up the phone, punched Merke's number. No answer. It was after five; he must have gone home. Rosten replaced the receiver and looked down at the desk. But it wasn't the desk he was seeing, it was that first day on pathology rotation twelve years ago. There had been only one postmort in progress when Susman had guided the clutch of them in. "Well-nourished white female," he remembered Bailey muttering with a snicker as they neared the whalelike shape. The Y incision had already been made, and whoever was doing the work was clipping the rib cartilage with a tool that looked like something meant to prune rosebushes. The whole scene made him want out. But slinking off was not the Rosten style. He'd forced himself to push his way toward the front. He should remember the corpse, but he didn't. He couldn't even recall the pathologist.

What he remembered was Kiernan, the green scrubs hanging loose on her small body, her dark eyes focused entirely on the corpse. What was it about her that had hooked him? He remembered her firm breasts, the round of her hips . . . but that was later. Then it was all intensity, that passion vibrating just below her skin. Other guys had found her obsessed with medicine, too fascinated with forensic pathology, too bright, too abrupt, too unyielding. But he had seen a passion that matched his own.

The light through his bedroom window had been filtered by a maple tree then. He could still see the lines of yellow and gray as they cut across . . . He shook his head sharply. This was not the time to think of that.

He went to the cabinet and extricated the Delaney file. After twelve years she calls him out of the blue, and what does she want? The Delaney file. He laughed soundlessly. Well, the other guys in that internship class wouldn't be surprised, would they?

But what could she want to know about Delaney, the drowning? He pulled the coast guard report and scanned it. Thirty-foot waves the day Delaney's boat must have capsized. Perfect weather to drown in. He had the cause of death, and the contributing factor. No question on this one.

No question—and yet he'd already had two other calls on Delaney. One from a Dwyer Cummings from Coastal Oil Group asked for the Delaney autopsy protocol. Who was this Cummings, and why did he want to know about Delaney? And Jessica Leporek. He'd heard of her, naturally. Woman running the local campaign for that initiative to impede oil drilling. She didn't ask for the autopsy report, just left a request to call her back re: Delaney. No, not a request; a demand that implied she was a powerful woman, or would be if the initiative passed— which seemed pretty doubtful from what Rosten had read. The coroner's office got calls about autopsies all the time, but from relatives or the press, not people like these. They'd made him uneasy enough to take a second look at Delaney.

He could, of course, not let Kiernan in. It was tempting. Who the hell was she to say he owed her? So he hadn't come to her rescue when she got herself fired from the coroner's office up north, but that was years ago. And she of all people should not have missed a single indicator in a single autopsy. All right, so he was the only pathologist in the area who'd said that. None of them knew her like he did. She hadn't changed their lives.

At eight o'clock he could leave her standing at the back door. But he knew he wasn't going to.

11

Kiernan could have taken the freeway, but this late in the afternoon the coast road was just as fast and much more appealing. The Jeep was a St. Bernard, a savior in mud or blizzard, but the Triumph—she sighed, yearning for her sleek black convertible—the Triumph was a greyhound. She knew she was driving the Jeep too fast. It's not a game, Tchernak had said before finally refusing to ride with her on roads like this. But for her it was—a dumb game, a lethal one. And the rush she got screeching out of a hairpin curve next to a two-hundred-foot drop was right up there with sex.

Past Monterey the road flattened. She passed Ano Nuevo, where the elephant seals came to mate, and headed on into miles of fog-laden dunes, cold, secret places washed by the sounds of eternity. The scenery reminded her of the Great High-way farther north, where Robin Matucci had left Garrett Brant for dead.

Why? Kiernan asked herself again. Take the evidence at face value: Matucci had struck Garrett with her car, stopped, got out, looked down at him, and then simply walked away. But why even stop? Remorse? To see if she could help? Apparently not. Why leave him to die? Panic? Possibly. And what about Delaney? Did she kill him, or was that Maureen's wishful think-ing? After she'd had a look at the body at the morgue, Kiernan thought, she'd have a better idea.

Tendrils of fog floated across the two-lane road. This part

of Highway 1 was empty except for the illegally parked campers
pulled off in beach lots. She turned on the radio, slowly twisting
the dial, ear cocked for the moan of guitar strings. The words
"Proposition Thirty-Seven" stopped her hand. The offshore drilling initiative.

A male voice was saying: ". . . debate between Dwyer
Cummings of the Energy Producers' Group and Jessica Leporek,
Northern California Director of the Initiative Campaign. Good
evening. Our first question will deal with the issue of offshore
drilling itself. What's at stake here? Mr. Cummings?"

"Lots, Barry." Cummings's voice held traces of a southern
accent. "The D.O.I., that's the Department of the Interior for
those of you who aren't on a nickname basis with these guys,
well, they estimate that there's one point three billion barrels of
oil out there on the Outer Continental Shelf. We need that
supply for virtually everything from driving our cars to heating
our houses, cooking our food, and warming our bathwater.
Our—"

"Let me interject here," a woman, presumably Jessica Leporek, insisted, "that one point three billion barrels is merely
seventy-seven days' worth of oil. Are we willing to endanger our
beaches for less than a three-months' supply!"

Cummings let a moment pass before saying, "Well, Jessica, that just shows you how critical each drilling site is. But to
get back to my point: we in the oil industry are frequently
painted as the bad guys in this. I'll tell you right now, we hate
that. We don't want oil spilling any more than you do. We go to
the beach, we care about the birds and the otters just like
everyone else. And, added to that, we have a big investment in
that oil. With the cost of gasoline skyrocketing even if we cared
nothing about the environment, we still wouldn't want our supply wasted in a spill."

"Wanting is one thing, Dwyer, but here's the record. Spills
the size of the one from the Exxon *Valdez* in Alaska—that's
eleven million gallons—occur every single year. Spills of one

million gallons occur every single month. And nobody, Dwyer, neither the coast guard nor the petroleum industry, believe we can clean up more than a few thousand gallons."

There was another pause. "I'm glad you raised the clean-up efforts. Let me tell you what we are doing. The—"

Kiernan moved the knob. She'd heard all this before. It didn't matter what they were doing, Tchernak had insisted, because no one could clean up a bad oil spill. "It'd be like having someone dump tons of molasses down your chimney. It fills the whole house. There'd be just enough air space for Ezra to keep breathing," he'd added quickly. "Now, your problem is to clean it up without letting that molasses get outside the house, where it will wreck something else. You can skim off the liquid, but how are you going to get the hardened gook off the ceiling, the carpets, the mattress? How will you clean your papers, your computer keyboard, and Ezra? All that and keep him from tracking goo back over every spot you've already cleaned, getting himself sick in the process? You can't, of course. That's the bottom line."

She glanced across the sand to the breakers, now almost hidden behind the thickening fog. The latest pole listed the initiative as too close to call. She turned the radio knob until she heard guitar music. The moan of the strings moved down her spine. After a while it echoed between her breasts and she thought not about the Spill Initiative, but about Marc Rosten and what a dangerous decision it was to see him again.

Twelve years ago, with him everything had seemed fine, then without warning, it was rubble.

The coast road widened to eight lanes by the outskirts of the city. The dark and the fog billowing in from the Pacific made it feel unnaturally cozy. She pulled over at the top of Upper Market Street and looked down the slope at the lights of downtown San Francisco: ropes of yellow beads glowing against the silky blackness, diamond sparkles as the trolleys switched overhead power lines, blue and salmon neon outlining new highrises. She loved this view of the city, the promise of freedom.

The morgue was a gray stone building in a low-rent, low-safety area, a place where the elderly and the poor slide into death. The lot behind it was nearly empty. She pressed the bell at the back door and waited.

The night guard was a stranger to her. "I'm Dr. O'Shaughnessy," she said. "Will you tell Dr. Rosten I'm here?"

The guard raised an eyebrow. "Just a minute."

Kiernan glanced down at her jeans and black Shaker-knit sweater. Lots of places, she wouldn't have looked like a doctor, she thought, but in San Francisco—well, she just might be overdressed.

But not for this night. The Pacific wind chilled her neck, ruffled her short hair and made her sorry she'd left her jacket in the Jeep.

It had been in this parking lot that she'd first noticed Marc Rosten; he'd been grabbing the lapels of a Mercedes owner who'd stolen "his" parking space, a guy half a foot and fifty pounds bigger than he was. Rain dripped from the ends of his curly hair, his eyes seemed huge and fierce behind his rain-splattered glasses. He'd looked like a madman. Clearly the owner of the Mercedes agreed, as he backed out of the spot and watched Rosten pull his battered Nash Rambler in. Rosten had turned to her, grinned, and said, "We got to keep these rich bastards in their place, right? Or at least until we become rich bastards ourselves." They'd been in the internship program just two days. Later they decided she was the only other intern who would have shared that opinion. Had he instinctively known that, as he had insisted, or didn't he care? Marc Rosten had never been without do-or-die opinions, without ebullient enthusiasms, always eager to talk over his cases, to try everything for every patient, to be three places at once. After the Rambler died, also in this parking lot, he rode a ten-speed and made it to the lot faster than she did driving. Hospital administrators hated him, patients adored him, and other interns kept a wary distance away.

Yet in the dark of that turret room on the top floor of his

brother's Victorian house, all the energy had been focused, calm, patient. The thin, fierce lips had been surprisingly soft and giving. And his hands, with their long tapered surgeon's fingers, stroked so lightly that it nearly drove her out of her skin. They were hands that were wasted on the dead.

That year had been the most exhausting of her life, when thirty-six-hour shifts were the norm, when the two-month rotations moved from O.B.-Gyn to Surgery, to Neurology, to Ophthalmology/Otolaryngology to Pathology. The life-and-death scene on each new ward called for knowledge she didn't yet have, intuition for which she had no basis, and an alertness so long gone she could barely remember what it felt like. She should have spent every one of her free moments sleeping. But she'd spent them in that turret room with Rosten. Moments so intense that now, twelve years later, if she closed her eyes she could trace his whole body by touch. She could still recall the alkaline smell of his sweat, feel his thick wet curls, see those dark eyes staring down, demanding, celebrating, an inch from her own.

She could see just as clearly the front porch of his house, the pale blue paint merging with the thick fog, as she stood there waiting for him to come down. The door to the lower flat had opened. "Gone," Marc's brother had said. "His residency in Boston came through. He left this morning."

She had blocked out the scene that followed. She could only recall that blue paint and the distant sound of shouting that she realized, now, must have been her own. And she remembered quite clearly the next frantic week before her own residency began, calling every medical school in the East, rage growing with each call. At first she'd expected to get Rosten on the phone and hear his apology. As the week progressed, she'd readied herself to fly East and demand an explanation. She had never reached him at all.

That was twelve years ago.

The door to the Bryant Street building opened. She realized she hadn't heard the footsteps coming toward her. She hurried through into the wood-paneled lobby, then stopped, and looked at him.

Marc Rosten was still as magnetic as ever. The streaks of gray merely made his hair seem blacker. There were lines now around his eyes and mouth, but they lent a new and appealing steadiness to his features. He hadn't changed, and yet was entirely different.

"You remember where the morgue is?" he said, turning and moving quickly down the hall. His eyes still had that burning intensity. For the first moments of any meeting they had always focused exclusively on her, "sucking you into me" he had said. Now he didn't look at her directly. He spoke with a tight control that was the antithesis of the Rosten who had flung covers, sheets, and pillows in all directions as he made love.

The hallway was icy, the hum of the air-movement system was louder than the refrigerators would be in the morgue. She followed him into the elevator and rode down in silence. He could have commented that she hadn't left him much choice when she'd said he owed her, but apparently he wasn't going to deal with that one. And her first loyalty, she reminded herself, was to the case, not to old grievances.

She stepped out into the basement. The sharp smell of Clorox struck her. The first time she had come into an autopsy room she had expected it to reek of formaldahyde like the anatomy labs in college. She'd been surprised when the dominant smell was ammonia.

This autopsy room was just as she recalled it, a large rectangle with five porcelain tables surrounded by troughs. She wouldn't have been surprised to find a body on one of the tables, the water running pink in the troughs, and a pathologist speaking into his microphone as he removed the heart for examination or sectioned the liver. The dead don't choose their hour of death; pathologists don't choose their hour of call. There had been weeks when the autopsy room was never empty. Now the room was silent and dark, and as Marc turned on the fluorescent lights one after another, they seemed to highlight the anonymity of death. And the immediacy of life. Or perhaps it was Marc himself who did both.

"Number eight," Rosten snapped, without looking at her or stopping to check the register. He yanked open the metal door with the same angry tug he'd used on the Mercedes owner's lapels. He hooked the chains around the slab, wheeled the corpse over by the autopsy tables. Then he waited, arms crossed, eyes at half-mast. He wasn't tapping his foot or looking at his watch; he didn't have to.

Who are you to be angry at *me*? Kiernan clenched her teeth to keep from blurting it out. She looked at the body on the slab.

Carlos Delaney was past the aid of Clorox and cold. The time he'd spent in the Pacific had turned his skin a sickly white. She knew that if she were to take his hand, the skin would slough off like a stretched-out rubber glove. But there wasn't enough skin to come off. The crabs had seen to that. They'd eaten through to the plates of the skull. The ears were almost gone, as was the tissue above them, and the lips and cheeks. There were thick purplish rings around his eyes.

"Not too palatable," Rosten muttered.

Glancing over, she could see him tightening his shoulders, forcing himself to keep looking at the partially decomposed corpse. After all these years, Marc Rosten still had not come to terms with his profession. "Crabs waste no time," he said. "Guy falls into the sea and it's Thanksgiving for them." He turned away from the body. "Crabs eat us just like we eat them, take the easy parts first—hands, feet, ears, eyes, whatever they can get their choppers into. Us, we can't be bothered with the hard stuff, the meat under the shell. Not unless we're hungry enough."

"Is that part of your opening remarks to new students?" she asked, fighting to keep her voice from betraying her anger. She would *not* allow him to condescend. Taking a deep breath, she looked back at Delaney, noting that there was no telltale discoloration that would have been caused by the blood settling in the dead body. "No specifically localized lividity," she said. "You figure he was batted around in the water for a while after death?"

Rosten nodded abruptly.

"How long was he in the water? Five or six days at least, from the look of him."

"Five," he admitted. "The activity of the crabs and bottom feeders tells us he spent about a couple of days down there."

Kiernan stared at the white skin of Delaney's midsection. The waist was the most likely spot to find lividity, but there wasn't any. She looked back at Delaney's face. "How'd you ID him? Teeth?"

"Couldn't find a match. Not every sailor or deckhand elects to spend his free time at the dentist's."

Another time she might have laughed. Now she simply asked, "So how?"

"The eyes!" There was a fleck of excitement and pride in his voice.

Kiernan nodded, feeling the pull of his enthusiasm, remembering how easy it had been to be caught up in it.

"Damned good thing he had the goggles on. Eyeballs are the first things crabs go for."

"Also the first thing to decompose. You were lucky."

Rosten nodded sharply. "They were in reasonably good shape. But, I started to wonder, just why would a deckhand be wearing tinted goggles at night?"

"To keep the spray from the storm out of his eyes?"

"*Tinted* goggles. Except for the mast light it was pitch black out there."

"Very odd. What did you find in the eyes?"

"Premortem damage to the foveal cones and the choroid layer of the eye."

"So the insult to the eyes, or the disease, happened while he was still alive," Kiernan said, giving up any effort to restrain her excitement. That same rush of the chase they'd shared here before. She pushed the memory away, and tried to call up a picture of the eyeball. It was not an organ usually sectioned in an autopsy. It galled her to have to say, "The sclera covers the outside of the eyeball. Beneath that is the choroid, which is heavily pigmented, right?"

Rosten nodded, the barest hint of a smile curling his lips.

"And internal to that is the retina, and the foveal cones in the retina are sensitive to color and provide visual acuity, right?" she went on.

"Right. So we checked with local ophthalmologists and found one who had seen a man fitting Delaney's description. He mentioned that Delaney had listed a broken femur on his history form. He recalled Delaney said he'd been treated at Kaiser Hospital in Oakland before. I checked there and matched my femur to their X-ray!" He smiled with satisfaction.

The same smile. The smile that had misled her. This is not a contest, she cautioned herself, this is my only chance to find out about Delaney. "What about cause of death?"

"Asphyxiation," he said. "Blood chloride levels *un*equal in both sides of the heart. There was aspirate material in the heart, stomach and microscopic flora in the lungs." His smile had faded but there was a look of confidence about him, "the witness-stand look" they'd called it in med school: that expression of pleasant forbearance that said to juries, "Rest assured, I am the expert."

"So Delaney took in a lot of seawater. What about a secondary cause? Did you find ecchymoses around the eyes?" she asked, wondering about telltale broken blood vessels.

"Not enough to say he was strangled first."

"The damage to the foveal cones and the choroid layer? Just how bad was it?"

Rosten flinched. The expert witness was piqued at being asked a question he'd hoped to avoid. Kiernan fought back a smile. So much for keeping it merely an interview. The old competitiveness was too ingrained. Rosten could, of course, stop answering her questions, but she was willing to bet he wouldn't. Too much like throwing in the towel.

He didn't. "All the foveal cones had been compromised. That fitted with the ophthalmologist's report. The choroid was ninety percent dysfunctional too."

"Did the ophthalmologist say what had caused that? Heredity? There are no signs of albinism."

"The ophthalmologist guessed scotoma, but couldn't say what disease caused it. He did say it wouldn't be something communicable."

She wasn't surprised that had been Rosten's first concern. One of the goals of the coroner's department was to spot a contagious disease before a second body came in with it. "So Carlos Delaney had poor color vision and little acuity, right?" That would explain the tinted goggles, Kiernan thought, but not why he was wearing them at night. Maybe he hadn't been able to take them off? If Robin Matucci had tied him up earlier . . . She'd need to think about that later.

Kiernan realized she'd reached the limit of Rosten's knowledge of eyes. She stared again at Delaney's disfigured face, trying to refocus herself, then asked, "What did toxicology show?"

"Point two three alcohol in the bloodstream.

"Point two three! Serious drinking."

"Right."

"So we can assume maybe six, seven ounces?"

"The level in the stomach was noticeably higher than in the liver."

Kiernan nodded slowly. "He did his drinking so close to his death that the alcohol didn't metabolize. Was he an alcoholic?"

Rosten wagged a finger just above Delaney's liver. His hand looked brown against the white of the corpse. The familiarity of the movement suggested a bond between him and the deceased. Or did it indicate possession? *His* case.

"Well, now, that's an interesting question. There was some fibrosis in the liver, nothing significant, but enough to make me wonder, so I checked the striated muscles." He paused.

She could tell he was waiting for her to ask what he found, but she couldn't bring herself to cheerlead. She waited.

Finally, he said, "Rhabdomyolysis."

She nodded, impressed. Finding that microscopic change, the distortion of the fibers of the skeletal muscles, was good work indeed. "So signs of heavy alcohol consumption, but not necessarily recently." She wondered if Delaney's brain had shrunk away from the skull, leaving excessive liquid, as was the case with many long-time alcoholics. "Given the length of exposure he'd been subjected to, I suppose there was no way to check for wet brain?"

Marc's hand stopped midair. "The tissue was like tapioca; nothing was firm enough to section."

"Did you preserve it? You can section it after it firms up in the formalin." She could hear the sharp edge to her voice.

"Of course I've preserved it," he snapped. "I am very thorough."

He didn't have to mention the conclusion she had not reached in the autopsy that led to her firing. No other pathologist had called that a lack of thoroughness. But then no one else had refused to support her. She tried to relax her steel-tight neck muscles before asking, "Did you check—"

"Look, the guy was loaded and he drowned in a storm that capsized the boat. It's very straightforward."

Kiernan struggled to restrain her annoyance. "Okay, so Delaney had been a heavy drinker some years back, but his physical symptoms hadn't progressed as would have been expected had he continued. Is that a safe guess?"

"A guess, yes." Another unstated rebuke.

"And yet, Marc," she said turning to face him, "Delaney had a real hard fall off the wagon right before he died. How do you explain that?"

"It's not my job to justify behavior; I thought you'd remember that."

Betting that he couldn't deal with silence, she forced herself to wait.

She won. He said, "If you want my *opinion*, the drinking was a reaction to the storm. The coast guard said there were thirty-foot waves. That's nearly three stories high. It'd be enough to drive me to drink. You done here?"

"For now." So he *had* talked to the coast guard, or at least read their report. Chances were he had information he wasn't giving her, information he wasn't likely to offer now.

She watched him push the gurney into the freezer. Was he still the man she had known? His passion, the exuberance of a man who flung the bedclothes aside to get to her, was that entirely gone? Or had it been leashed and taught obedience? She felt a great sense of relief knowing that in a couple of minutes she'd be walking toward her Jeep, and her contact with Marc Rosten would be no more than a phone call in the morning. "I need to read the autopsy report."

He shrugged. "Public record. *When* it comes back from typing."

"Which will be?"

"A week, maybe."

"Ah, the bureaucrat's cloak!"

"What's that supposed to mean?"

"You can get me a copy of your own notes."

He slammed the freezer door, turned and put a hand on her arm. She recalled the warmth of his touch, in this very room, but there was no warmth now. "You've seen Delaney. The debt's paid."

She shook off his hand. "This is not a contest, Marc. Delaney's not lying half-eaten on the slab because he took a wrong step. You've got a guy here with no recent history of alcoholism who gets himself so loaded he can't see straight, who does it in the kind of storm where he could barely free one hand, much less drink, and he's out there in the dark wearing tinted goggles. And you call this accidental drowning? Obviously you are no longer the hotshot diagnostician I remember."

"I'm a lot of things you don't remember."

"Right. And sloppy seems to be one of them."

He glared at her, then, in one of those split-second changes of mood she recalled as so characteristic of him, he said, "I'll call you in the morning. Give me the number where you're staying. And after that we're quits. Got it?"

"Right. Fine." She pulled out a card, wrote down Skip's phone number, slapped the card in Rosten's palm, and walked out. Once in the Jeep, she admitted she'd allowed her rage to run the interview. That could have cost her any number of vital findings. Not a contest, indeed. Who was she kidding? The last time she'd let passion rule her behavior was twelve years ago. She slammed into reverse and backed into the fog.

12

Hours after Kiernan O'Shaughnessy left, Maureen Brant's heart was still pounding. She'd been terrified that Kiernan would refuse the case.

She waited until dinner was over, then walked rapidly over to the studio, stuck a note on the inside of the door, closed and locked it behind her. Then she ran back across the yard before Garrett could react to the sound of the key turning.

She grabbed her purse, ran for the car, and drove as fast as she dared along the rock-strewn, rutted dirt road. By the time she got to Highway 1 she was tense and her back was filmed with sweat despite the evening chill.

She pulled into the Barrow's Grocery lot, ran inside, nodded at Jannie Barrow sitting behind the counter. Did the woman ever get up from that easy chair? Or had she been there so long the chair would move with her if she did?

Maureen could tell Jannie wanted to talk. Quickly, she picked up the phone and dialed. As she waited for the number to ring, she thought how odd it was that Jannie Barrow had had this public phone installed at the far side of the shop rather than close enough for her to eavesdrop on her customers.

"Olsen," the voice said.

"Skip, it's Maureen."

"So what d'you think of Kiernan O'Shaughnessy?"

"She's sharp, no-nonsense, just what I need. And, Skip, she's going to look at Delaney's body."

"Good," he said, relief clear in his voice. More relief, Maureen thought, than was appropriate in a man who had assured her there would be no problem getting his associate on the case. It made her uneasy. "Skip, she didn't say definitely she'd take the case, she just said she'd check the body."

"It's the best we could hope for. If anyone can find something suspicious on that corpse, Kiernan O'Shaughnessy can. Believe me, I had a couple of stiffs she worked on years ago. When it was over, she'd spent more time with her hands on liver, heart and kidneys than a French chef. She checked every single inch of skin of one guy under the magnifying glass—and he was a three-hundred pounder. The guys at the tox lab hated her; she must have doubled their work load."

"Skip, don't tell her about Delaney. Not until she's committed herself."

"Well—"

"Please, Skip. I can't take the chance. She has to take the case."

There was silence on the line, and then a groan. Olsen lowering himself into his chair. "Okay, Maureen. Once she's committed herself it won't matter. It'll be too late."

13

Kiernan drove through the Mission District, thinking of the morgue and of Marc Rosten. How could she ever have been attracted to that niggling, tight-assed . . . Her head throbbed, her hands were sweaty against the wheel. The strength of her passion for Rosten had not diminished. It just had a different name. But she couldn't allow herself to be as angry as she had been when she was—what? In love? Lustful? Or just caught up in the drama of it all?

She had to be realistic. Which, in this case, meant admitting that she wasn't doing such a hot job of separating the present from the past. She turned right sharply, tires squealing.

At least she was done with Rosten, wasn't she? No. She knew better than that. She wouldn't be done with him until she'd made him say why he'd left without a word. There had been no promises between them, no plans for marriage, a family, or even adjoining offices. Adjoining offices least of all. He'd been planning to go into family practice in those days, and would scarcely have wanted his waiting room next to her morgue. Would he have made plans? A moot point, since she'd insisted on none. She'd seen her parents tied to each other by habit and fear, too deadened by her sister's death to care about the small cage of their own lives. Her two goals as an adolescent had been to get out, and to uncover the truth about Moira's death. She did not intend to get sidetracked by any man. And Marc Rosten had known that. It wasn't a demand for commitment that had caused him to vanish.

The Mission District gave way to Noe Valley. Fog obscured the street signs, and she had to come to a dead stop before she could read them. Dixie Alley was an unlighted wooden staircase leading from Grand View to Upper Market Street, several hundred feet higher up. Skip Olsen lived at number 17, which turned out to be a two-room "in-law" apartment, converted from the basement recreation room of a house that faced Upper Market. She must have been directly above it when she had stopped to stare down at the light of San Francisco a couple hours earlier.

She followed a cement path behind the house to the back steps—actually the front steps of this unit—and climbed to a tiny wooden porch. Sliding-glass doors opened onto a pine-paneled living room–kitchenette, with a stone fireplace the size of Maureen and Garrett Brant's. It was a hunting-lodge hearth, one that suited the black leather couches and thick rya rug.

It was Skip Olsen himself, limping toward the glass doors, who looked out of place. He was, Kiernan realized, as out of place here as he had been leaning against a patrol car. He was too short, too sallow, too balding, too toddler-plump to fit the hearty masculinity of the room. And his walk, she noticed, was a list to the left and then a painful pull-up to the right, as if his hip socket sat too low on the leg. Had he been in an accident? Had a car crushed his ilium into his spine? Or was it a gunshot that had severed . . .

"So you're out of the permafreeze now," he said, using the term she recalled him perpetually assigning to the morgue refrigerator where they kept the "stiffs." She felt as if no time had passed since she last encountered his adolescent bravado.

"And you're off the police force?"

He motioned to a round maple table next to the sliding doors. Kiernan pulled out a chair and sat. "Almost a year now."

"What happened? I knew you hated the morgue, but I assumed you liked being a cop."

"Maybe." He dropped into the chair facing her.

The smells of liniment, old cooking oil and long-settled

dust rose as if to reassert possesion of the tiny dining area. "So why did you leave the force?" she insisted.

"I took a fall wrong, landed on my butt hard enough to sprain a ligament. It never healed. Driving around on patrol all day was too much for it."

"You're on disability?"

"Nah."

She slammed a hand down on the table; the table was sticky. "Olsen, I'm a doctor. Don't give me this whitewash. If you have sciatica, or sacroiliac dysfunction, or a ruptured intervertebral disc, you apply for disability. Now what really happened?" She was giving Olsen what she hadn't thrown at Rosten, she knew that.

"I have a client who may not be telling me everything, an acting chief coroner who definitely isn't, and now an ex-cop who can't even be straight about his own history."

"Okay, okay," he said, slumping forward. "Look, you probably read part of this in the newspaper: One of the guys was leaving, so a bunch of us got up a send-off party for him at the Flamingo Club. A gang of locals crashed it. There was a brawl. That's when I landed on my tail."

Still not the full story. "What was the entertainment at the party, Olsen? Coke? Strippers? Hookers?"

He squirmed, sandy hair falling over his round face. "Couple of G-stringers. One of the guys from vice knew them."

"And word got out to the papers?"

"Yeah, but I didn't call them."

Olsen's pale blue eyes shifted continuously, side to side, as if checking for a sneak attack.

"But the rest of the guys at the station figured you did, right?"

"Yeah. And when it came time for the disability hearing, the only guys who testified said I seemed horse-healthy to them. Back problems don't always show up on X-rays, you know."

She nodded. "And you're probably not getting much business thrown your way now that you're private."

Olsen snorted. "I'm lucky to walk past a puddle and not have a patrol car spray me."

Kiernan leaned back, watching as he squirmed in his chair. Clearly the man was in pain, that dull pain that grabs the inside of the flesh and squeezes until it plucks excruciatingly at the sciatic nerve the whole length of the leg. She had seen those squirming movements, that expression of fear, anger, resignation often enough when one of Tchernak's old football injuries kicked up. But there was something about Skip Olsen that precluded any sympathetic pats. He wasn't a man she wanted to touch.

"What about the press? How are your relations with them?"

"You don't believe me, do you?" He was halfway out of his seat.

"Of course not."

Glaring, he lowered himself back down. "Well, you're wrong. I didn't plan to expose the whole affair, I just wanted to get two guys I knew would hang around later with the G-stringers. How could I know there would be a brawl, and the press guys would hear the squeal and come racing out while everyone was still there?"

"Olsen," Kiernan said slowly, "I don't care about your relations with the force. But I do need to know where you stand. If I am going to work with you, maybe entrust my life to you, I need to have some basis to assume that you will . . . tell . . . me . . . the truth."

He looked directly at her. For the first time, his eyes were still. "I don't have the luxury of tossing aside trust, not any more. I'm at rock bottom."

She leaned back. Did she believe his story, his *last* story? More than she would have expected. But not enough to bet her skin on it.

"Okay, Olsen, tell me about the Garrett Brant case. You're the expert."

"Yeah," he said, the adolescent belligerence gone, "the expert by default. No one else gave a shit. Just another hit-and-run to them."

"And to you, it was . . . ?"

"Someone left the guy to die there. It was June, coldest June in a decade. San Francisco summer. You know what it's like by the Great Highway, out there by the beach: icy cold, winds shredding flags on flagpoles. Sand could have blown over him in half an hour."

"How was he found?"

Olsen snorted. "Some lunatic jogger out to freeze his balls off."

Kiernan pictured the wind blowing hard across the beach, up the dunes. "The hairs that were stuck in the blood on Brant's face, how come they didn't get blown away?"

"Luck. Just blind luck." Olsen rested an arm on the back of his straight chair. "Brant was wearing a hood. It shielded him from the wind; that, and the dune beside him. Luck."

"And you were on patrol?"

"Yeah, I was hauling my bum butt out from behind the wheel fifty times a day. Cold and damp are hell on a bad back. Nothing ever dries out there on Great Highway. When I first saw Brant I thought he'd be DOA. I've seen a lot. On the force nine years. But that, it got to me. Then when I found the hairs and got the okay to run them, I thought I'd get the sucker who left him there."

"And you didn't find a match until now?"

"Yeah, ironic isn't it? I bugged 'em to run them every time they closed a hit-and-run, which, as you can guess, is not like every Tuesday."

"And when you found the match, what'd you do?"

"What could I do? I'm lamed out now."

Kiernan laughed. "Come on, you don't expect me to believe you got that bombshell and did nothing more than sit here next to your sliding-glass windows and watch the sun come up in Oakland."

He shrugged.

Kiernan stood up.

"I've driven from San Diego to Big Sur and Big Sur to the

city today, and then visited Delaney's corpse. My patience was low an hour ago. What there was left, you've killed. So either you tell me what you got me out here to talk about, or I pack it in!"

Olson gazed down at his hands. "Okay, so I did see the Matucci woman."

"You *saw* Robin Matucci? I thought she was dead, or at least missing by the time you got the DNA results."

He stared down at the sticky tabletop. "Well, yeah, I suppose she was. I guess I didn't give you the chronology straight."

"Olsen!"

"Well, see," he went on quickly, "like I said there are a whole lot more red convertibles in the city than there's any reason for. Whole lot more people who want to freeze their brains off driving. No cop would ever track them all down. But, like I said, I was lamed out. But I'd nothing else to do, so I got a friend at Motor Vehicle to run me a list, and I got hold of every single car on the list. Then when *Early Bird* went down and they got the hair—"

"So that's how come you got the results so fast—you could just check hers against what you found on Brant's body."

He nodded. "Called in what's probably my last debt on it, too."

"Tell me about Robin Matucci. And this time, Olsen, tell me everything."

A smile slithered across Olsen's round face. "One knock-out of a lady. Real beauty. Long red hair, a set of knockers like . . . Not a body you'd kick out of bed, if you know what I mean? First time I saw her she was docking, the wind was flapping that hair, pressing her shirt tight against . . . She was bringing back a load of geezers." He flicked a thumbnail against a finger. "Suppose you think that's what I am now."

"I don't think anything," she said, trying to hide her frustration. For someone with no bedside manner, this was a trying conversation.

"You want to know about Matucci, you're talking to the

right guy. I've done a background on her that'd make a D.A. kiss my butt." Kiernan expected him to reach under the table and produce a fat manila file. But he merely leaned back, rested his forearms on the table. "Robin Regina Matucci, age twenty-eight, born here in the city. Father ran an antique shop of sorts south of Market. Gentrified from 'collectibles' to 'antiques,' like the district's changed."

"Past tense?"

"Yeah, went paws up a year ago. Mugged, fell and cracked his head on a parking meter. Artery burst, and it's doggie heaven."

"And Robin inherited his shop?"

Olsen laughed. "No storybook ending. She didn't inherit nothing. Unless you call spending days helping her mother clean out the junk something. No, all Robin got from that shop was the need to escape, an itch for the sea. And a fleet load of ambition. I talked to every guy on the pier and they all say the same thing: Robin Matucci was one damned smart woman. Some say nice, some call her a good captain, some just say she knew which way the waves were breaking."

Kiernan nodded. She could sympathize only too well with Robin Matucci's reaction to childhood confinement. "And the customers, the guys who paid for the day charter?"

"To them she was a queen. She had good coffee on board, a good surface to stand on so they weren't falling all over the place, and best of all, every single one said nobody could find fish like Robin Matucci." He held up a hand. "Now, soon as I tell you, you'll catch on here. There's fish hiding out all over the Pacific. According to the captains, there's stuff you can watch for, radio chatter you can try to second-guess, but even if you do everything right you can still come up empty. Or you can motor out blind and hit a school of salmon. So you got the captains trying to second-guess the elements, and the passengers trying to second-guess the captains. The regulars decide a captain's lucky, and they follow. Some of these regulars fish three or four days a week. They're experts on rating the boats. And to a one, they swear Robin was the best."

"How'd she do it?"

"No one knows. Believe me, I asked."

"She owned the boat."

"Right."

With satisfaction, Kiernan noted the surprise in Olsen's voice. Suspicion that she might already have done some research would move him to truth a lot faster than any cajolery. "Boats cost a couple hundred thou. How'd Robin Matucci come by that?"

"A bank loan. And a bunch of summers in Alaska, working the fishing camps and the charters. You can make a bundle up there if you know what you're doing, and you're working so damned hard you don't have the energy to spend it, even if you're close enough to someplace that'll sell you stuff."

"Alaska. When?"

"Three, four, five years ago."

When Garrett Brant was there. But Alaska was a big place. "Do you have a Social Security printout on her?"

He nodded. But he didn't produce it.

He was waiting to deal. But it wasn't time for that yet. It was time to get what was free. "What did Robin Matucci say about the hit-and-run?"

"Now that was interesting," Olsen said, putting his elbows on the table. The movement made him wince, and he tightened the shoulder on the side of his injured hip. "The first time I ask, she denies knowing about it, but I was a cop long enough to spot a liar. So I go back, see. This time she 'accidentally' dumps a bucket of fish water on me. Not smart, because that really tells me I'm on the right track. So I go back the next day. And she pushes straight past me. Did I mention the woman's six feet tall?"

"Six feet?"

"Well, maybe five nine or ten. But she's strong. You don't captain a boat without muscles."

"So what's so interesting about her avoiding you?"

"That last time—it was right before she disappeared—she said, 'Why are you busting your butt about this, the statute's run out?' "

Kiernan nodded. "Interesting indeed."

Olsen beamed. "Yeah. She might've known the date of the hit-and-run. I might've thrown that in myself. But the length of a specific statute of limitations, how many people know that? How many civilians even know which one would apply to a crime like that, right?"

"Right," Kiernan said, extending a hand for him to shake. "And then she and Delaney go overboard."

"Or Delaney goes overboard."

"This your version, or does it come from the guys on the dock?" she asked.

"Mine alone." Olsen glanced through his glass doors at the fog. "Delaney washed up on the Farallons. What was left of the boat washed up south of the city. We don't know where Robin Matucci went over. Could be she jumped out and swam to shore."

"But the fishermen don't think so?"

" 'Cording to them they don't think anything. Maybe that's 'cause they're smarter than me."

Purposely ignoring his tacit demand for sympathy, Kiernan waited. God, why couldn't the man grow up?

"When I came back from asking around the last time, my windshield was bashed in. Slivers of glass all over the driver's seat. *Just* the driver's seat. I know what a sliver of glass did to Brant. So, with a rare show of smarts, I figure I got enough to worry about with this hip, without losing my brain besides. It's making me crazy to get this far and have to drop it, but that's what I got to do."

"And you're hoping I'll do the legwork?"

"Nah. I'm not looking for gifts. What I told you tonight, it's a loss leader."

Kiernan nodded. "Who's the best guy on the dock to tackle?"

He grinned. "What'd your *friend* Marc Rosten tell you about Delaney?"

"Grow up, Olsen. I am too tired and grumpy to deal with an adolescent."

"I'm asking about Delaney," he said archly.

She sighed. "Bad eyes and drunk."

Olsen smiled. "On the dock, talk to Ben Pedersen on *Nelda's Dream*. But watch out for him. Looks like a teddy bear. Could be a grizzly. He'll tell you a lot, but what he won't say is that he picked up a bundle of business after Matucci went over." He paused and waited to catch her eye. "Here's one thing he won't be anxious to tell you: He's in hock up to the gills."

14

Kiernan checked into a motel off Lombard Street, halfway between Olsen's and Fisherman's Wharf. She called Tchernak, said good night to Ezra, and set her alarm for 4:00 A.M.

At ten to five she parked across the street from Fisherman's Wharf. Before the hum of the motor died out, fog coated the windshield. As she hurried toward the wharf the wind iced her face. Streetlights offered a muted glow too weak to make it to the ground.

The wharf, one of the area's main tourist attractions, was no bigger than a city block. It was surrounded on four sides by souvenir shops, restaurants, and storage warehouses. A single narrow lane of water was all that connected it to the Bay. Although it was a working dock, it was so wedged in by pretentious honky-tonk that it looked fake and shoddy itself. Kiernan walked behind the row of restaurants that formed the connecting line of its reversed E shape, and stood outside the pale circle of light near the dock's center. A sea lion barked, demanding an early breakfast. She recalled complaints about sea lions who'd discovered the good life—the pro-lion newsmen had had a lot of fun with them. There had been complaints about everything here, including the restaurants, one of which—the Crab Cage Café—had gone so far as to attach a fake plywood crab cage to its roof. It was considered a fitting symbol of the wharf's pervasive tawdriness.

The cold wind cut through her sweater. The boats were half hidden in fog, but she could smell coffee, hear the slap of rubber boots against planking, and the splash of water being rinsed off decks. She made her way along the pier trying to see the names of the boats in the dim light, and finally spotted *Nelda's Dream*. It was the size of an eighteen-wheeler. The front two-thirds of it were enclosed. Kiernan walked out onto the slip. The cabin light was on, and through the mist-shrouded windows, she could make out a man looking at a clipboard.

"Ben?" she called. "Ben Pedersen?"

"Yeah. Who're you?"

"Kiernan O'Shaughnessy. I just need a few minutes of your time. To ask a couple of questions."

"I've got paying customers who'll be getting here in twenty minutes." He turned. In the light the bearlike form looked more like a grizzly than a teddy. The lines on his weathered face suggested snap decisions and little tolerance. And he was nearly the size of Tchernak.

"Being up at this hour is more painful for me than it is for you, believe me."

"You another reporter nosing around about Robin Matucci?"

"Private Investigator. It'll take you less time to talk to me than decide if you can be bothered. Can I come aboard?"

He tapped a meaty hand on the rail, considering. "Okay. Ten minutes. No more. Step's are back there," he said pointing toward the dock.

Kiernan climbed the three-step wedge in place next to the boat. Once aboard, the boat seemed smaller. The decking, which she had pictured as polished teak, was covered with rough gray paint, a non-skid surface. Pedersen motioned her forward, inside a room that resembled a small diner, with four booths and Formica tables. Farther forward was the room with the steering wheel and radio, was that the wheelhouse? Or the cabin? Or, dammit, was *this* the cabin?

Without asking, Pedersen poured a second mug of coffee, held it out to her and sat in the nearest booth.

"Thanks." She slid in across from him.

"Private eye, huh? The insurance company trying to squeeze out of paying? You working for them?"

"No. I'm no fan of bureaucracies. I get up at four in the morning so I can work for myself."

Pedersen took a swallow of coffee. He looked only slightly less suspicious.

On the radio a tenor voice said, "Probably be socked in all day. Whaddya think, Deke?"

Pedersen was watching her, but his head was cocked toward the radio. She said, "I heard Robin Matucci was the most successful captain on the wharf."

"Who told you that?"

Kiernan smiled. "Someone who didn't like her. So I paid attention. Why do you think she attracted so many customers?"

"Because her people caught fish, that's why! That's the name of the game." He rapped his fingers on the table. "She always had the best equipment, the latest in everything. Whatever it took, Robin would do it. She deserved her success," he said, bitterly.

For a man in hock "up to the gills," that bitterness wasn't hard to understand. Was this the time to challenge Pedersen about that? From the dock voices grumbled, muffled by the fog.

The voices on the radio cut in on each other. "What about up toward Bodega?"

"Windward of the Farallons?"

No, keep the finance question as an ace in the hole. "What was Robin doing out in such a bad storm?"

"She left the day before. The storm hadn't started then. It wasn't supposed to get that bad."

"So it doesn't surprise you that she could have drowned?"

"No. Not going out in a storm like that," he said angrily, but for the first time looked pained.

An abandoned lover or would-be lover? That threw a new light on Pedersen. "Would it surprise you if Robin didn't drown?"

He lifted his coffee mug, but didn't drink. And when he set it down it vibrated against the Formica. "Don't you think I've thought of that, wished for it, changed the weather in my head? Suppose it'd cleared instead of getting worse? What if the rain had started Monday morning instead of Monday night? Then maybe she wouldn't have gone. What if someone picked her up on their way to Hawaii? Dammit, do you think there's a possibility that you can come up with what I haven't already squeezed dry?" He lifted the mug with both hands and gulped down coffee. "She had a Zodiac, a rubber dingy, and survival suits on board. But a Zodiac would be useless in a storm and you don't swim in from the Farallons."

"We only know he went over near the Farallons. What makes you think *she* did?"

"She didn't have time to call for help. No one heard a call."

Kiernan raised a palm. "No, what we know is that she didn't call for help, not necessarily that she couldn't. Why would Delaney's body be on the Farallons, the boat have washed ashore south of the city and Robin Matucci's body be nowhere around?"

He banged the mug down. Coffee spilled in all directions. "Because Delaney was a drunk. Jesus! I could have told her that. Yeah, he swore he'd been dry for years. And then what do

I hear but that the guy's got enough liquor in him for New Year's Eve. If he'd stayed sober, maybe they'd both still be alive." He reached behind him for a rag.

"Why'd Robin hire him? Shouldn't she have known better?"

"Yeah, well," he said, mopping up the coffee, "Robin was sharp as they come dealing with city inspectors, and suppliers. She could scotch a fight on board *Early Bird* before the second guy realized he was being baited. But, damn, she was one pushover for half-assed deckhands." He flung the sopping rag into the sink behind him.

"How come?"

"Got me," he mumbled, his voice unsteady. "You can work with a bad deckhand, but it makes your job twice as hard. The worst deckhands are the ones who can't deal with people. They make their money in tips, so that kind don't last. And that wasn't the problem with Robin's guys. They were . . ." He fingered his beard. "Well, deckhand is not a career position. The biggest problem is guys who don't show up one morning and leave you shorthanded. The guys Robin took on, they couldn't get the hang of things. She used to laugh about it. Said when they were baiting a hook they were working to capacity."

"And was Delaney like that?"

Pedersen spun his mug around thoughtfully. "No, he wasn't dumb. Unless you call getting so drunk you can't stand on deck dumb. Dead dumb. And he never did that till that last day. There was no way she could have known he'd fall apart like that. No way any of us could have warned her. No one on the dock ever saw him drunk."

"How long had he worked for her?"

"I don't know. A month maybe."

"Did he work for anyone else?"

"No. Robin was the top of the heap."

The sea lion had moved closer, barking impatiently. On the dock more voices called back and forth, buckets and chains clanked more insistently. Feet slapped the ladder beside the boat and a lanky man stepped on board, hauling two buckets after him. Pedersen glanced at him, then at his watch. To Kiernan, he said, "I have to get moving. But look, if there's anything funny about Robin's death, I want to know."

Kiernan nodded. "And, I can take it, you'll help me however you can?"

"Right."

"Okay, who was her closest friend?"

"Girlfriends? Not many women here. Sometimes her sister'd meet her across the street, but she never came on the dock, just waited over there. Then they'd go get Robin's car and drive off in that red car with their red hair flowing out behind them." He swallowed hard.

"Where does this sister live?"

"Don't know. Never met her. For some reason Robin never wanted to talk about her."

Odd, Kiernan thought, but there was no time to press him for speculation. "What about friends here, on the dock?"

"Everyone liked Robin. She was everyone's friend."

"Including the deckhands?" Kiernan asked skeptically. Nobody is everyone's friend.

"Oh, yeah. She started as a hand herself. It's not easy for a woman. Back-breaking work, you leave here at six. You've got guys tanked up by the middle of the day. If they don't catch anything, they're hauling off at their neighbor. If they do, they're celebrating by grabbing ass. Keeps a woman deckhand on her toes." He laughed. "Robin told me that was the joy of being captain, when things got bad she had the wheelhouse to keep her butt in."

The lanky man stuck his head in the cabin. "I got three quarters worth of bait. That okay?"

Pedersen looked at his clipboard. "Plenty."

"Time to find Harpoon, huh?"

"Time to check the damn poles. Go on," he snapped.

The deckhand shrugged off Pedersen's anger and stomped

to the stern. Pedersen turned back to Kiernan. "Okay, detective, your ten minutes are up."

Kiernan downed the dregs of her coffee. What was the significance of this particular Harpoon, and why had the mention of it gotten to Pedersen? A look at him told her she'd fare no better than the deckhand with that line of questioning. Instead, she said, "But if Robin was as careful as you say, why didn't she hire more than one deckhand?"

"*Early Bird* was smaller than the *Dream*. A helluva lot more elegant. Going out in *Early Bird* was like sitting in the front parlor. Robin took corporate groups, maybe only five or six guys. Corporation pays as much as twenty guys do. Lot less work. Look, I've got to—"

"Okay." Kiernan stood up. "You inherited some of the corporate groups. Who're the contact people?"

He wasn't prepared for that, she could tell. It was a moment before he said, "I can't give out their names."

"Ben, you said you'd help me however you could. You cared about Robin."

He glanced toward the dock and back. "Okay, I'll check. Call me tonight."

"Come on. You can remember one or two."

"I'd rather check and be accurate."

"Ben. When someone dies suspiciously, the trail gets cold real fast. You can't afford to have me sitting around doing nothing all day today while the trail freezes. Just do the best you can. Give me the names you remember."

A woman in a beaked cap clambered aboard, pole in one hand, a red and white hamper weighing down the other.

"Hey, Teresa. Good to see you," Pedersen said, suddenly more jovial-sounding than she could have imagined.

"Ben." Eyeing Kiernan, she said, "This your new lady?"

"No, hon. She's just leaving. And the only lady in my life is Nelda here." He patted the boat.

Kiernan didn't move. "Names?"

"Okay," he muttered. "Dwyer Cummings."

15

So Dwyer Cummings had been a frequent passenger of Robin's. And now of Ben Pedersen's. Pedersen might be sorry Robin was gone, but it sure hadn't inhibited his business sense. Pedersen, Kiernan thought, was a man she'd trust a lot more in the ocean steering a boat than here on shore.

Dwyer Cummings, spokesman for Energy Producers' Group. From what she'd heard of Cummings in the radio debate with Jessica Leporek she could picture him, leaning back in one of those swivel chairs in the rear of a boat, pole in the holder, beer in hand, a grin on his sunburned face as he explained to the guy next to him that offshore drilling platforms made great habitats for fish. No wonder Ben Pedersen hadn't had a sign supporting the initiative in his boat. If Pedersen was in financial trouble, he wouldn't be about to offend a source of income like Cummings.

Kiernan walked back to the restaurant end of the dock and looked wistfully at the dark windows. Why couldn't just one of those places be open? Eating eggs, ham, muffins, home fries, and keeping surveillance on the dock at the same time—that was the right way to investigate. Sighing, she pulled her jacket tighter and settled in to watch one of the still-unemployed deckhands as he made his rounds from boat to boat.

The crowd around Pedersen's boat had moved on board. He had indeed benefited from Robin's absence, Kiernan thought. But had it been enough to pull him out of his financial hole?

By six-fifteen, the sea lion had been joined by two others,

and the barking sounded like a kennel at feeding time. The jobless deckhand—Zack, she'd heard him called—ambled toward the sidewalk, hands dug deep into the pockets of his too-large jeans. There was an uncertainty to his step, not quite a shuffle, which, if Kiernan hadn't known better, she would have sworn came from a couple of days on a rolling boat.

"No luck, Zack?" she asked.

He shrugged. Like his jeans, his windbreaker was too large. A gust of wind caught the faded blue fabric and it flapped against his narrow ribs. For a moment it looked as if he'd be blown off the dock. "It's a long haul back to my room," was all he said.

Kiernan smiled. This was a man ready to deal. "Did you know Robin Matucci?"

"*Early Bird*? The one who went under? Sure."

"Tell me about her over breakfast."

"And a ride back to my room?"

"Done. Come on."

The fancy restaurants may have been still closed, but a tourist mecca was not without its advantages—plenty of motels with 24-hour restaurants or coffee shops. The nearest was two blocks away.

As Kiernan walked in, she noticed almost automatically that there were no closed phone booths. The blatantly fake "nautical" decor looked as out of place as the people in the room—mostly white-clad tourists who were used to humid mornings in Cape Girardeau, Missouri, or warm nights in Lakewood, New Jersey, folks from normal climates who hadn't believed the warnings they'd got about the chill morning fog in San Francisco. Now they sat shivering in shorts and thin tennis sweaters. In contrast to their crisp, clean whiteness, Zack looked like a sack of garbage left behind by the last shift. His frayed wool cap and salt-stained windbreaker seemed ridiculously out of place behind the lime-green tablecloth and pink napkins.

"I've traveled enough to know the safest bet for breakfast in places like this," Kiernan told him, glancing at the menu. "Eggs scrambled medium—it's hard to screw that up, but get lots of ketchup in case they do; wheat toast and plenty of jelly. Lots of coffee, regardless of what it tastes like."

"Bacon?"

"Right, bacon or ham." She smiled. "Never order sausage if you haven't counted the strays."

"How about a beer?"

What he did to his liver wasn't her business. Who was she to . . . But she knew no amount of arguing could erase the memory of all the cirrhotic livers she'd seen in bodies too young to be dead. "The offer was breakfast."

"I have beer with breakfast."

"Don't wheedle. You want breakfast and the ride, or not?"

He scowled. His skin wasn't puffy, but he had the look of old, weather-exposed wood—gray and sere, all resilience gone, held up by the support posts of familiarity.

When they'd ordered, she said, "So tell me about Robin Matucci. You ever work for her?"

"No."

"Ever try?"

"Yeah," he muttered, mostly to his napkin.

"Why?"

"Pay."

"Why didn't you get on?"

He shrugged. Clearly he was going to give as little as possible in return for his nonalcoholic meal. His face tightened in anger, but Kiernan couldn't read him well enough to guess whether it was a reaction to her continued questions, or something else. Zack was one of those sources who needed to be coddled. But "bedside manner" had never been her strong point. She'd have to make some effort, though. "Robin had a reputation for hiring deckhands who weren't too bright."

Zack laughed. "Not too bright, that's a good one."

"But why, Zack?"

"She had to be the boss. She was real nice around the

dock. But on *Early Bird* she couldn't stand a guy who could bait a hook without her permission."

The food arrived. Zack glared down at it. Ignoring him, Kiernan mixed the bacon in with the eggs, lathered the jelly on the toast and dug in. After Tchernak's breakfasts all others huddled together in mediocrity, but that didn't keep her from downing them. When she looked up, halfway through, Zack had finished the bacon and toast. His face looked less gray, and the fearful squint of his eyes had relaxed.

Kiernan put down her fork. "Tell me about Carlos Delaney. Was he as dumb as Robin liked?"

"No way. Delaney was a bright guy. I'll tell you how bright he was." Zack leaned forward conspiratorily. "He sized her up real quick. And she probably never caught on."

"How'd you catch on?"

Zack grinned, exposing a space where a left lateral incisor had once been. "His questions. He may have got her number—he had to do that if he planned to keep his job—but he didn't bother to get mine. He figured just what you did, that Zack's an old alky with slosh for brains, right?" He stared at her until she nodded and smiled. "He used me like a textbook. Where was this on the boat, where's the best place to keep that? Asked me how the loran worked, for Chrissakes. Didn't even know about triangular navigation." He laughed. "He even asked me what a harpoon was."

Harpoon. That was the second time that word had come up this morning.

"Do you use harpoons with party-boat fishing?"

Zack laughed louder, a surprisingly raw sound. At the table behind him a couple turned to stare, then eyed each other as if to say, "Only in San Francisco." Oblivious, he said to Kiernan, "Jeez, you're no Einstein either. If we gave harpoons to some of the geezers we take out, they'd be over the side with them."

"So why did Carlos ask?"

Zack leaned across the table. "He didn't say."

"But you figured it out?" Kiernan prompted.

"Oh yeah. He asked me three times. Probably thought I wouldn't remember. Robin made calls to 'Harpoon' on the ship-to-shore radio. Delaney thought it was a place, like a lighthouse or a cove, or maybe it had some kind of code meaning."

"Why'd he think that?"

"I don't know. Delaney wasn't a big talker."

Maybe he just hadn't talked to Zack. "Where'd he live?"

"He spent a week at the Neptune. A lot of us stay there. But that was a month and a half ago. Then he moved. I don't know where."

"Why did he move, Zack?"

He shrugged. "Maybe he learned all he wanted to know about us by then."

Kiernan signaled for the check, paid it, stopped in the bathroom—another rule of the investigator: never pass up an indoor privy—and met Zack at the Jeep. It was light now, the sun had risen high enough to expose the lid of gray over the city.

She started the Jeep and pulled into traffic. "Zack, what do you think of Ben Pedersen?"

"It'd take a lot more than a meal to make me rat on Ben. Ben's father and grandfather fished from the wharf. Ben's been on boats since he was a kid. He's more 'wharf' than that bastardized bunch of boards they've got left there is. The wharf used to be a working dock; used to be home to the fishing fleet. No more. Only enough boats left to con the tourists into thinking it's real. Don't you go saying nothing against Ben. He'd give up his balls before he'd let anything happen to the *Dream*."

"What would he have given up for Robin Matucci?"

For the first time Zack looked surprised. "He tell you about him and Robin?"

"No way else I'd know. Way it sounded," Kiernan said, embellishing her suspicions, "he was crazy about her, but maybe she wasn't so sure."

"She coulda done a lot worse than a guy like Ben Pedersen. With him, she'd never have had to worry. He'd have done anything for the boat."

The light turned yellow. She stepped on the gas and pulled hard on the wheel, cutting off a sports car revving up to jump the light. Good thing Tchernak couldn't see this. "You won't buy the guy a beer because you don't want him to die of cirrhosis," Tchernak would be saying. "Never occurs to you people die in crashes?" She looked at Zack, but if he had any qualms he was concealing them. "Zack, did you ever hear Robin talking to her sister?"

He sat up. "She didn't have a sister."

"The red-haired woman who met her at the wharf from time to time?"

"That wasn't her sister," he said as if announcing a herring wasn't a salmon.

"Who was she then?"

"Pull over here. On the right. Behind that truck."

"Do you know who she was?"

"Yeah. But that's not part of breakfast."

"Fair enough. How much?"

"Hundred."

"A hundred! No way, unless the redhead was Dan Quayle in drag."

"Okay, seventy-five."

She extricated two twenties and held them out.

"Jessica Leporek."

"Jessica Leporek, the head of the Initiative Campaign here? *She* was Robin's friend?"

But Zack had already snatched the bills and left.

"Jessica Leporek," Kiernan said to Brad Tchernak, "was Robin's friend."

"*Our* Jessica Leporek, head of the initiative drive in San Francisco?" Tchernak whistled.

Ezra howled.

"Then Robin Matucci must have supported the initiative. From everything I hear around headquarters down here, the initiative is Jessica's whole life. She wouldn't waste her time with someone who isn't for it. And, frankly, I don't think anyone who wasn't a fanatic could put up with her."

"Would you like to guess who one of Robin's main passengers was?" Kiernan leaned back and pictured Tchernak at the other end of the line, his tan, beautifully muscled chest half visible over the blankets he'd never admit he was still under at seven-thirty in the morning. But she could interpret Ezra's whines in the background.

"Who?"

"Dwyer Cummings."

Tchernak whistled again. Ezra howled louder. "Did Jessica know that?"

"I'll ask her as soon as I see her. She's not at the office yet."

Ezra whined.

Kiernan pictured Ezra, his wiry muzzle resting anxiously on Tchernak's bare arm, his skinny gray tail wagging hopefully. She could hear canine toenails scraping the floor, then a more distant whine, faint enough to mean Ezra had crossed the room and was waiting at the door. "Tchernak, you clod, you haven't taken him for his run yet, have you?"

Ezra whined louder. He had already had his customary phone "talk" with Kiernan.

Turning back to the question that had been gnawing at her, she said, "Robin Matucci's smart enough to make herself the most successful captain at the wharf. But she made a point of hiring the dumbest deckhands, and she played both sides on Prop. Thirty-Seven. What was she up to?"

"Got me. But I'd be willing to bet, if Jessica found out about Dwyer Cummings, Robin would have heard about it. And so would everyone within a hundred yards of the dock."

"Get the word on both of them. And run background checks on the following: Ben Pedersen, Skip Olsen—"

"Skip Olsen? Hey, what's going on up there? Can't you trust even him?"

"Probably. This is just insurance."

She hesitated so long Tchernak said, "And?"

"And while you're at it, get one on Marc Rosten, M.D."

Tchernak guffawed. "The old boyfriend. Never split from a private eye, huh?"

Kiernan started to protest, realized there was no good protest, and said, "I'll call you back at noon."

"Hey, remember. No fenestration. Stay out of other people's windows."

"Tchernak, nagging is such an unattractive quality in a servant."

16

Kiernan parked on Upper Market Street, at the top of the Dixie Alley staircase, and walked down the twenty or so steps to number 17.

Skip Olsen was standing on the narrow deck outside his door, staring out at the panorama of Oakland and Berkeley across the Bay. He was wearing a red-and-gold Forty-niners' sweatshirt: Back-to-Back Superbowls XXIII-XXIV. Glints of sun broke through the fog, highlighting his cheekbones. For a moment Kiernan felt she was looking at a much younger man—a Skip Olsen who was angular, healthy, and almost handsome, she realized with a start.

"Kiernan," he said as she opened the gate, "you don't waste any time."

"I don't have any time. I've been up since four."

"Come in. Coffee?"

"Unless you've got straight adrenaline," she said, following him through the sliding glass doors to the dining area.

"Cream?" he asked, already pouring. He handed her the cup.

She took a swallow, trying hard not to scowl in disgust. She was a coffee snob, and she knew it. It was one of her few food snobberies that predated Tchernak. Many more had been added since he'd taken over her kitchen, but none equaled her distaste for weak coffee.

"Doctor told me to cut it out," Olsen said, "but I figure the vices will still be there when I get around to curing them. So what've you got to report?"

Kiernan laughed. A little jockeying for control? "You first."

"Okay. Maureen Brant just got off the horn."

"This early? I arranged to call her at ten."

Olsen shrugged and took a swallow of coffee. "She couldn't wait. Called the minute the grocery opened."

"What'd she say?"

"The obvious. She wants to know if you'll take the case. I told her I thought so. Right?"

"As it happens, you *were* right. But I might have found something at the wharf that would have made me decide differently. Don't presume for me, okay?"

"Sor-*ry*," he said, in an adolescent cadence that negated the apology.

"Is Maureen waiting at the store for me to call?"

"Yeah."

"I'll get back to her before I leave." Sliding into the chair across from him, she told him what she'd learned.

Olsen leaned forward eagerly, settling forearms on the table, never taking his eyes from Kiernan's face. "Dwyer Cummings, huh? Very interesting."

"What do you know about him?"

"Only what I read in the paper and the business magazines.

I've got a lot of time to read. I figured I'm not going to get any boost from having been a cop, but I grew up in the city. I dare you to find anyone who knows San Francisco better than me."

"So, Skip," Kiernan said impatiently, "what is it you know about Dwyer Cummings?"

"Dwyer Cummings is probably in his late forties. Big, blond, football-hero type," he said with undisguised scorn. "Career oilman, went from engineering to administration. Been on the pipeline. Now he's spokesman for the Energy Producers' Group."

"What's that?"

"PR wing of the oil companies, all the ones that deal in the state. They've got professional PR people; what Cummings does is speak on technical issues with the authority of someone who's been an engineer in the drilling areas. He's the point man battling this initiative business." Olsen laughed decisively.

Kiernan raised an eyebrow.

"Well, Dwyer Cummings does have a kind of folksy charm, intelligent folksiness. He's a damned good speaker, well-informed. But don't let his charm snow you. The word in the industry is that Cummings was involved in something no one is willing to talk about."

"Specifically?" Kiernan said, surprised at the edge to her voice.

Olsen caught it too. He picked up his cup, but continued to stare belligerently as he drank. Then he said, "Best I can tell you is that something happened in Alaska and then Cummings was sent down here."

"Sent down here to be spokesman for an initiative that could be devastating to the oil industry, and not only in California? Environmentalists in every coastal state are watching Prop. Thirty-Seven. So whatever Cummings was involved in up there, it couldn't be important enough to endanger the 'No' on the Thirty-Seven campaign."

"I said I didn't know what it was yet."

"Okay. Maybe it's nothing. Cummings seems pretty peripheral to Delaney's death, and even more so to Garrett Brant's accident. But we've got so little we're going to need everything."

"I'm working on it. Stuff like this, it's not info you get off the wires. For this you need to cozy up to one of his rivals."

"Cozy away," Kiernan said with a smile, realizing as she said it that this was exactly the kind of work that would appeal to Olsen. "Okay, what have you heard about Ben Pedersen and Robin Matucci?"

Olsen leaned forward, eyes widening. "As a twosome?"

Clearly, Kiernan thought, this is a man who loves the whispered word. "Sense I got from Pedersen is he would have liked that."

Olsen nodded knowingly. "Could be. I didn't hear anything when I was down there. Saw the two of them together once, but nothing lovey-dovey going on. You want my opinion, it's all in Pedersen's head. Understandable, set of knockers like that. If he was banging her, there wasn't any reason to keep it a secret."

"None we know of," Kiernan said irritably. Working with Olsen was a big mistake. The man was driving her crazy. "I need someone undercover on the dock," she said, shaking off her irritation. "Maybe nothing more to be got there, but then again . . . You know anyone?"

"Let me think. My contacts aren't too good yet. It's not the best way"—Olsen fingered his cup thoughtfully—"but I guess I'll have to do it myself."

Kiernan stood up. "Skip, you've already been spotted."

"I'll go after the boats leave. Or I'll catch the deckhands off the dock."

"They've already broken your windshield."

"Guess I'll just have to be more careful."

"No." Kiernan put a hand on his shoulder. "This is my case. I decide who does what. And I'm telling you, this isn't a wise plan."

Olsen shook off her hand.

"I'm serious, Skip. Either you work on my case my way, or we don't work together. Got it?"

It was a moment before he grunted out what she took to be a yes.

Kiernan smiled. "Good. 'Harpoon' is something or someone Robin called on the ship-to-shore radio. Delaney asked Zack, the deckhand, about it. Zack figured Delaney thought it was a place. Pedersen's deckhand said something like 'time to find Harpoon' as they got ready to leave, and Pedersen nearly took his head off. See what you can find."

Olsen grinned, showing square yellowish teeth. "If it's there, I'll find it. Come this way." He limped into the bedroom.

All Kiernan had seen of this room the previous day was the end of the bed. What she had missed were three walls covered with bookshelves, one of them entirely filled with phone books and directories. A computer, two phones, Xerox, and fax were lined up on a counter, while a clothesline strung above them held three streamers of drying negatives.

Kiernan laughed. "I hope you didn't have all this here to shake free during the earthquake. You'd have been so far under that they'd have sealed the house and left it, like in Pompeii."

"It was here, or most of it. Took me the better part of a day to get everything back in place. And San Jose and Eureka"—he pointed to two phone books—"took it hard."

"When can you find me Harpoon?"

He glanced at his watch. "It's almost nine now. Noon, no problem. Depending on what else you need and how fast."

"My office is getting background on the principals. But that'll only be current to last month. I'll probably need you to search records downtown."

"I could have done the background for you."

"You didn't tell me. Last night you were only an ex-cop. This morning you're Sherlock Holmes on line."

He shrugged. "What's an out-to-pasture cop to do?"

She nodded, pleased not to have to explain that she didn't farm out work if she could help it, particularly not to a man who hadn't been completely honest. On the other hand, some things had to be farmed. "Can you get me a list of Robin Matucci's and Delaney's addresses, and their heirs? Also their lawyers. Robin's not married, right?"

"Not unless it was to *Early Bird*."

"Then maybe that one will be easy." She glanced out the window over his bed. A slice of sun glistened on the feathery leaves of a jacaranda tree, cut a swath across the steep ivy-covered hillside and disappeared. Olsen was still at the windowless inside wall, straightening his out-of-town directories, which, Kiernan noted, were in neither alphabetical nor geographical order.

She leaned against the doorjamb. "What do you know about Jessica Leporek?"

"Married a pile of money," Olsen said, turning around and resting his hips against the edge of the desk. "Been a volunteer with Bay Watch and the Marine Mammal center, a docent at the Asian Art Museum, and probably worked with a couple other environmental groups. She's fanatic about the antidrilling initiative. No one questions her sincerity. She'd cut off her right leg to get this thing passed. But . . ." There was a different quality to Olsen's speech now, none of the condescension he'd shown when discussing Cummings.

To just what kind of person would Olsen feel kinship? Kiernan wondered. "But what? What's her flaw, Skip?"

"Not lack of knowledge, that's for sure. It's more subtle than that." He hiked up one shoulder and caught his hip higher against the edge of the desk. "Thing is, she's not a girl the boys like. Know what I mean?"

She nodded.

"She's one of those women in public life people make fun of. You know? Like Margaret Thatcher." He tapped his foot nervously on the carpet.

"Go on."

"Like the clumsy kid the other kids don't want on the team. No matter how hard he tries, he's never going to be one of them. They're going to snicker at everything he does, and make it so everyone in school understands he's the goat." He turned around to face his computer. The movement was too fast. He gasped and grabbed his hip.

Kiernan could see only part of his face, but it was enough to reveal the telltale flush. Another person might have reached out, but, instinctively, she left him his privacy. Her childhood neighbors had shunned her, too, but that was because she rejected the church. At thirteen, it merely fired her adolescent rebellion, and she'd stomped past them, gone to public school, and taken out her anger perfecting gymnastic routines till she made the state championships. But that was hardly the same as Olsen and presumably Jessica Leporek's experience of being scorned for themselves, she thought. There would have been no righteous anger for them. She waited till the color faded from Olsen's face, and said, "So Jessica Leporek is fighting an uphill battle?"

"Yeah. The initiative might win, but it'll be in spite of her."

Kiernan stood up. "Get me an appointment with her, for tomorrow morning if you can. Eleven would be best. And Cummings, see if I can catch him after work, at home. Maybe about six."

"Where you off to now?"

"Delaney's. You have a current address for him?"

"Coast guard had zip. If they hadn't known the deckhand was missing and had a name to begin with, he'd still be a John Doe. Manager at the Neptune wouldn't tell the coroner's investigator zip." He smiled.

"But you got his forwarding address, right?"

"Olsen Investigations at your service. Twenty-sixth and Noe. Green six-plex, sixth from the corner. You planning to take a look in there?"

"I might have to. What about Matucci?"

He stepped carefully to the desk, extricated a file, flipped to a Xeroxed page and read off an address on Northpoint Street.

"I'll call you at noon."

*   *   *

Skip Olsen watched her walk down the stairs. So lightly. Her feet almost didn't touch the steps. Life isn't fair, the doctors had kept telling him, as if that would make everything fair on a grander scale. He walked slowly across the living room. Half his ass was skin-numb, and he could feel the bone grinding up into the hip joint like a pestle in a mortar.

He dropped onto the sofa. Too quickly. The icepick pain—cold, sharp, fast—running into the joint and then lightninglike down both sides of the leg. Going back to the wharf would be a bitch. Dumb. But he didn't have any choice.

Kiernan climbed into the Jeep, and dialed the number Maureen Brant had given her at the grocery store.

"She had to leave," the proprietor said when Kiernan asked for Maureen.

"She just called me ten minutes ago."

"She waited as long as she could, you know." The unspoken accusation was clear. "She was real worried about that husband of hers."

"How so?"

"Like someone might get to him."

"Did she say that?"

"Not in so many words."

Rumors and suspicions she might accept from Olsen, but she was damned if she'd discuss them with a stranger. Still, it made her uneasy. "When is she coming back?"

"She'll call you at three."

"Fine." She hung up and dialed the coroner's office. When she'd identified herself, Marc Rosten's secretary said, "Dr. Rosten is in a meeting. Can I take a message?"

"He was to have a copy of his autopsy notes ready for me. Would you check to see if he left it?"

"He didn't leave anything for you."

Kiernan took a deep breath. Rosten had always been

mercurial and impulsive, but he had not been unreliable. It was a rotten time to start. She said, "When will he be available?"

"Not till after lunch."

"Fine. Tell him I will call him then."

Noe and 26th, downhill from Dixie Alley, and just south of the 24th Street bookstores, galleries and coffee houses, attracted singles, gay couples, and newly marrieds. It was a neighborhood that Zack could only dream of. And Delaney? He'd gone out of his way to keep a menial job for which he was overqualified. And here he lived in an area most deckhands wouldn't choose and couldn't afford.

Delaney's building was a typical San Francisco six-plex, with outside central staircases front and rear. Kiernan checked the mailboxes. She wasn't surprised to find his name absent.

She knocked on the nearest door: Wilson. No answer. That was the problem with a working-adult neighborhood—people were at work.

She tried the second door: Yamana. It wasn't till the second floor that she got the gift of winter, a man in his thirties (Creswell) with the reddest nose she'd seen since the previous Christmas. Thank you, cold season, she thought.

"You frun da drug sto'?"

"No. 'Fraid not. I'm looking for Carlos Delaney."

"Who?" He yanked a tissue out of his pocket and honked into it.

"He lived here up until two weeks ago."

"No Delaney here." Keeping the tissue at the ready, he put his hand on the door, about to swing it shut.

"Maybe you'd remember him if I described him." She pushed away the picture of Delaney lying on the slab, his scalp eaten, his eyes ringed with bruises from the goggles. "About five ten, dark hair, blue eyes."

He shook his head.

Recalling Delaney's day blindness, she said, "Always wore dark glasses."

"Oh, him! Chet Debbewo. Hey, dat an alias? Dey both sou'd like aliases."

Debbewo? "Devereaux?"

Creswell affirmed with a nod and a titanic blow into the tissue.

"He lives upstairs. Right above me," he said, quite clearly this time.

"Where can I find the landlord?"

"Yuma! Left right after da eartquake last year. You want his number down dere?"

"Thanks."

He was halfway through writing it when the boy from the drugstore plodded up the stairs. Kiernan took the paper, waved thanks, and hurried downstairs.

The good news was that she now knew where Delaney/ Devereaux lived. The bad news was that it was above the one person home all day with nothing to do.

Breaking and entering was rarely a good idea, as Tchernak was so eager to point out. It was a practice that created ex-licensed, injured PI's, incarcerated PI's, dead PI's. Sensible PI's shunned housebreaking at all costs. She knew that. Housebreaking was like seducing a man you work with. You know you'll be sorry in the morning, and probably for a long time after, but that makes it all the more tempting. She should have learned that from Marc Rosten.

But patience was the last thing Rosten was qualified to teach, and at the bottom of the list of skills Kiernan seemed likely to master. She could call the landlord in Yuma. Would he tell her to go right in and search Delaney's flat? Not likely. When he found out what was going on, he'd tell her to get lost. Then he'd call in a cleaning crew, sweep away any evidence, and rent out the flat before she could hunt up a relative of Delaney's and get legitimate access.

Kiernan glanced up toward the third-floor flat. She was

sorry she'd ever admitted it, and to Tchernak yet, but she did love housebreaking. She got a rush, an almost sexual rush from loiding a lock, or climbing through a carelessly left-open window. Penetrating it. Standing alone in the space someone had created to suit himself, sifting through closed closets, secret papers, revealing medicine cabinets, excited her. The pressure that forced total concentration, pitted her against alarms, police, neighbors, chance; it made her tingle all over. That was the real turn-on, not unlike the feeling she remembered from walking up the steps to Marc Rosten's flat at shift's end, wondering if he'd be there by his rumpled bed, waiting. She'd only had one close call, in a house in Rancho Santa Fe. She could still feel that as clearly as she could remember the feel of Rosten's flesh pressed into hers. And then she'd managed to escape through the very door her nemesis had entered. That was the orgasm.

But at ten on a clear morning, housebreaking would not be a prelude to orgasm. It would be a ticket to jail.

Still, even from the outside, Delaney's building had raised questions. Why had the man from this very middle-class neighborhood posed as a deckhand, and gone to a lot of trouble to do it? He was too smart for Robin's tastes, but, obviously, not smart enough to survive.

Maybe Robin's home, in the pricey Marina district, would give some answers.

17

Kiernan crested the steep hill of Pacific Heights, with its pre-1906–earthquake mansions lined up like matrons at a reception. The fog had burned off entirely here, and sunlight glistened on maples and magnolia trees. At the foot of the hill, the Marina district stretched flat and sparkling white to the edge of the Bay, and a tanker glided under the bright red arches of the Golden Gate Bridge.

It had been here, on a morning just like this, that Kiernan had had her first thoughts of wealth. She and Rosten had speculated that two doctors could afford to live anywhere they chose, but "be wasted on us," she'd muttered. "We're both too exhausted to be able to enjoy it." Later, alone, she pondered the prospect: Pacific Heights, the antithesis of her childhood row house in Baltimore. She'd admired the colorful Victorian houses on Divisadero Street, but she hadn't acted on her impulse to buy one, even when she was with the cornoner's office north of the city. Instead, she'd bought a modest house and furnished it in rattan, as if at some level she had known part of her life was temporary, that someday she would be gone from the coroner's office and another day, months later, that she would give up her life there and buy a ticket to Bangkok.

She had returned from Asia after two years to discover her house was worth triple what she'd paid for it. Which was a good thing, because by then she had contemplated the prospect of wealth long enough in the abstract: she was ready for a beach house in La Jolla. And a houseman.

She drove across Union Street and Lombard and into the Marina, wondering whether Robin Matucci's route to high-style living had been as circuitous as her own.

The last time she'd been here had been only a month or so after the big earthquake; the road had still been torn up and ropes blocked off the crumbling streets. But now the sidewalks were busy and the curbs jammed with cars, parked within an inch of every driveway, in front of garages, blocking entranceways.

Kiernan pulled up by Robin Matucci's house, parking at the angle of the corner. The curb was gone, replaced by macadam, and next door a jagged crack still bisected the bricks in the facade. But Robin's house looked unscathed. It sat flush between its neighbors, a stucco marina row house with a bay-windowed living room above a garage, a stairway leading up beside it. The house was built atop the rubble from the 1906 earthquake, manmade land that had turned to mud and sucked buildings down just as Garrett Brant's Alaskan mud flats had pulled its victims into their depths. And still, Kiernan knew, the house was worth half a million.

A plump, gray-haired woman opened the screen door to shake a mop outside. Robin's mother? Cleaning out a dead daughter's house was exactly the way a mother might handle her grief. Kiernan remembered her own mother after her sister's sudden death: so stunned she couldn't bring herself even to speak. But this woman was not in such bad shape; surely she would be able to help fill in Kiernan's sketchy picture of Robin, or at least explain her daughter's friendship with Jessica Leporek.

Kiernan walked up to the front door just as the woman was shutting it. "Mrs. Matucci?"

"Yes, I'm Maeve. And you are . . . ?" There was a firmness to her square jaw, and shaky defiance clear in the lines around her eyes.

Again Kiernan thought of her own mother. At least Mary O'Shaughnessy hadn't been beset by private investigators, slimy, deceitful creatures for whom the truth was merely one option and the end always justified the means. . . . Kiernan could feel her face flushing. She swallowed hard, pushed away the accusing stereotype, but failed to dislodge the flush of guilt. "Mrs. Matucci, Robin is probably alive. My name is Kiernan O'Shaughnessy. I'm a private investigator. And I'm the only one trying to find her."

The color drained from Maeve Matucci's face, and she stood stone-still. "Prove to me who you are."

With relief, Kiernan showed her license.

In the same show-me tone, she said, "What makes you think my Robin's alive?"

Kiernan relaxed. Maeve Matucci was no Mary O'Shaughnessy crying silently for protection. "Delaney went overboard by the Farallons, thirty miles out. Just because one person is swept overboard doesn't mean another is. The boat didn't sink till it was three miles offshore, so Robin could have been on board for hours after Delaney's death, and what would she have been thinking about all that time? How to make it to shore, right?"

Maeve Matucci was probably unaware that she was leaning toward the door—toward hope, Kiernan thought. But she obviously realized her lips were trembling, because she sucked them in and pressed them tightly together. If Robin Matucci was still alive, wouldn't she have let her mother know? "Robin was a good sailor, wasn't she?" Kiernan asked.

Maeve Matucci looked closer to tears than to words.

Giving her time to get control of herself, Kiernan gazed past her at the lavish anteroom. Unlike the simple exterior of the house, it sported a Bokhara rug, a gilt-framed mirror and an elaborate table displaying a huge arrangement of irises and other flowers too dead to identify. Definitely not the place into which a ship's captain trudges to pull off her salt-encrusted boots. The door to the garage was open. Kiernan shot a glance into the dark space. From what she could tell, it was empty— there was no car, and, more unusual for a Bay Area garage, none of the kind of junk that would normally have filled the attic, had these houses possessed attics. Nothing that suggested permanence. She couldn't imagine Robin Matucci in this house.

A cardboard box stood by the door. On top of it lay a framed photograph. "May I?" she asked, reaching for it.

It was a family portrait taken maybe twenty-five years earlier. Kiernan recognized Maeve, younger then, a slender, dark, stylish woman. And Robin, sitting on her father's lap—obviously her mother's daughter, with the same deep-blue eyes, the same air of determination in her small face, and a mass of red curls that nearly overwhelmed her. She must have been about five years old. Her father had been dark, too. The bond between father and daughter was so evident that Kiernan found it hard to focus on anything else in the picture.

Handing it back, she said, "It looks as if Robin and her father were very close."

Maeve laughed, a startlingly bitter sound. "Like two peas in a pod, they were. Johnny was always looking for the pot of gold at the end of the rainbow. And when Robin was born, from the first moment he set eyes on her it was like she was the leprechaun that was going to lead him to it." Her voice softened. "Such a dreamer, that man. He'd sit in his junkaporium—that's what I called it, his antique haven in a storefront surrounded by pawnshops—all day long. Of course, *he* didn't think of his stuff as junk. He—"

"What about Robin?" Kiernan wondered if the decor in this house stemmed from Mr. Matucci's fondness for "antiques."

Maeve's face tightened momentarily. "She had too much sense. She loved him, but not enough to make his mistakes. She wanted to take care of him, get him out of that shop south of Market, him like a sitting duck for any punk with a Saturday night special. Johnny got held up there more times than he could count." She shook her head in exasperation. "From the time she was twelve, Robin always had a job. Gave up all her team sports. Never had time for girlfriends. It was always work to get

Johnny out of that shop. She was a deckhand as soon as she was old enough for working papers." She picked up another picture from atop the carton and thrust it at Kiernan. "Robin on *Early Bird.*"

The picture didn't surprise Kiernan. Robin stood on the bow of the boat, a tall, tan woman smiling confidently, her long red hair blowing behind her. Olsen hadn't been exaggerating about Robin's beauty. She was a woman who would draw stares anywhere. And the boat itself was sleek, freshly painted, brass fixtures gleaming in the sun. It was to the other party boats Kiernan had seen at the Wharf as Robin was to deckhands like Zack: both were a different class of beast.

"Was Robin always so sure of herself?"

Maeve took the picture in both hands. Looking at it, her eyes misted slightly; she seemed to be speaking directly to it. "Nothing that girl couldn't master once she put her mind to it." The edge that had marked her voice was gone. Now she was just the proud parent. "Took ballet through the YMCA and starred in the one performance, she did. Got a brown belt in their karate class. In junior high she made the team in every sport she tried. She could fix anything. Just like her father. She rewired the back porch when she was still in high school. Never took her car to the mechanic unless she didn't have time to deal with it herself, and then"—Maeve shook her head—"she spent as much time getting on them for their mistakes as she would have doing the work herself. When Robin set her mind to something, you could consider it done."

"But she didn't get her father out of the store south of Market."

Maeve laughed, the bitterness back. "She wasn't as sharp as she thought. Johnny refused to move. She was so mad at him she yelled—only time I've ever heard her do that. She said some crackhead would break in and shoot him. Said he'd die in that shop." Maeve shook her head. "But he passed on naturally; she's the one who died on the job." It was a moment before she could continue. "Johnny had no intention of moving. Robin called him a liar. She never could understand that what Johnny valued was the dream. And that if he moved, he risked destroying it."

"Maybe she was afraid—"

"Not Robin," she snapped. "Robin wasn't afraid of anything. And she never panicked."

Maeve was close to falling apart. Kiernan hesitated, then forced herself to say, "Surely she must have panicked at that hit-and-run accident of hers?"

"No! Robin never had an accident. Robin was too good a driver."

"But there's proof. Perhaps she was too ashamed to mention it?"

Maeve's hand went to the door.

"Maybe Robin talked about it to her friend Jessica Leporek?"

"Maybe you haven't been listening to me," Maeve said, with a surge of anger that took Kiernan by surprise. "Robin never had girlfriends. She didn't have time for other women." She slammed the door shut.

Kiernan walked slowly down the path. Investigating was supposed to clarify cases. But everything she uncovered created new questions. Those deckhands of Robin's, did they remind her of her father? Was she trying to protect them as she had failed to save him? A compassionate woman?—not if she ran down Garrett Brant and left him to die.

Why did Robin, who had never had time for girlfriends, suddenly start seeing a woman who even Tchernak found trying?

And what about Harpoon? Why was Robin calling it, Pedersen defensive about it, and Delaney curious? And what the hell was it?

18

Kiernan pulled the Jeep around the corner. It was past ten. She picked up the phone and punched in a number.

"This is Dr. O'Shaughnessy, calling for Dr. Rosten."

"I'm sorry. Dr. Rosten is out of the office."

"Did he leave a copy of the—"

"He didn't leave anything for you." The exasperation was so clear in the woman's voice that Kiernan wondered just what Rosten had said. Had he described her to his secretary as a badgering former lover, a pain-in-the-ass private investigator, or had his tone of disgust in itself been enough to get the message across?

"When will he be back?"

"He has a meeting till noon. And he'll be out all afternoon."

Kiernan put down the receiver, careful not to slam it. Why was Marc Rosten making such a big deal about the autopsy report? It would be public record as soon as it was typed. Was he reconsidering his findings? Or was he just digging in his heels?

Her motel, the Western Sun, shoddy at best, had one saving grace—it was within walking distance of a decent coffee shop. She ran the four blocks, bought two pounds of beans, grinder, filter, and filter papers with which to educate Olsen, and a large container of Major Dickason's blend to drink on the way back.

There was still an inch or so of coffee left when she got to her small, pinky-beige room and picked up her one message: Olsen had made her appointments: Jessica Leporek at 11:00 A.M. and Dwyer Cummings at 6:00 P.M. the next day. Leaning back against the scarred maple headboard, she savored the last aromatic drop. Caffeine had no redeeming qualities, she had informed patients in medical school. It is an alkaloid drug that can overstimulate the central nervous system . . . ; it increases blood sugar, causing insulin to be released only to bring it catapulting down . . . But one of the credos of that same medical-school class had been that acceptance of the Hippocratic oath conferred immunity to the dangers of caffeine.

She dialed Olsen's number. Maybe he'd gotten word back on Robin Matucci's heirs.

"Olsen Investigations."

"Skip, it's Kiern—"

"Good news!" Silence followed.

"You've come up with something?" Kiernan prompted.

"There's a Carl Hartoonian in Marin County. He's connected with something called Atmospheric Analysis, which provides aerial printouts of the ocean."

"You think he's Harpoon?"

"Worth a try."

"Good work! Give me the address and I'll check him out."

"I could go see him." There was a whiny quality to Olsen's voice.

"I'll do that this afternoon." She wasn't about to pass up the opportunity to see Harpoon herself.

"I've got the time. I—"

"No you don't." She had the urge to send him to his room. Control! she muttered to herself. You need this man. "Skip, order in some pizza and we'll have a business meeting tonight."

"Pizza! I can't eat cheese, you know that."

"No, Skip, I don't." The man had an incredible ability to irritate. "Order it without cheese."

"You don't want anchovies, do you?"

"Get whatever you want on it. I like everything. I'll stop for beer and see you at seven."

"Okay, it's a date," he said, sounding considerably more cheerful, either from the catholic array of topping options or the prospect of beer.

Kiernan hung up. She was near the Golden Gate Bridge, probably half an hour away from Atmospheric Analysis and maybe the unveiling of Robin's secret. *If* Hartoonian was Harpoon. She felt as frustrated as Ben Pedersen. So close, but she couldn't go until she'd dealt with Rosten's autopsy notes.

"What are the chances," Kiernan muttered aloud, "of Marc Rosten having those notes for me?" About the same, she decided, as the Western Sun Motel making the cover of the *Condé Nast Traveler*.

Begrudging every moment taken, she pulled on her "professional woman" costume: a suit made from the darkest green Australian tweed her dressmaker could find, straight, fitted, but not quite severe; black heels that made her almost normal height; silver stud earrings inlaid with slivers of malachite. She raced for the Jeep. Makeup she'd deal with at the red lights.

At ten to twelve she pulled into the morgue parking lot and walked up to the back door. The night watchman's job at the morgue is not a sought-after position. The morgue at night was a lonely place, and cold. A place that nurtured fears. Night watchmen came, and went fast. But Angus Labcatt, the day man, had been at the back door when Kiernan started medical school. He prided himself on knowing every intern who had done a rotation here.

As she rapped on the glass door, he looked her up and down and smiled. "Dr. O'Shaughnessy. My, don't you look beautiful. I'll have to tell Millie tonight that you look like you could be running the place. Not just the morgue here, but the whole city. My, my, you look good."

"Well, thank you, Angus," she said to the old man. "You don't look bad yourself. Is Marc Rosten treating you well now that he's running the joint?"

"Jes' fine. But he's only got another two weeks to treat me fine. Then the chief gets back." He laughed, and Kiernan couldn't gauge whether his amusement was in expectation of his chief's return, or because Angus, who collected rumors and observations about his doctors to take home to Millie, recalled her affair with Rosten.

She didn't wait for him to tell her. "I'm here to see Rosten. I'll tell him he should use the powers of his temporary position to get you a Barcalounger, so you can lean back and contemplate who you can let in."

"Well, if anyone can tell him—" He grinned.

"Would you call his secretary and let her know I'm coming? No, wait, don't give her my name. Just tell her his luncheon date is coming."

"Done." He grinned. "You have a good time."

Kiernan hurried along the hall, heels clicking like playing cards against bicycle spokes. Unlike the night before, the hallway was crowded. Interns in green scrubs, technicians in lab coats, and pathologists rushed back and forth between morgue and lab. Lawyers hurried out, headed for the courtroom, and uniformed police officers sauntered in from the main office. She paused at the counter there, located the sign that identified Rosten's secretary, and called out, "I'm here to have lunch with Marc, uh, with Dr. Rosten."

The woman looked up with a curiosity that suggested luncheons with strange women were not the norm for Rosten. "He's not back yet."

Kiernan restrained a sigh of relief. "He told me to wait in his office."

The woman hesitated.

A metal cart clattered down the hall. "He said it would be quieter in there," Kiernan yelled over the din.

With a shrug, the woman motioned her around the counter and opened Rosten's door. "If you need anything I'll be here till twelve-fifteen."

"Thanks. But Marc assured me he'd be back by noon. If

he's not here by then I'll leave without him." She smiled. "We can't let these men think they can keep us waiting."

She got a defensive nod in return. Rosten, she recalled, had always been a favorite with the secretaries. Apparently he still excited their maternal protectiveness.

The door clicked shut. She let out a sigh. It was already five to twelve. Rosten had better not be back till noon. Where would his autopsy notes be? She had only been in this office a couple times. But there'd been a new coroner since then. He had rearranged the entire office. Try the files first. She pulled open the top drawer and looked toward the back. Nothing on a Delaney.

Those maternal secretaries, they'd check on their Dr. Rosten's guest. All they'd need to see . . . Quickly, she looked in the bottom drawer, the John and Jane Does. Only two now, both Johns. The first was black and the second dead of hypothermia in a doorway in the Tenderloin.

11:57. But punctuality was not Rosten's strong point. He could be back later than planned. Or earlier. The office was eerily silent, almost as if it had been sealed. Just as it had been on her first visit, with the class. She'd gotten in early, sat alone for five minutes; she'd not so much heard the lack of sound as felt the pressure of the unmoving air, and wondered if this was how it would feel in the freezer, if the tenants were not beyond feeling altogether. Rosten could clomp up to the door unheard. If he caught her he'd make sure she never got in another morgue in any city in the state. Tantamount to taking her license.

Hurriedly, she circled Rosten's desk and pulled open the top drawer. A preliminary report from the coast guard was on top. Coast guard letterhead with handwritten notes. She stared at the Xeroxed page. The coroner's office never requested copies of the coast guard reports. Things worked the other way around. The coast guard requested final copies of the autopsy, after all the lab protocols were in, which usually was not until two months after the body had been found. The coast guard could tell how the boat had sunk, but they needed findings from the corpse to figure out why: drugs, alcohol involvement? The state of the boat did not clarify the state of the corpse. In her years here, Kiernan had never once heard of a coroner or medical examiner worry about what was in that report.

She read: "The autopsy was performed on the body of Carlos Delaney by Marc Rosten, M.D. at 1:45 P.M." She skipped the list of observers present and read: Final Diagnosis: 1. Asphyxia due to drowning.

Exactly what Rosten had told her. No reason to hide that.

She flipped to the next page "Gross Examination of Autopsy," scanning the paragraph headings: Lungs, Heart, Liver, Gallbladder, Spleen, Pancreas, Gastrointestinal Tract, Adrenals, Kidneys, Bladder, Prostate. Nothing that wouldn't be expected. Head: "Small subdural hemorrhage interior to left anterior, proximal temporalis muscle."

She pictured a bruised spot above Delaney's left ear, where he had been hit hard enough to have produced bleeding beneath the membranes that cover the brain: not surprising in a man who had died in a small boat on exceptionally rough seas. She read on, looking for indications of contrecoup: broken blood vessels on the right side of the brain opposite the left subdural hemorrhage—the type of damage Delaney would have sustained had he been moving and struck his head against a hard object. At the moment of impact his skull would have been stopped abruptly, and for a split second the force of movement would have impelled the soft brain tissue onward into the left temporal and partial plates of the skull, snapping blood vessels as the brain tore away from its moorings on the right.

There was no mention of contrecoup. Hadn't Rosten thought to look for it?

The doorknob creaked. It was turning.

Kiernan shoved the report in, closed the drawer and turned to look at the picture behind the desk.

"Everything okay?" the secretary called. "Can I get you some tea? Sometimes Dr. Rosten gets held up."

"I was afraid of that," Kiernan said, making a show of

looking at her watch. She headed toward the door. "I'm on a tight schedule. I'll just go ahead to the restaurant and if he makes it, he makes it."

"I'm sorry," the secretary said.

"Can't be helped." Kiernan strode out the door and clicked down the corridor.

She was at the door when she spotted Rosten in conversation with a gray-haired man. She waited till he noticed her, waved, and left.

She smiled as she pulled out of the parking lot. The hemorrhage to the anterior proximal temporalis muscle could have been a bruise sustained while Delaney fought against drowning. That would be the natural assumption. Clearly, that was the assumption Marc Rosten had made. But it could also have been the result of a chop to the head, a chop made by a woman who had studied karate as a child.

If Delaney had banged into the boat as he drowned, he would have sustained bruises. Bruises, plural! A smattering of bruises would have been consistent with violent drowning. One bruise was not.

Could Robin have subdued him with a single karate blow to the head? Not likely, not in that spot. The best such a chop to the skull would do would be to stun. Still, in an open boat in high seas, being stunned might equal being dead. Particularly in a victim with a blood alcohol of .23.

Kiernan pulled into a parking spot, picked up the phone and punched the coast guard number. Going to the Alameda Naval Station in person would have been better, but was no longer an option. Her smug little wave to Rosten had blown that. By now Rosten would be in his office looking through his desk, and suspecting she had seen not only the autopsy report, but the coast guard's as well. She needed to get to them before he did.

"Marine Casualty Investigations, Zimmerman speaking."

"Hello. This is the San Francisco coroner's office. We just got your notes on the sinking near the San Mateo County line, boat called *Early Bird*."

"Sure. Glad to oblige."

"We appreciate your cooperation. And the fact that you sent us your notes. But I'm afraid we're having a little trouble deciphering them."

Zimmerman gave an embarrassed laugh. "Well, I did warn the coroner that he'd be better off waiting till I got them typed."

So in this already abnormal request, Rosten had not taken the normal route and had his secretary call; he had handled it personally. Very abnormal indeed. "He should have listened to you. But can I impose on you again? I've got our copy here. Could you just read me yours and I'll make the clarifications on mine? It's only a page long."

"Sure. Hold on. Look, it's going to take me a couple minutes to get it. Why don't I call you back after lunch."

"It'll be a madhouse here then," Kiernan said quickly. Zimmerman calling the coroner's office was the last thing she wanted. "It would be a great help if you could do it now. I know I'm cutting into your lunch—"

"No, no problem. Hang on."

A truck passed. Normally she would have worried about the noise carrying over the phone lines, but she recalled other conversations with the coast guard, some on sea-to-shore lines that crackled and rumbled. Anyone who'd survived working at the coast guard station would be used to blocking out background noises.

"Here we go," Zimmerman said. "These are really just notes to myself. You understand?"

"Of course."

"Okay. 'Evidence of explosion. Engine not found. Cabin top separated—' "

"Separated from the engine, you mean?"

"Right. Any commercial vessel of this kind over twenty-six feet has built-in flotation devices. Once the engine breaks loose and that weight is gone, the cabin's almost impossible to sink."

"What did you find?"

"Part of the cabin, most of the wheelhouse. Smaller pieces

of the rest of the top. Here, line three. Teak decking, brass fixtures. Normal expected navigational equipment for a boat of this type, plus the Dytek Seawater Temp Indicating System, and FloScan fuel monitoring system."

"Nothing else?" Kiernan asked, thinking about the Harpoon question and what secret equipment Robin might have used to find fish.

"The explosion took care of a lot, like chairs and ovens and doors."

"Nothing abnormal?"

"Nothing except the wires for the listening device I mentioned in the last sentence."

Controlling her excitement, Kiernan said, "Read that to me."

"Found unusual listening device, semicolon, wires running from cabin to wheelhouse. Turned over to coast guard Intelligence for investigation."

"So this is like a wiretap?"

"Looked like it to me. I called the guy in Intelligence this morning—this isn't in the report—and he agreed. Simple wiretap that anyone with a basic knowledge of electrical wiring could install. Ran right under the moldings in the cabin."

"Where was the recorder?"

"Gone. Dammit. I'd be real interested to hear what was on that tape. But because the wires were exposed, the ends were jarred loose in the explosion and the recorder could be anywhere between Pescadero Beach and the Farallons."

She heard the clang of a cable-car bell in the distance—down here it would have to be one of the motorized ersatz cable cars used for publicity. But the bells sounded the same. And they did not sound as if they came from inside the coroner's office. Quickly she said, "Thanks for your help," and hung up.

Wiretapping! Who would want to know what went on on *Early Bird*? The first name that came to mind was Ben Pedersen. Ben Pedersen would still be at sea. But he'd be back by the time she finished with Hartoonian.

19

"Who is this guy Olsen?" Marc Rosten barked, waving the scrap of paper he'd just written on. Bad move to snap at the Medical Examiner's secretary, he knew that, but he was so goddamned furious. How could Grace have let Kiernan into his office alone, let her root through whatever she wanted?

Two phones were ringing, but the clerks could answer them. Grace Ulher looked up at him from the oversized looseleaf book into which she was inserting a file. She shook her head—the silent treatment.

Rosten forced a laugh in response to what her tone should have been. *If* Kiernan hadn't driven him to snap at her. He valued his good rapport with the support staff, particularly these older ladies who had been with the department since this morgue had been a blueprint. Walking over to Grace's desk, he smiled. "Grace, I spend my days with the dead. And dead men don't talk about who's who. But I know I've heard this name before. Harold Olsen? It doesn't ring a bell with you? I thought you knew everyone who's anyone here in San Francisco?" He grinned and waited, hoping that his smile was still boyish enough to wield some power.

"Well"—Grace put the looseleaf on the corner of her desk and looked up at Rosten—"I can't be sure about the 'Harold' part, but there used to be a cop named Skip Olsen we'd see in here. 'Course that was some years back. You were probably still in school then"—she paused—"or maybe you weren't. No, it's within the last ten or fifteen years."

"What happened to Olsen? He retire?"

"Too young to retire. It seems to me there was some kind of scandal. You know, one of those after-hours parties the police keep getting caught at, with drugs or sex or whatever. Olsen was on the outs with the rest of the cops after that. Then he was gone." She looked up at him quizzically. "Why do you want to know, Dr. Rosten?"

"I knew I'd heard the name. It was going to bug me till I could remember where." He grinned. "You've saved me the trouble."

He was still grinning when he walked into the Medical Examiner's office and telephoned an acquaintance at the Hall of Justice. "Dr. Rosten, Acting Coroner, calling for Inspector Hernicki."

"Would you hold, Mr. Rosten?"

Dr. Rosten, he wanted to insist. Instead he waited. That was the problem with being a public servant, dealing with other public servants. Everything moved like the dead. He fingered the Delaney file on his desk. There was nothing questionable in it, just as there'd been nothing odd in the autopsy. And yet Kiernan had been looking for something. He'd have to read it over again.

The phone line crackled. "Hey, Marc, how you doing, boy?"

"Live and kicking. You, Fred?"

"Live, but not kicking as hard as I used to."

Rosten waited another moment, hoping Hernicki would ask what he wanted, *offer* his services. He hated this business of begging for favors, knowing he'd get a call in a month or two from Hernicki that would make him scurry around for paperwork, or force him to pressure the lab techs and get them pissed off at him, or jolly them along and end up owing them, too. If he were in private practice . . . Patients weren't perfect, he knew that. There would be things he'd have to put up with. But they wouldn't be this Tammany Hall of favors and back pats. "I need a favor, an easy one."

"Shoot." Hernicki was giving nothing.

"Guy named Harold Olsen. Used to be with your department. Got in some kind of hassle then left. I gather he's none too popular down there with you guys."

"You could say that." Hernicki's voice was crisp. "You asking what he was up to?"

"In part."

When Hernicki relayed the tale of the Flamingo Café, Rosten smiled. "Olsen's a private eye now, Fred."

"We know that. We haven't forgotten him. You're not thinking of hiring the asshole, are you?"

Rosten laughed. "No, just the opposite. He's working with another PI who's badgering me."

"You want us to keep an eye on him? See if he's jaywalking? See if the other guy's parking illegally?"

"The other guy's a woman, Kiernan O'Shaughnessy." Rosten held his breath, momentarily afraid that Hernicki had been around long enough to remember him and Kiernan.

Hernicki said, "Constables of the Peace at your service. It'll be a pleasure to serve you."

Rosten put down the receiver. In the silence of the Medical Examiner's office, his skin felt warm with the rush of power, of control. And underneath was a cold swirling fear, as he realized just how easy it was to step inside Tammany Hall!

20

Nearly one o'clock. With luck, Kiernan thought, she'd make it to Hartoonian's and back across the Golden Gate Bridge before rush hour began. She followed the cable-car tracks up California Street. The bright sun of the morning was gone and thin clouds obscured the horizon. Winter weather.

By the time she hit the Golden Gate Bridge, the mist was blowing strong across all six lanes. She held the wheel firm against the wind and glanced down at the choppy water below. In the fifty-some years since the bridge had been completed, nearly nine hundred people had jumped off it—San Franciscans who ended their downhill skids there, New Yorkers, Carolinians, Kansans who'd moved inexorably west, as if pulled by the magnet of death. They'd stood, almost all of them facing not the vast cold of the Pacific, but looking toward the skyline of San Francisco. The wind at their backs, for once. Then they jumped. When their bodies rose after three days, bloated from the gasses of decomposition, the coast guard brought them to the morgue. Despite—or perhaps because of—their condition, the floaters had produced more than their share of jokes among the irreverent pathology residents, the mildest of them being that resurrection was not what it was cracked up to be.

At the north end of the bridge, the mist had turned to rain. The houses were smaller, older, reminiscent of the Bay Area she remembered from twelve years ago. On the ocean side of the narrow, two-lane road, the ground dropped into arroyos of tall tan grasses flecked with green. It was a road made for the Triumph, she thought grumpily, as she yanked the Jeep into the turn.

Atmospheric Analysis sat near the crest of the hills, a rain-streaked, brown-shingled geodesic dome about forty feet in diameter. Kiernan recalled briefly considering the dome-home kits ten years ago, well after the height of their popularity. "Roll with the quake," the brochure had promised. But somehow a house that flipped over to bobsled down the hillside seemed hardly more appealing than one that lurched off its foundation and crumbled. "How do you drag it back up?" she had asked the salesman.

Apparently it was not a question that had bothered the folks at Atmospheric Analysis.

She pulled up next to a white Bronco, hurried across the bare ground to the decking and pushed the buzzer. There was no portico to protect the waiting guest from the blowing rain.

She was about to ring again when the door opened, revealing a soft, sallow man in a brown flannel shirt and ill-fitting cords. His short brown hair lay flat against his bony skull, and the only roundness in his thin face came from the lenses of his black-rimmed glasses. Through them his dark eyes seemed too large, too intense for his pale face. It was hard to believe that this nervous, ashen man was the sought-after Harpoon. He looked like the closest he'd come to a fish was a tuna sandwich.

"I'm Kiernan O'Shaughnessy," she said extending a hand. "I need to talk to you about Atmospheric Analysis."

He noted her hand but seemed hesitant to touch it. Keeping a firm hold on the door, he said, "Yes?"

"Are you Carl Hartoonian?"

"Yes?"

"Great. I just need five minutes of your time. Inside," she added, giving her soaking hair a quick shake.

Hartoonian's hand tightened on the door. "I'm pretty busy right now. Can you tell me—"

"Simple insurance questions. But look, you're getting soaked too." When his hand dropped, she stepped inside into a circular room that had been sliced in half by a wall parallel to the front door. To the right, a kitchenette fitted under the sloping wall. No dishes in the sink, not even a pan on the stove. To the left, a mattress, with blankets squared at the corners. Two low bucket chairs squatted next to it. The spareness of the room and its obsessive tidiness suited its owner. What would Hartoonian have thought of Robin Matucci's house? Kiernan wondered.

A black plastic desk stood midway along the central dividing wall, and covering the top half of the wall were computer-generated maps; those to the left represented the entire West Coast; the other four were even larger blow-ups of the Bay Area. Waves of greens and yellows and blues spread vertically along the ocean. Against the drabness of the room, the colorful maps stood out like impressionist paintings on a gallery wall.

Kiernan hung her slicker on a rack next the door and moved closer to study the coastline as it emerged through the varying colors. Hartoonian stood behind her, hands on hips, beaming like a proud parent. It was as if he had squeezed all the colors from his life and happily splashed them onto his maps. What matter if he were left dull and lifeless?

Turning to him, Kiernan said, "You're Harpoon, aren't you?"

Behind the thick lenses, his eyes widened alarmingly. He seemed even smaller, even more unsure of himself.

Struggling not to reveal her own excitement, she said, "It was you Robin Matucci was calling on board *Early Bird*. These maps, did you read them and advise her where to find fish?"

He shrank away from her. "I didn't say anything about that."

"I know you didn't *say* it. I'm an investigator. Figuring things out is what I do." Kiernan smiled to cover her irritation with herself. She'd been too impatient with him; now she'd have to backtrack, let him talk till his suspicion passed. "I've heard enough about Robin's uncanny ability to find fish. Guys who've been fishing the Bay all their lives can't figure out where the fish'll be, but Robin comes back full. I'll tell you, Carl, I've gotten real anxious to see this set-up. You've done one fantastic job for her. But I guess you know that. So how does this all work?"

He looked at the maps and back at Kiernan, the war between pride and protectiveness magnified by his thick glasses. Taking a step between her and the wall, he said, "Private investigator? Just what are you investigating?"

"Like I said, a couple insurance questions about *Early Bird*. The company needs to clarify them before they can settle the paper work. Actually," she said, "how you find fish isn't one of them. I just got so fascinated with it that I couldn't resist asking." She hoped she wasn't spreading it too thick.

But Hartoonian's look of pride told her that too thick a spread would be virtually impossible. He turned to the maps, beaming. "These are images from the satellite; color-coded for temperature. See the boundary lines where one temperature comes up against another?"

"And water temperature tells you where the fish are?"

"Well, it's hardly that simple," he said protectively. "The fish tend to be on the warm side of the boundary. But different fish prefer different temperatures. And the boundaries themselves differ. Because of the topography below, and the currents, and so forth. Some boundaries have stayed in one general area longer than others, while some have moved with the water. The more stable ones have been in place long enough to attract more fish."

Kiernan nodded. "But, Carl, there's more to it than that, isn't there? I mean, fishermen can test for water temperature themselves."

"Sure they can, once they get there! But they can't do it before they leave the dock, and if they make the wrong decision and go south of the Gate when the right water's north, their day is shot."

"So why haven't they all gotten these printouts?"

"Too shortsighted and too cheap." His voice had an uneasy bravado to it.

How had Robin Matucci found this man, and where? Had she seen through his insecurity and chosen to nurture the defensive disdain beneath it? Kiernan could imagine his eyes widening with wonderful disbelief as Robin asked about his work. He would have been bowled over by a woman like that.

He turned back to the printouts, standing straighter now, wrapped in the aura of his expertise. "The thing is that the ordinary printouts aren't worth a whole lot. They're only good within a mile, and a whole degree. A mile's a big place to troll back and forth across. And you have to remember that the printout reflects that mile of water as it was when the picture came off the satellite. You get a six A.M. printout and you don't get out to the spot till ten . . ." He turned his hands palm upward. "Water moves."

Kiernan stared at the printouts. Hartoonian seemed like a man Robin could count on, one she could turn to for help. What was behind the wall that divided the dome? Maybe Robin had called him, had come here. Since the accident. Maybe she was still here, on the other side of the wall. Was there a door to the outside back there?

"Anyone can get the charts from the National Weather Service and the National Oceanic and Atmospheric Administration. They're free. You can get them over radio facsimile or even mailed to you." He laughed comfortably. "But not these," he said beaming at his work. "These are the highest resolution, done from satellite lasers that shoot light pulses over five hundred miles down to earth. On these, I can spot upwellings that bring up cold deep water full of nutrients. And I can tell you what was there yesterday, what was there an hour ago. I can tell you what the right spot is now, and if you call me in an hour, I'll give you an update."

"And Robin called you every hour or so for help?"

"If she needed to, I was there." His smile was as intense

as when he'd first started talking about the maps. And yet there seemed to be a flicker of fear in his expression. Fear or grief.

She had to know. She turned to face Hartoonian. "It must have been very hard for you hearing that Robin died."

The question seemed to startle him. His eyes narrowed behind his thick glasses, and there was a catch in his voice as he said, "Yes, well, of course."

"There was more to your relationship than just business, wasn't there?"

He shook his head stiffly, and looked toward the door. Kiernan suspected his mouth was too dry to protest, or, as he clearly yearned to do, tell her to get out.

"What about Robin and Ben Pedersen?"

"There was nothing between them!" He sputtered with outrage. The outrage of a lover, or at least a wannabe.

Robin was used to being in radio contact with Hartoonian. She could have called him at the last moment before the *Early Bird* sank. Hartoonian surely would have dropped everything to help her. But there was no sign Robin had been in this main room. Whatever there was would be behind the wall. And Hartoonian was hardly going to let an investigator trot back there. When he got control of his breath, he would certainly tell her to leave.

Shifting to a less threatening subject, Kiernan said, "You've known Robin a long time, right?"

"Five years."

"In Alaska?"

He nodded. "Met her at the California Tavern up there." The expression in his eyes relaxed.

Kiernan waited a moment, letting the pleasant image comfort him. "The California Tavern? I've heard about that." She decided embroidery couldn't hurt.

"Great place, the ol' C.T. . . ." He smiled, with the same not-quite-sure expression he had had talking about Robin. "No matter where you're from, after you've spent a few dark, twenty-below months up there, California-anything sounds pretty good. Of course, to Californians it sounds good right away, or at least they all stop in there."

She eased toward the door to the back room. "All the transients? Like the guys who do temporary work on the oil-company cleaning crews?"

"Sure."

"Carl, did you know an artist on the cleaning crew?" When he didn't respond, she said, "Garrett Brant? Blond guy with brown eyebrows, about six feet tall? He was working on a series of paintings that represented the life of the people in various parts of Alaska through their landscapes."

The tentative smile, which had given the stiff lines of his cheeks and jaw softness and color, had left his face. Again, his eyes looked too large, too suspicious. "He might have been there, but I don't remember. Look, I really do have to get back to work."

"Okay." Kiernan reached for the doorknob. "But let me see those fabulous computers of yours."

"No!" He grabbed her arm. "They're very sensitive."

"I won't touch." She opened the door.

"Looking isn't going to tell you anything," he muttered as she strode through the door.

But Hartoonian was wrong; the room told her Robin Matucci was not there. It was full of computers, printers, phones; it could have been Olsen's office. There were no closets or trunks, no place to hide anything, or anybody.

When she turned, she found Hartoonian smiling smugly. "Disappointed?" he asked.

When she nodded, his smile faded, and he looked a little taken aback. Whatever his relation to Robin, he seemed to be basically a nice man. A nice man she was going to use, as she suspected Robin had. "Carl, you knew Dwyer Cummings, didn't you? At the California Tavern?"

"Yes, but, look I really—"

She walked to the front door and reached for her slicker.

Maybe he knew why Cummings had been exiled. Scandal, industrial spying, embezzling? She played the odds. "You remember the fuss before he left there, about the theft?" She poked her arm into the sleeve and waited.

Hartoonian didn't reply.

She insisted: "He stole something."

Hartoonian's expression lightened. "No, you've got it all wrong. Dwyer Cummings had a problem with the bottle, and he didn't know when to keep his mouth shut, but he wasn't a thief. He didn't steal anything. He wasn't the culprit, he was the victim."

"What did they steal from him?"

"Nothing they could sell. It was just some memo that could have made him look bad."

"What was it about?"

Hartoonian laughed. "Cummings could be indiscreet, but he wasn't a fool. He never said."

"Who took it?"

"I don't know. No one ever found out. The memo just disappeared."

21

Skip Olsen trudged back across the wharf to his car, gritting his teeth against the pain. He refused to limp like some worn-out codger. No one cared how he walked, that's what the physical therapist said, but he knew different. In this business, you look weak, you get zip. He smiled. He must have looked pretty damned strong. The Big Bench Presser of the trade. He grinned wider. The rain struck his face and the wind made his jaws ache, but Skip Olsen didn't care.

O'Shaughnessy had told him not to come. He was too well known. He wouldn't find out anything. Well, the first thing *she'd* find out was that she was wrong.

The second, when he chose to tell her, was a juicy little fact. A nautilus of a find. He liked that smile. Nautilus machine, the thing that transforms a small bit of force into a big muscle. A find like this was going to pump him right back in control of this case. A real nautilus, all right: Jessica Leporek was on the dock with Robin Matucci two days before Matucci went under. And the two of them were looking daggers at each other.

It was a good find. Important. And just as important, it would give O'Shaughnessy a new route to follow, keep her from looking too closely at Delaney.

Olsen reached for the car door.

An arm wrapped around his shoulders. A hand slapped over his mouth. He tried to look up; couldn't move. The hand slid off his mouth, grabbed him by the hair. The orange paint on the car was the last thing he saw as his head slammed into it.

22

It was after four when Kiernan got back to the motel. The phone was ringing.

"Kiernan? It's Maureen. I'm calling to check in. What have you found?" Maureen was panting.

"Just a minute. Why did you leave the store before I called this morning?"

"Oh, sorry, Kiernan. Garrett had been acting funny, and I just got nervous, and I couldn't wait. I knew the call wasn't a big thing with you."

"You're wrong, Maureen, it *is* a big thing. It's important that you be there when you say you will, so I don't have to wonder what happened and whether it's something connected with this case that I should be concerned about."

"Oh. I'm really sorry, Kiernan. I guess I didn't think— That doesn't affect your decision, does it? I mean, you're still on the case, aren't you?" The beginnings of panic were clear in her voice.

"Yes, Maureen, I'm still on the case," Kiernan reassured her. "There was enough of a question about Delaney's body to make me wonder."

"What did you find?"

"There was a horizontal bruise above his ear. The only significant mark on his head."

"Like he could have been hit with a poker, or something like that? On a boat?"

"Or a karate chop. Seems Robin knew some karate."

"Ah-hah! What else? Tell me everything."

"Slow down. I'll make a full report." Kiernan laughed. She settled back on the newly made bed. "I found Harpoon, who turns out to be a scientist who used sophisticated satellite analysis to guide her to more fish than any other boat captain."

"You don't waste any time. What did you find out from this Harpoon?"

"Dwyer Cummings, Robin's most faithful passenger, left Alaska under the shadow of a theft from his office. A memo. Hartoonian—that's Harpoon's real name—heard about it in the California Tavern up there. Ask Garrett if he remembers hearing anything."

"Okay. Anything else?"

Kiernan laughed. "It's a good thing I don't waste time."

"I didn't mean to press you. It's just that I'm so anxious. I didn't realize how much I was counting on this investigation. I guess I couldn't let myself think about it, not when it still wasn't clear if you'd take the case. Look, I'll call you later tonight."

"No, not tonight."

"You don't have to worry about going out. I've got the number for your cellular phone."

Tonight of all nights she did not want the car phone buzzing. "Call me in the morning, at ten. If we don't connect then try me again at noon."

"The store opens at eight."

"I don't." She could hear Maureen's quick gasp. "Look, Maureen, most investigator's reports are made once a week. I know you're anxious—"

"That's okay. I won't be a pest. I'll wait till ten. Kiernan, I'm just so relieved you're with me on this."

Kiernan put down the phone, thinking not of Maureen and Garrett but of Carlos Delaney. Had Robin hired him and all his predecessors because she was so insecure that she needed to surround herself with deckhands as bland as the furniture in her apartment? Why had she chosen to take him out in the Pacific with storm warnings posted? What had she been using him for?

Rain streaked the motel window. Kiernan smiled; it was rain that would grow stronger as the night progressed. The kind of rain that provides a shield for housebreakers. Thinking of Delaney's waiting apartment, she felt her body grow tense. She'd planned to wait till after midnight, but in this weather she could go earlier.

She called Skip Olsen and got his answering machine. "Skip, something's come up tonight. I have to cancel dinner. Don't call me. I'm going to take a nap. I'll get back to you either later tonight or probably tomorrow morning."

The world was swaying. Olsen couldn't see. His eyes refused to open. Or maybe they were open, and it was night-black.

Where were his arms and legs? Couldn't feel them. Couldn't
hear anything but a kind of swishing and thumping.

Slowly sensation returned. Cold. Damp. His head wedged
between rope and metal. Barking outside.

His arm pricked numb. He still couldn't feel his hands.
His mouth was Sahara dry. Wedged open. Gagged. Pain swept
down his leg. He shrieked; nothing came out but a shallow
groan. And the sloshing of water against the sides of the boat,
the crunch of footsteps above. Pain again, burning his leg.
Move! Get off the leg!

He couldn't move his feet, his legs, his arms. He rolled
side to side with the boat. The boat! He was in a boat, just like
Delaney. Oh shit, Delaney! God, he didn't want to think about
Delaney.

Pain. White-hot!

Blackness.

8:17. The hell with it. Kiernan got up, put on jeans and a
green turtleneck, grabbed her slicker and headed for the Jeep.

Rain hit her face, blown at an angle by the strong wind off
the Pacific.

As she waited for the engine to warm, she ran through the
list of reasons not to break into Delaney's apartment. None
dissuaded her. A second list called "Why to wait till midnight"
fared no better. Tchernak, she thought smiling, would have had
plenty of good reasons for her. Harry Scott, the investigator she
had worked for in San Diego, had insisted that a licensed private
investigator had no business breaking the law. "It's too dangerous. Takes too much time. And it makes us look sleazy." All
that warning without her even having mentioned the sexual rush
she got from it! Lock-picking for the erotic woman! She laughed,
shifted the Jeep into first, and pulled sharply into traffic, cutting
off a Mercedes.

She drove slowly down 26th Street. Rain streaked down,
blurring lights in windows. In Delaney's six-plex lights shone

in only the first-floor windows. On the third floor, Delaney's windows were dark, as were those of the flat next to his. Perfect!

Now, she thought, for the hard part—finding a parking spot. Can't make a fast getaway if your car's been towed.

The spot she finally squeezed into was a full three blocks away. She thrust her arms into her slicker, hefted her fanny pack, and walked quickly down the gentle slope of 26th Street. The tarry smell of wet roofs filled the air.

She paused for a moment near Delaney's building and shook her hair sharply, spraying water in all directions. She allowed herself a brief smile as she surveyed the building. The foreplay had begun.

Delaney's staircase was empty. She walked quickly up to the first landing, past the side-by-side doors, climbed the seven stairs to the half-landing, then paused to check the second-floor door—she did not want to run into Delaney's neighbor again. His front lights were off. With that cold he should be in bed. Probably in back of the apartment. So far, so good. She hurried on to the third floor, breathing faster.

There were no lights in the apartment across from Delaney's, and no outside light. All the better. She pulled out what looked like a credit card, but wasn't. A credit card might work in a lock, but the chances of opening a door were not half so great as snapping the card. This piece of celluloid was more flexible. Flexible but firm under pressure, always a good combination. She stood perfectly still, listening to the hiss of cars, the grind of low gears, the groaning of brakes, the slamming of car doors. Not a housebreaker's paradise. But it heightened the tension. She liked that.

Despite the chill air, Kiernan's face was still warm. Rain that had previously tapped gently on the windows now seemed to pound. But there were no footsteps on the stairs. As she pushed the card between tongue and striker plate, her fingertips tingled and the skin across her cheeks felt taut. She could feel the touch of her nipples against the fabric of her bra. The edge of the card was against the tongue. She pushed, the tongue gave. Slowly, she turned the handle.

The door didn't move. The deadbolt was on. Damn! The card felt limp in her hand.

She sighed. Lightless or not, this was no place to try anything fancier. No surprise Delaney had left the deadbolt on, any sensible city person would. But if this building was a standard San Francisco six-plex there would be a similar staircase and door arrangement at the back. Walking softly, she made her way down the stairs.

The walkway was beneath the first story, open to the sky only once in the middle, by way of the narrowest airshaft Kiernan had ever seen. But at least it was dry. She took off her slicker, folded it small and stuck it in her fanny pack, moving the pack around to her stomach. There was no rain in the backyard, either. It took her a moment to realize that wind-slanted rain couldn't reach the ground here; the whole backyard was a larger version of the airshaft. In the pale trapezoids of light from the first-floor windows and the brighter one from the second story she could make out a yard no more than ten feet deep, ending at a three-story blank wall. The yard would be useless for growing anything more sun-hungry than ivy, but for a woman needing facile entrance to a flat, that arrangement could not have been better—except for the sick man in the bedroom under Delaney's window.

She could wait. Go back to the motel, sleep, come here in the morning and try the "woman friend locked out on a cold, rainy morning" routine. Common sense . . . But it was too late. She was too far into the foreplay now.

She made her way up the stairs, walking to the sides to avoid squeaking steps, listening for sounds of TVs or stereos. Her breath came faster. The apartment below Delaney's was silent: not even the honk of a nose blow. But the light was on. The guy had to be reading. Damn! She moved on, placing a foot, pausing, stepping up.

She recalled that Rosten's flat had had a three-window bay

like these. Occasionally, when she'd lost her key, she'd opted to go through the window on the far side of the bay, the one residents assumed was safe from burglars. In those days, knowing she was legit, she'd given no thought to the police—her only worry had been of falling, and years of gymnastic training had turned that into simple care not to misstep and humiliate herself.

The stairs here protruded beyond the bay. A glance at the catch on the nearest window showed it was locked. She leaned out to examine the second. Rain chafed the side of her face, and the backyard enclosure provided no protection. The second window was locked, too. But the top of the far window was down a couple of inches.

She leaned back under the stair roof, listening. The house to her left was only two stories high, too low to be a problem. It was the one to the right, next to Delaney's apartment and a duplicate of this one that bore watching. The windows there were dark. All she needed was three minutes.

Her skin tingled, her breathing was shallow. She looked back at the windows, gauging her moves, running the tape through her mind as she'd done with gymnastic routines. The windows were wet, the sills slick. One of the first things she'd learned in gymnastics had been how to mount the uneven bars: grab the bottom one, catch a knee over it and swing up; then, using the momentum she'd gained, get both feet on that bar, balance, and grab for the top one. The only time she'd stopped midbalance had taught her the properties—and the pitfalls—of inertia.

She wiped her sweaty palms on her jeans, climbed onto the railing, leaned out over the three-story drop, and placed her right foot on the middle windowsill. No stopping now. She pressed her hands against the moldings, brought her left foot onto the sill, pushed off and grabbed for the top of the far window. She pulled it down; it creaked, but gave. Hands poised on the top, she paused momentarily, savoring the thrill, then thrust herself through headfirst, hanging onto the top till her thighs were on it and she could bring her hands to the floor. She slid her legs down slowly till she could bend a knee and bring one foot down. Then she pushed the window back up.

Her heart beat faster, her skin tingled. She was aware of a tightness in all her muscles: arms, legs, chest, groin. She felt alone against the apartment and its hidden contents, against the ghost of Carlos Delaney, against the curiosity of neighbors, the ambush of noise, the police, the universe. She loved it.

She stood still, focusing her whole being on the flat. The windows rattled, rain played on the glass. The water heater rumbled on. The place smelled of crackers, old chocolate, stale sweat.

Her eyes had adjusted; the rooms were not dark so much as dim. She extricated a flashlight from her pack and walked carefully, stepping along the sides of the hallway rather than the middle. Couldn't the man have bought rugs! At the end of the hallway was a living room, in the middle, a kitchen and bathroom, and in back the bedroom through which she had entered. Exits: living-room door, bedroom window, kitchen and bathroom windows on the narrow airshaft.

If the flat had not come furnished, then Delaney had spent some time at Busvan or the Salvation Army searching for threadbare pieces of a beige sectional. The living-room carpet was equally worn. A long, tall bookcase covered the outside wall. She moved closer to it and shone the light on the titles: legal works, novels, books on plumbing, travel, beginning electrical repair. *Electrical repair!* On the floor beside the coffee table was a pile of magazines—*California Angler, Sports Fishing, Cruising World*—magazines suited to the novice deckhand Zack had described Delaney as portraying.

Along the far wall was a piano, with sheet music open to a Scott Joplin rag. Not music for a beginner.

The kitchen revealed nothing but Delaney's taste for chocolate. The sink held one dirty cup, stained not with coffee but with cocoa. The image of Delaney's crab-gnawed head flashed through Kiernan's mind. She shut her eyes to keep that image separate from the cozy picture of a man drinking one last cup of cocoa before going out to drown.

Moving toward the window, she listened for voices coming up the airshaft. No sound but the clatter of rain on the roof and water gurgling down the drainpipe.

She moved on to the bedroom. If there was anything to be found, it would be here. Even in the dim light, the bedroom had the look of a place left in a hurry: sheets and quilt in a tumble, dirty T-shirt, shorts, socks in a heap beside the Murphy bed.

The thickness of the dust made it clear that Delaney had lived here for a while. So why did he rent that sleazy room in the Tenderloin? Why the pose that he was just another deckhand who needed a place to live? Why the alias?

In the closet into which the bed was intended to fold was a fold-top desk. Locked. She pulled out a penknife and forced it.

The cubbyholes were stuffed with bills: P G and E, Sprint, Pacific Bell, Mastercard, Visa: all in the name of Devereaux. The bills went back over two years.

The drawers held nothing but clothes, clothes that suggested a better life than Delaney had on the dock. Another life.

She bent down and shone the light under the Murphy bed. Boxes crowded together to the edge. Twelve, maybe even sixteen of them. She moved to the end of the bed and shone the light across the floor in front of the boxes. More dust. At the far side, she found what she was looking for, the dust-marked trail of the box someone had pulled out. She yanked it out and pawed through. Sweaters. She pulled out the box behind it. Manila files. Files with case names and number on the left, with a log of transactions, and a billing log. Files like she had in her own office. Private investigator's files!

Investigator's files, a book on electrical repair, and a job on a boat on which the coast guard had found eavesdropping wires! Odds were then that Devereaux, a.k.a. Delaney, had been spying on Robin. What was he waiting to hear? How she found fish? No. Bright as Delaney might be, well prepared as his books suggested he was, he wouldn't have spent six weeks listening to

Robin and not come up with Hartoonian. Finding Hartoonian had taken Skip Olsen just a couple of hours. So what was a private investigator doing on Robin's boat? Who was he working for?

The wind rattled against the windows. Kiernan jumped. She searched the box of files for "Matucci." Not there. "Damn," she muttered. Whatever Delaney was investigating, it must be listed under the client's name, as indeed it should be. She started through the files again, more slowly this time.

Then the doorbell rang.

23

Bent over Delaney's box of files, Kiernan froze.
The doorbell rang again.

A log of cases? Delaney should have one. She grabbed the loose sheets at the front of the box and stuffed them down her shirt.

The doorbell kept on ringing. She shoved the file box back, pushed the carton of sweaters in front to hide it, and stepped into the hallway, jamming the flashlight into her fanny pack.

"Police! Open up!"

Was it really the police? She could always insist Delaney had lent her the apartment.

"Police! You got thirty seconds, lady!"

Lady! That skewed the odds. It was too late to brazen this one out.

"Twenty seconds and we're coming in!"

We're! Too risky to try the back stairs. Kiernan raced for the kitchen, yanked down the top window, climbed up on the sink, and slid through the opening, hanging by her knees in the narrow airshaft. Her heels brushed the bottom part of the window. So much for the erotic thrill of housebreaking. No wonder there'd never been a good word about coitus interruptus!

"Open this door! You want it smashed in?"

Light from the windows below and from the one opposite threw yellow smudges on the filthy stucco walls of the airshaft, highlighting the snails and slugs clinging to the sides. Tensing her abdominal muscles, she swung her arms up and grabbed for the edge of the roof.

Missed.

Her back hit the wall. She jammed her heels into the windowpane to keep from falling. From inside she heard someone pounding on the door. The voice yelled, "Okay, that's it!"

Pushing off the side of the building, she swung up again. And missed again. Her head smacked the wall.

The front door crashed open.

She took a deep breath, swung, reached, and shoved her feet against the glass. The glass shattered. She heard men running in. Grabbing the gutter, she yanked herself up and braced one foot on the window. Someone grabbed for the other. She kicked, pulled the foot out, pushed down hard with both arms and hoisted herself over onto the roof.

She could hear men's shouts from the airshaft. They wouldn't follow her—the space was too narrow. They'd head for the fire escape. She glanced at the roof of the house to her left. Too low; too long a drop. The only way down was over the roofs to the right.

The voices inside were louder. Two men, three?

The roof was barely canted to the side. She moved near the front. No flashing red lights below. No double-parked patrol car. No back-up units wheeling in. These guys weren't cops. Who the hell were they and what did they plan to get out of her? Who sent them? Who knew she'd be here?

No point in prolonging this. She shook the rain from her

hair, and stomped back across the roof to the fire escape, squatted down, pulled out her flashlight, and waited.

The stench of dirt and tar clogged her nose as she stared down at the edge of the roof. Rain pelted her back. In the distance sirens shrieked. She could still hear voices coming up the airshaft. But they were softer. Then louder. It was a moment before she realized the back door had been opened.

"Up there," a male voice shouted. "Move!"

She stood up.

The rain looked like a wall of water shielding endless black. A wall of water coming at him, was that the last thing Delaney had seen as he went over the side? Kiernan's soaked sweatshirt clung to her back. Icy rain pelted her face, ran down her neck, down her back, mixing with the sweat of fear. What was taking them so long?

Feet hit metal. One of the men climbing the fire escape. She waited for the other to flash a light along the edge of the roof, but none came. The fire-escape ladder came just to the edge of the roof; from there it was a matter of scrambling over. She backed off a yard. A hand came over the edge, grabbed onto the gutter. She waited. Another hand appeared. Then the head.

She flicked the flashlight onto high and shone it in his eyes.

"Hey! What the— Turn off that light!" In the piercing light the man looked deathly pale. Meaty cheeks, dark, stringy-wet hair, blue eyes blinking furiously. A face she'd never seen before. "Turn that goddamned thing off!"

"Who sent you?" she demanded.

His eyes were nearly closed. His left hand swung around, grabbing blindly.

"It's a long way down. It'd be real easy for me to shove you back. Now, who are you working for?"

He swung again.

Sirens cut the air, nearer now. Had the neighbors called the police? She had to get out of here. But not without an answer. She stamped on his hand.

He screamed, and let go of the gutter.

Bracing her feet, she seized his hair and yanked his throat against the edge of the gutter. He gagged.

"You've got one more hand. Little bones, real easy to crush. Now, who sent you here?"

The siren was higher pitched, louder, closer. His hair was slick. He was taking too much time, thinking instead of blurting out the truth.

"Who?"

"Olsen," he muttered.

"Don't lie to me. Who?"

"Olsen!"

She jammed his throat into the metal gutter. "Prove it!"

The siren screeched to a stop.

"Olsen!" He snatched at her ankle.

She kicked, slamming her heel into the bridge of his nose. Screaming, he fell back. She heard him thud on the landing.

The siren stopped midshriek. A door slammed.

Kiernan turned and ran across the roof, feet slipping on the wet tar. She scrambled for balance and raced on, over the building's edge onto the next roof, across it, to the next. Ahead were two more roofs this level, then a space, a shorter house. *Don't try the farthest one, that's what they'll expect.*

She stopped, panting, then moved as quietly as possible to the rear edge of the next roof, and felt around for the fire escape. Her hand hit metal. She peered over. Damn! There was a light on inside. Couldn't be helped. She swung her legs over the side and half climbed, half slid down to the back stairs.

Behind her an apartment door opened. She tore down the stairs to the second-story landing. A man upstairs was yelling. She reached the first landing, leapt over the railing to the yard. Footsteps clattered on the stairs behind her. She dashed under the house, through the passageway to the sidewalk.

Across the street she spotted a van parking. She ran toward it, unzipping her fanny pack. Crouching beside the van, she slipped on her slicker.

Voices shouted down the street. In front of Delaney's building. Reacting to the clatter of her assailants.

Forcing herself to move slowly, she walked in the other direction. This was why Harry Scott decried housebreaking. It was, she thought, enough to promote a vow of chastity.

Once around the corner she broke into a run, splashing through puddles, racing as fast as she could. The Jeep was still where she had left it. She climbed in, turned the key and waited for the engine to warm. Now that she had stopped, the fear caught her; she sat shaking in the cold car. She clutched the gear knob tight, desperate to put the Jeep into first and drive to someplace safe. But where? Her motel? Would they know about that too? Olsen's?

Olsen!

She hadn't believed the guy when he'd come up with the name, but still . . . Could she go back to Olsen's? Would he have returned by now, smugly content at having set her up?

She pulled out. There was no reason why Olsen would set her up. What could thugs get out of her that she wouldn't tell Olsen on her own? Nothing *before* tonight. Now, she knew, that would be different.

Olsen lived less than ten blocks from here. She drove north to 24th Street. Even in the rain the commercial street was crowded. Cars lined up to turn into the Bell Market parking lot, blocking the single-file traffic behind. She looked at her watch. No wonder. It was only nine-thirty. It seemed unbelievable that these people were out shopping after a leisurely dinner; it was as if they lived in a parallel reality, sitting calmly in their cars, strolling into the store, deciding between Riesling and zinfandel.

She parked at the bottom of the staircase and ran up the wooden steps of Dixie Alley, through the gate to Olsen's porch.

The apartment was dark. She knocked on the glass. "Skip!" She shone the flashlight through the sliding door onto the dining table. Olsen's mug sat on the stained table. "Damn you, Olsen," she muttered.

She climbed back into the Jeep and drove a couple of blocks, watching for signs of a tail. If there was one, he was real good. She could go back to the motel. Instead she pulled up under a streetlight to look at the sheet of paper she'd taken from Delaney's apartment.

She stared at the damp, curling page. It was a Xerox of a check for a thousand dollars, actually made out in Delaney's real—presumably real—name, Charles Devereaux. In the lower left-hand corner was noted "retainer." It was signed by Delaney's employer: Harold Olsen. Skip Olsen!

"What in hell is going on here?" she muttered aloud. "He insists on hiring me, doesn't tell me that he's already hired a PI who's bought the farm. And then the fucker Olsen disappears. Or was kidnapped. Or is lying next to Delaney in the Great Closed File in the sky."

24

He was choking. He couldn't scream. He couldn't see. He couldn't even feel his damn hands. Skip Olsen groaned.

Suddenly more awake, he tensed. He was tied up. Gagged. Blindfolded. He was going to throw up. And, goddamn it, he needed to take a shit.

His eyelids strained against the tight cloth. He couldn't throw up: he'd choke.

But the sway. Christ, he was in the bottom of a boat. He always did get seasick. What a way to die. He could see the guys at the station, one of them toasting his memory, the rest of them doubled over, laughing their guts out.

Who had conked him? He remembered the hand touching him, but that was it. No memory of the blow. Par for the course, right? Victim never remembers the blow. Brain goes out before pictures hit the memory. Anyone who says he remembers is lying. He tripped more than one felon up on that.

But he'd found out something . . . about Jessica Leporek. The thought lurked in the back of his mind, but he couldn't grab it.

Where was he? Was this a police launch? Coast guard? His feet tingled. Wait: they were propped up against the end of the boat. His head hit something hard. And the stench! He gagged, heard the noise, tried to stop, couldn't. Pain smashed against his skull. His hips and legs were numb. He was grateful. Once he started to feel that bum leg, no amount of self-control would help; he'd choke for sure. He groaned; didn't bother to stifle the noise this time.

Then he heard footsteps on the ladder. Rubber shoes. He smelled brine, beer, and old, rancid sweat before someone smashed his skull hard against the bulkhead.

25

Morning sneaks in to San Francisco. The dark of night fades slowly to the dimness of fog. Fog, Kiernan grumbled as she hoisted herself out of bed, is supposed to be a summer phenomenon.

Eight o'clock might be too early to call Olsen. The thought pleased her. "Olsen Investigative Services—" She slammed the receiver down on the message. Dammit, why had the man hired

Carlos Delaney and not told her? What else hadn't he told her? There were probably things he hadn't told Delaney, and now Delaney was crab delight.

She glanced at the dresser she'd shoved in front of the door and felt the draft from the bathroom window she'd left wide open in case she'd had nocturnal visitors and needed a fast exit.

Impatiently, she dialed Olsen again. Not there. Maybe he'd come in late and left early. If Skip did hire Delaney, it must have been to find out about Robin. And, instead, Robin had found out about him. Maybe they scuffled. Maybe both of them drowned. But not likely. She pulled on her slicker and walked to the coffee shop for Viennese blend and muffins.

It wasn't till she got back that she spotted the envelope on the Jeep's window. A parking ticket! Dammit, why hadn't she chosen a motel with an adequate parking lot? She stuffed the ticket in her pocket and stalked back to the room.

By ten she'd spoken to Olsen's machine twice and her own once; called the Big Sur grocery twice. Where was Maureen Brant? Any other time, she'd be hanging on the phone. But now, when Kiernan had a vital question to ask her—did Olsen hire Delaney?—where was she? Angrily, Kiernan paced the floor. She should abandon the case. Principles— But it was too late now. She wasn't working for Maureen, or even for Garrett, anymore. She was hooked by her own need to know. She left word at Barrow's Grocery that she'd call Maureen at noon.

Now, at last, it was time for Jessica Leporek, who, just maybe, had been Robin's friend. It would be interesting to get Leporek's take on Cummings and the memo theft. And more interesting to get his. Later.

It was just eleven when she parked by a green curb on Market Street about a mile and a half down from Skip Olsen's flat. The rain had retreated to a heavy mist that cloaked the city in drabness.

Proposition Thirty-Seven was housed in a narrow store-front. "Block Offshore Drilling!" demanded a huge sign in one window. Smaller posters filled the other: "Save California

Shores," showed a postcard-quality photograph of the rocky cliffs and dramatic breakers at Big Sur. The scene could have been five miles west of Maureen and Garrett Brant's house. Kiernan stopped, staring; Garrett Brant would never see that beach again. "Protect Our Otters!" "Protect Our Seals!" bumper stickers insisted. "An Ounce of Prevention . . ." loomed over a poster-sized shot of Alaska: a snow-covered peak pierced the pale blue sky, dark green pines tufted with white crowded to the edge of the shore. But the beach was black. Tar-covered sand, rock, the corpses of birds and otters. Kiernan's breath caught. The poster was trite and a bit dated; it pandered directly to sentiment. She knew that intellectually, but it didn't lessen the effect.

It was a moment before she was aware of the cars and trucks rushing past her on Market Street, the bursts of chatter from couples in raincoats hurrying on their way to stock up at the giant Safeway, or to lunch at one of the radicchio-to-chanterelle cafés. Tchernak, she thought, would go wild over all the culinary possibilities on display here.

She opened the door to the headquarters. A tsunami of ringing phones and noisy banter washed over her. Every square foot of the office held a campaign worker, and every worker seemed to be doing three things at once. It was like the ER on a Saturday night—the ER without the blood.

"How can I help you?" a sandy-haired boy shouted from behind a desk.

"Jessica Leporek. I'm here to see her."

"She know you're coming?"

"Yes. I'll just go on back." Before he could protest, she headed for the door in the partition. It was marginally quieter and noticeably messier back there. The sink was hidden by a tower of unwashed cups. Boxes of papers were stacked precariously along the walls and in haphazard rows throughout the room.

To the right was another door, partially opened. She stuck her head around it and looked into a white room with posters, notices, and schedules, tacked up on every wall. A red-haired woman crouched over the phone. Kiernan had seen photos of Jessica Leporek in the campaign literature Tchernak trailed through her flat at home. Unlike most candid shots, those had flattered the subject. In person Jessica looked more like the mother of the vibrant redhead pictured washing down an oily bird or striding up the Capitol steps. Sunbursts of lines surrounded her eyes and two deep, painful-looking grooves marked the space between her eyebrows. Her red hair was streaked with gray, and in need of a wash that she looked too frantic to give it. She held the phone between ear and shoulder, using both hands to root through a pile of papers. Absently, she motioned Kiernan to a chair.

"Of course it's important," Jessica insisted. "The Department of the Interior, not known for its environmental concerns, estimates the oil producers will build twenty-two drilling platforms off northern California alone. Try to take a boat out to sea and it'll be like rush hour on I-80. They—"

For a moment Jessica's mouth hung open as if she couldn't decide whether to regroup and fight to finish her sentence. Her shoulders drooped defeatedly as she pushed aside the piles she'd been excavating and started digging through another.

"So they say," she countered, obviously interrupting the person at the other end of the line. "So they say. If you believed their propaganda, you'd think drilling platforms were nothing more than fish playgrounds. They don't mention that the drilling itself creates tons of toxic waste—seventy-five thousand to one hundred fifty *thousand* tons of toxic waste for every single platform. Multiply that by twenty-two! And that's not taking into account the contents of the contaminated waste water—oil, grease, cadmium, benzene, lead. All this is in the fish's little playground. Do *you* eat fish? Do your kids?"

Listening to her, Kiernan sat back, recalling Olsen's evaluation of Jessica Leporek: the clumsy kid no one wants on his team. But Olsen's assessment wasn't quite right. It was Jessica's freneticism and overwhelming intensity that would give her enemies grounds to mock her. Kiernan found herself eyeing the door with longing.

"Those toxic wastes get dumped on the sea floor. They suffocate the organisms there. We're talking the basis of the food chain. It's— Fine. Yes. Okay. Right. 'Bye." She banged the phone down, yanked out a sheet from the second pile of papers, looked at Kiernan and said, "Yes?"

"Kiernan O'Shaughnessy, Private Investigator. I have an appointment to talk about your friend Robin Matucci."

For an instant Jessica Leporek sat dead still, and the ringing of phones, the questioning shouts from the front room seemed to resound in the silence. Then she turned back to the pile. "Yes?"

Not the reaction of a friend. The reaction of a woman intimidated by an appointment she couldn't recall. Employing the confident manner she'd honed for her court appearances as an expert witness, Kiernan said, "What was your relation to Robin?"

Addressing her words to her papers, Jessica said, "Friends of sorts. Not close. We met at an event I organized."

"You run events, too?"

"*Run*'s too strong a word now. I don't run anything but this, and I've hired a clutch of efficient assistants to keep things in line here"—smiling, she shook her head and waved both hands at the office—"My house is a disaster. I haven't had my hair cut in months; my husband could have a new wife for all I know. She could have dinner with him every night and sleep in my bed three nights a week."

"But you do organize events, and you did meet Robin at one of them," Kiernan said, feeling as if she were translating a tongue foreign to logic. Still, she couldn't help but like Jessica. "When was that?"

"A little over three years ago, in September."

"It must have been a memorable occasion, for a woman as busy as you to recall the date."

Jessica laughed, and momentarily the grooves between her

eyebrows relaxed. "You sound like my husband, only a helluva lot more tactful. He'd say it was a memorable occasion when I wasn't carrying on about a two billion-dollar fishing industry in danger of permanent damage, or—"

"Was Robin one of your supporters?"

"Just like Bill, my husband. Plow on through, he says; it's the only way."

"Robin?"

The smile faded. "No, she wasn't working for Prop. Thirty-Seven. She was a fool not to spend every spare hour down here. What do you think it will do to the charter-boat business to have the shoreline marked with drilling platforms? And one big spill, what's that going to do to the recreational fishing trade? How many guys are going to lay out big bucks to spend the day floating in muck, pulling in fish they'd be afraid to eat?"

"So why wasn't she here? Because of Dwyer Cummings?"

The grooves deepened. "Cummings?"

"I heard part of your debate with him. Did you know he was one of Robin's most frequent passengers?"

"Well, I shouldn't be surprised, but I'll admit I am. Still, it makes sense." Noting Kiernan's puzzled expression, she said, "Robin was totally committed to her boat, her business. She wouldn't have done something that damaged it. Now I know what you're going to ask: then why didn't she support the initiative? The answer is because she didn't think ahead."

Kiernan held up her palm. "That doesn't square with what I know of Robin. She saved her money to help her father. She worked hard to buy *Early Bird*. She considered the future a lot. Do you think she was planning to *not* have the boat in a year or two?"

Jessica picked up a paper clip and began pulling the curves straight. "I can't imagine her without it. But, look, what difference does that make? She's dead."

"Maybe. Possibly not."

"Alive? You think she really could be alive? I can't believe it. That's great. Where do you think she is?"

Despite her public position Jessica Leporek hadn't learned to be much of an actress. "If Robin survived, she hasn't contacted anyone."

"So where could she be hiding?"

Interesting this immediate assumption that Robin was not injured but hiding. "Hiding from whom?"

"Well, you know, if she screwed up and caused the boat to sink she wouldn't be able to face anyone. She told me when she was a kid she learned success was everything: to be a failure, or even average, was to not exist. You're a pretty big failure if you sink your boat."

No mention of Delaney's death. Was Jessica's focus on the loss of *Early Bird*, rather than Delaney, her bias or Robin's? Kiernan lowered her voice. "Jessica, I've heard a rumor that Dwyer Cummings was involved in a theft, probably as victim, just before he left Alaska."

Still clasping the paper clip with both hands, Jessica leaned forward, as if pulled magnetically. "Just what do you know?"

"A memo of his was stolen."

Jessica shook her head, remarkably unconvincingly. "Damn! I've heard that rumor for three years, ever since Dwyer got here."

"Three years? He couldn't have been working on the anti-initiative campaign that long. The initiative campaign committee was formed only last year, wasn't it?" Kiernan asked, trying to recall those facts with which Tchernak had sprinkled dinner night after night, facts she'd tried to tune out.

"Officially last year, but the initiative's been on our minds for closer to five. We just had to wait till the time was right. And nothing's secret. The oil guys had their spies. I don't know what Dwyer's job was until this year, something low profile."

"The kind of job they might give him to get him away from Alaska and out of sight?"

"Maybe." Jessica shrugged, a forced, phony-looking movement. "Are you sure you don't know anything more about it?"

"Not yet, but I will. And I'll find out quicker and more

accurately if you tell me what you know. Like what could that memo have said."

The boy from the front desk leaned in through the doorway. "Jessica, what about the rally at Stinson Beach tomorrow?"

Jessica grabbed a clump of papers from her In box. "Wait, I've got something right here on that."

"I mean: Are you going?"

"What time?"

"Two."

"Let me—"

"You're free. I checked. I'll drive you, and get you back here in time for your meeting with"—he glanced from Jessica to Kiernan and back—"your meeting. Okay? You'll go?"

"Right, but we'll have to move fast."

"Gotcha," he said and left.

"You were about to tell me just what you know about Dwyer Cummings and his memo," Kiernan prodded.

Jessica glanced suspiciously at the doorway, then around the room. "Okay. But promise you won't repeat this, not that it's specific enough to do any harm. I just don't want anyone to be able to say we're mudslinging."

Kiernan nodded.

"Well, the word I've gotten on Dwyer is that he's careful about what he says. He drinks, but he can hold it. He's at his best bringing together groups of guys and getting them to talk. If he has a fault—what *they* think of as a fault—it's that he can be indiscreet in that kind of setting."

Jessica's evaluation of Cummings's drinking was more benign than Olsen's. "Are you saying the memo that was stolen was indiscreet?"

"I don't know. But whatever it was they shipped him out of Alaska headquarters fast."

"What was the memo about?"

"Kiernan, if I knew, I'd tell you. I don't know. It's not for lack of trying to find out, believe me. I've virtually lived in these offices for nearly two years. Any sensible person would vote for

Prop. Thirty-Seven. But the truth is we could still lose this election. I'd saw off my right leg to anyone who'd give me damning secrets about the Energy Producers' Group's spokesman. I've told you everything. I'm counting on you."

A woman peered in through the door hesitantly, then noting Jessica's expression, turned and left. In the front room the phones seemed louder, the talk more urgent. Her time with Jessica was running out. Kiernan said, "You've known Robin for three years, but you and Robin weren't friends at all, were you?"

Still clutching the stack of papers, she said, "Look, I'm sorry she's dead, or missing or whatever, but—"

"No, you're not. This is a woman you describe as being interested only in her own boat. You don't care about charter boats; she didn't care about the initiative. Neither of you is the type to go shopping together. And yet you went to see her a number of times. Why?"

When Jessica didn't answer, Kiernan demanded, "You met her at an event you planned. What kind of event?"

"An opening at my gallery."

The phone rang. Jessica grabbed it. Kiernan blocked out the content, listening instead to the rumble of conversation from the front room, the ringing phones, the door opening and closing. She was smiling. So, Jessica Leporek, the environmentalist, ran an art gallery. Not an unlikely hobby for a woman with energy and drive, who'd been a docent at the Asian Art Museum, and who, if Olsen was to be believed, had "married a pile of money." What kind of art would a woman with her interest in the ocean environment choose for her gallery? As soon as Jessica put down the receiver, Kiernan said, "Did you handle Garrett Brant at your gallery?"

"Garrett? We talked about it. But it never worked out."

"Was that three years ago, at that opening?"

She nodded.

The phone rang. Kiernan put a hand over the receiver. "This is important. Right after that opening Garrett Brant was hit and nearly killed. He was driving back to the city to see a woman about arranging a show. That was you, wasn't it?"

"No. We never got as far as that. I never promised him a show."

"But he was coming to see you, wasn't he?" The phone stopped, then started ringing again.

"I have to answer—"

"Answer me first."

"I don't have to talk to you."

"Jessica, Garrett Brant was coming to see you the day he was hit. Helping with this investigation is the least you can do for him. So tell me about Garrett."

"Okay, okay. He said he'd bring me something. But not that day. He was to come up two days later. I waited, but of course, he never showed. It took me a week and a half to find out he'd been in an accident."

"What was he bringing you?"

"I don't know."

"Jessica!"

"I *don't*. He just told me it would be something useful to the campaign."

"Not a painting?"

"I said I don't know." She wrenched the receiver free and picked it up. "Okay, okay. Right. Yes, now." Putting down the receiver, she said, "It's nearly noon. I have to go."

"Okay. Here's my card. I'm at this motel. If you think of anything, no matter how minor, call me." Leaving the card on Jessica's desk, Kiernan raced through the office to the Jeep. Noon! At noon she was supposed to call Maureen Brant. And this time she was probably more anxious to talk to Maureen than vice versa.

26

Garrett Brant looked at the redwoods beyond his studio window. He smiled happily. *The trees . . . just like they were when I was a boy here. Almost as if time had stopped.* He moved closer to the window. *There's the scar in the bark, where my swing hit it—*

He turned and noticed the wall of photographs. *Odd that the edges should curl so soon. I just put them up when Maureen and I got here.*

Tomorrow I'll be in the city. Should I bring it? He smiled, remembering Jessica Leporek's face, those slate-gray eyes of hers opening wide, her pale—salmon mixed with ocher?—lips stretched sensuously in that big smile, her burning-ember red hair. Her hand ice cold on his arm. "It's vital," that's what she'd said. He could see those tentative lines that were just starting to take hold between her brows—they'd be deep grooves someday. Intriguing. He could paint her. She'd like that. But she'd be more interesting in ten years when those lines . . .

He turned and caught sight of his painting.

Maureen Brant hunched forward, clutching the wheel as the old Dodge Colt bounced from rut to ridge on the dirt road. She pictured Garrett in his studio, staring at his easel. Trying the doorknob. Frustrated, slamming his shoulder into the door. *Just as long as he doesn't think to get his pistol and shoot out the lock, and wander off.* She shivered as she fought the fear that rode with her every time she got in the car. *He'll be alone for* over an hour. *I hope he'll be alone! But it's too soon for danger. And it's not even dark.*

The small tan car hit a rock. She grabbed the wheel tighter and stepped on the gas, as if speeding over the problem would smooth it out. A wave of fear filled her. *Why didn't I get a better car when I had the chance? What'll happen when they can't patch this together anymore?* She could picture Garrett's surprise at discovering a new car, his delight, his questions. But how many times could she play out that scene without shouting, "We've had it for a month, a year, a decade! Goddamn it!" She could see his eyes narrowing in disbelief, then his whole body sucked into that fear he could neither understand nor rid himself of. That deep gnawing fear, always ready to ambush him.

How long could she protect him from the world? From herself?

27

Kiernan was in the driver's seat before she noticed the envelope on the windshield. Another parking ticket. "Damn Olsen and his rotten relations with the cops!" she muttered.

Before she could reach for it, the phone rang.

"Kiernan? It's Maureen. I was afraid I wouldn't be able to get you before I had to leave. I'm sorry I couldn't get here at ten like I said, but—"

"Okay. That's not the issue we need to talk about. This is: Did Skip Olsen hire Carlos Delaney to investig—"

Maureen gasped.

"Olsen hired him for you, right? You knew about Delaney."
Maureen didn't answer.

"And you lied to me."

"I couldn't—"

"I can't trust you. I—"

"No!" she shouted. "No, please listen, Kiernan. I felt real bad about that. It was just that I was so afraid you wouldn't take the case. Don't be mad at Skip, I made him promise not to let you know. I was just so afraid. You know how much this means to me."

"Maureen, you let me stumble around blind. Delaney knew the truth, and he's dead."

"But Robin killed him. She's not going to get to you."

"Why not? Are you saying now that she's dead?"

"No. But, look, she could be in Oregon, or in Alaska, or even Europe, or . . . anywhere."

"Or in San Francisco, right? Right, Maureen?"

"Kiernan, please," Maureen sobbed. "It was a rotten thing to do. If it'd been anyone but you, it wouldn't have mattered so much. That's not a great excuse, is it? But, look, I'm really sorry. You saw how nervous I was. You probably figured it was from the life I lead. Well, that's pretty much true. But it was also because I felt so awful not telling you about Delaney. And Delaney, oh God, how do you think I feel about him? I never met him, but still. . . ."

"The crabs ate away the skin on his head," Kiernan said, unable to control herself. "They ate down to the bone, Maureen. They ate his ears and his nose and his fingertips."

"Oh my God!" She sounded as if she was choking.

Kiernan flushed, disgusted with herself. Her bedside manner had dropped to a new low. "Maureen, what did Garrett tell you about Dwyer Cummings?"

"You mean you're going to stay on the case?" Her voice broke. "Thanks."

"Okay. About Cummings?"

"I asked Garrett five or six times, but Garrett didn't remember him. Is there anything else you want me to ask him? Kiernan, who have you talked to? What did you find out?"

Quick recovery, Kiernan thought, but maybe all those years of social work had taught Maureen to read the person she was talking to. If so, she'd know getting right to the point was her best move here. "I just saw Jessica Leporek. She said that Garrett was going to bring her something useful to the campaign."

"Campaign?"

"Proposition Thirty-Seven, to block any onshore support for oil platforms. She's in charge of the northern California operation. But she also runs an art gallery. Garrett was going to bring her something. What was it?"

"Was that the gallery opening Garrett went to before his accident?"

"Right. They met there and he promised to bring her something important."

There was a pause before Maureen said, "This is the first I've heard about it. Are you sure?"

"Jessica sounded sure. Ask Garrett."

"I will. But don't expect much. If he remembered, and if he was willing to tell me, he'd have done it by now. We've lived in the day before his accident for three years.

"Ask anyway."

"I'll ask him all afternoon long. What else did you find out?"

"Wait. Let's use a little scientific method here. In a pathology investigation you run various tests, check the results and on that basis decide whether your premise was correct, and what other tests are called for. In our investigation, these interviews are those tests. Let's look at the results before we go on. Your premise was that Garrett went to San Francisco to arrange a showing with some woman, probably Jessica. The test result, the interview, indicates otherwise. According to Jessica, she never offered him a show. But Garrett was going to bring her his gift two days later. The next day he was hit."

The phone crackled and it was a moment before Maureen said, "Maybe he did give her something. Maybe she's lying about not getting it."

"Whatever Garrett was going to bring her, she wanted it a lot. If she'd seen him, she'd either have it, or know she wasn't going to get it. No, Maureen, she didn't see him. She figures whatever he had is still around. Maybe Garrett mentioned it unintentionally. Think!"

"Kiernan, I've had three years to analyze every word he's uttered." She lowered her voice. "Garrett works on the same, never-changing input. If I didn't vary the small things—make us a picnic lunch, bring in flowers from the market—he would follow the same routine, make the same observations every single day. If there's any variation in activity, in comment, it sticks out like a flashing light. And he hasn't said a word to suggest he was planning anything except seeing a woman about a gallery show."

Kiernan swallowed and said, "Sometimes in an investigation you run the same tests, but because you have newfound knowledge, outside knowledge, you can judge the results differently. Think about it."

"Of course," Maureen said. "What are you going to do now?"

"Maureen!"

"Sorry, I didn't mean to press you. I just wanted to know. I'm getting so nervous. I think about Delaney, and my skin turns to ice. I hear things . . . outside the house."

"What kind of things?"

"Branches crackling. I must have called Garrett ten times on the intercom in his studio today." She laughed nervously. "If he weren't in the shape he is, he'd think I was crazy. Probably there's no one in the bushes. Probably I'm just thinking of Delaney. But I'll be okay. I've got a rifle. I know how to use it. And there's probably nothing outside anyway. I'll call you tonight."

"Wait. Don't dismiss your worries. Skip Olsen's had his car window broken. Delaney's dead."

"Nobody knows where we are. Only you, and you're not going to tell."

"I could get someone to come down to protect you."

"No! Look, it would make me even more nervous to think anyone else knew where we are. Besides, Garrett can handle a gun, too. If someone attacked us he'd shoot. We'll be okay, really."

"Okay," Kiernan said slowly. "But let me know if something else happens. And if Garrett remembers anything about what he promised Jessica, call me at twenty after four this afternoon. If he doesn't, I'll call the store tomorrow morning. At ten."

"Okay, and thanks. And, Kiernan—"

"Yes?"

"Be careful." She hung up.

Kiernan put down the phone, reached through the vent window to grab the parking ticket. She flung the envelope in the back and started the engine. The first order of business was lunch. She could turn south into the Mission district for Mexican, Peruvian, or Guatemalan food. But unless the city had changed, she could end up devoting the rest of the afternoon to finding a parking space. Or risk another ticket.

Instead she headed back to the motel, walked down to a Vietnamese restaurant on Chestnut Street and picked up an order of chicken satay. All the way back, the spicy smell of the satay mocked her decision to wait and eat in the room. Wasting time in restaurants during a case drove her crazy. In the motel she could be talking to Tchernak. He'd have the background reports now. He'd . . .

She walked into the room, pulled the bedside table next to the middle of the bed, deposited the lamp on the floor and the paper bag on the table.

Leaving the bag unopened, she dialed Olsen. She wouldn't unhook the lids until he answered.

"Olsen Investigations—" She hung up on the recording. Dammit, where was the man? He had plenty of faults, but she sure hadn't expected a disappearing act. She leaned back against the headboard and glanced down at the faded leaf motif of the bedspread. He'd threatened to go to the Wharf. Had he ignored her and machoed on down there? Fool! He'd not only get himself conked on his most expendable part, but he could screw up the whole case. Damn him to hell! She didn't have time to run this investigation and track him down too.

She unpacked the bag, and opened the containers of satay and rice. Both were full. No room to mix. And this was not the type of motel room that included extras, like dishes. She dialed her own office. Delayed Gratification, round two.

Her message came on. Tchernak did not interrupt it. It was lunch hour, Kiernan reminded herself. Tchernak and Ezra were probably lunching on the beach. If she was ever going to eat, she'd have to change the rules of the game. The tape buzzed. "Tchernak, it's me. Call me as soon as you get in."

28

It had still been sunny when she left the motel, but a few miles away the dunes along the Great Highway, San Francisco's westernmost road, were cold and soggy. Kiernan looked at the ocean. She could see the breakers spitting foam, but the fog had turned the water pale gray, the sand a dirty gray-brown, and curtained off the horizon. It seemed as if the world out here was all made of one drab, dank fabric.

She drove slowly along the highway, passing through the metal gate that would be closed if sand covered all four lanes. Garrett Brant had come to the city on the day of his accident for a reason still unknown. Not to arrange a gallery show, as he'd told Maureen. Why had he lied? What had he come for? What he *had* done was get himself hit as he walked along this road.

Raised ten feet above the city streets behind it like a miniature version of China's Great Wall, the Great Highway protects the low-lying streets of the Sunset District from the blowing sand dunes to the west. It parallels the beach for two miles, a no-access, no-parking stretch. The alphabetical streets of the Sunset District—Judah, Kirkham . . . Ulloa, Vincente, Wawona—dead-end at the embankment leading to the raised highway. Garrett Brant had been hit on the wind-streaked dunes across from Noriega Street on a chillingly gray day just like this.

The highway department had put in pampas grass and ice plant in this year's hopeful attempt to hold back the encroaching sand. Had these shivering little bushes been here three years ago, when Garrett Brant lay abandoned? As Kiernan neared Noriega, the grasses gave way to sand and the hard-packed path angled close to the road. It was an easy place from which a car could veer off, strike a pedestrian, and race away.

She stopped and gazed along the dirt-and-sand pathway through the dunes down to the ocean. Four o'clock on a Wednesday afternoon; the beach was empty. It was a Tuesday when Garrett was hit. He was lucky a jogger had run up the path from the beach, scared off his assailant, noticed the red convertible. But which was better? To be dead or to be stuck forever in one uneasy moment?

Kiernan shook her head. Had he elected to live in his moment, Garrett Brant might have been willing to forego the truth of normal life. He might, like one of the sadhus Kiernan had seen in Nepal, have found bliss in his awareness of the trees, of the sharpness of the rocky path under his callused feet, of the still air grazing his naked shoulders. He might have taken pleasure in experiencing his moments of life as no westerner seems able to do. But that had been a choice Garrett had not made. His moments were no different from those of Maureen or

Kiernan or Robin Matucci, moments given meaning only as preludes to significant ones to come. Except that Garrett's were preludes to nothing.

Kiernan shifted into first and stepped on the gas. The convertible the jogger had spotted that day . . . Odd, a car with its top down on the Great Highway. But not so odd if Robin had come from another part of the city. If she had left Fisherman's Wharf—according to Olsen, it had been sunny there—in a hurry and hadn't wanted to waste time dealing with the top.

The dunes on the ocean side of the highway disappeared, leaving a cement walkway and flat beach. Then a new rise of sharp dunes, twenty feet above the road, spotted with cypress and bright orange ice plant, blocked the view of the sea. Kiernan felt a shiver deep in her chest. It was secluded in those dunes that she and Rosten had lain, huddled in his sleeping bag, making love as long as they could stay awake. Passion and exhaustion, sleep and lust had woven together seamlessly. More than once she had woken up with him inside her, pressed her naked body harder against his as if to remove the space of thought, and drifted back to sleep.

Automatically, she shook off the memory. Then she smiled. She had driven the Great Highway several times each year, every year since Rosten left. Those dunes had always triggered the same memory, and the memory had led to surges of fury. But this time the thought of Marc Rosten didn't anger her, not since she had raided his office and read that autopsy report. Not since she'd won a round.

She and Rosten had never played games, even at parties. Early on they'd realized they were both too unwilling to lose. But unless he had mellowed, she thought, this game wasn't over yet.

She came to the end of the Great Highway, pulled across the street and parked. On impulse, she scrambled into the back of the Jeep, extricated her running shoes from her bag and pulled them on. Then she walked across the street and up onto the top of the dunes. The fog had thickened, settling in around the dunes, covering the water, muting the sounds of traffic. What had Delaney felt out there on the last trip of his life, he who was not a sailor? Had the thirty-foot waves panicked him? Had he grabbed for a bottle he'd avoided for years? Had he slipped and banged his head, sustained that single bruise, and fallen overboard? Or had he looked at Robin Matucci and realized he was going to die?

But why? Why would Robin Matucci have run down Garrett Brant? And what would have induced her to jettison her beloved boat—and her life—just to murder her deckhand?

In the few minutes Kiernan had been standing on the dunes, the fog had congealed into heavy mist, as San Franciscans would call it. Anywhere else, it would be called rain. Rain that was doing her green wool businesswoman suit no good at all. She hurried down the slope, half running, half slaloming in the wet sand. By the time she got to the car the "mist" had soaked into her jacket and her hair was dripping.

It would have been more impressive to arrive at Dwyer Cummings's house dry, but so be it. Given what she had to ask him, he wasn't going to be pleased anyway. She climbed into the Jeep, turned on the engine, and sat shivering until the heater blew out warm air.

The Forest Hill section of the city where Cummings lived was a twenty-minute drive from the Great Highway. It was one of San Francisco's most exclusive districts, an area where finding a parking spot did not in itself signal a banner day. She pulled up in front of Cummings's house, toweled off her hair and penciled on eyeliner, a hint of shadow and a brush of blush. The effect, she noted, was not what it would have been before she'd seen Garrett Brant and Carlos Delaney, but it was better than nothing.

She walked up the stone-slab path to Cummings's house, only five minutes late, pressed the bell, and stood under the portico, listening to the mist splat on the walkway stones.

The house was not outstanding for the neighborhood. A

large beige stucco rectangle with portico pillars guarding the door and Spanish tile work around the windows, it was an appealing mixture of exotic and homey. The single yellow rectangle of light in a downstairs window was a good sign. More lights might have meant more people, interruptions, and avenues of escape for the Energy Producers' Group spokesman. A single light on the second floor would have suggested a timer.

Cummings sure was taking his time to make the twenty-foot walk from the light to the door. He was supposedly expecting her. And even if he'd forgotten, it wasn't yet six-thirty. He should still be in decent enough shape to make it across the living room. She pressed the bell again. Olsen had described Dwyer Cummings as a company man, bright, single-minded. "Don't let that folksy charm snow you."

The man who opened the door was a six-foot blond.

"Dwyer Cummings?" Kiernan asked.

Someone not assessing the man might have missed the momentary hesitation before he smiled and said, "You're the investigator?" His voice had the same easy welcome she recalled from the radio debate she'd heard driving up to the city.

"Right. Kiernan O'Shaughnessy. Thanks for taking the time to talk to me."

"Sure. Come on in. You're getting soaked out there." Cummings smiled easily. His hair was styled to the side now and seemed to have been finger-combed recently, possibly the cause of his delayed arrival at the door. Cornflower-blue eyes were set over wide, flat cheeks. It was a face that said "relax, trust me." Which, Kiernan realized, made her suspicious. He could have been the social director of the second best fraternity on campus—twenty-five well-preserved years later—welcoming an assistant dean for his annual inspection, hoping he didn't find what?

Kiernan followed him into a living room that ran the width of the house. The decanter sat on a round table between two leather chairs. He motioned her to one, settled into the other and said, "Drink?"

"Thanks."

"Scotch okay?"

"Fine."

"Water? Soda?"

"Water."

His hand was steady as he poured. He added a dash of water to his own glass, brow tensing as he flicked the pitcher back up to stop the diluting effect. It made her think of her uncle Amon, taking her aside when she was too young to care and explaining in studied seriousness how to mix a highball. "Kerry, lass," he'd said, slurring his sibilants, "after you stir the rye and soda always add a dash of rye on the top. Gives you that good taste of strength right off."

Cummings saluted her with his glass, but seemed careful not to drink until she had. It was good Scotch, and she felt the heat of it flow down her spine. She said, "I heard you Monday on the radio. You handled it well."

He leaned back and crossed his legs. "I'll be the first to tell you it's not easy debating that woman. It's like fending off a pack of hounds. You toss a stick and while you're watching one race after it, another's got its teeth in your ankle."

Kiernan couldn't suppress a grin at the accuracy of his observation. "From what I hear, Prop. Thirty-Seven is still up for grabs."

He smiled. "I take that as a testament to the good sense of northern Californians."

"And to your own handling of the campaign?"

He shrugged. "Hardest market in the country. Out here they're all environmentalists, even if they've never seen an unpaved street. You talk about offshore drilling and they think one end of the pipe's in the well and the other opens directly into the ocean. I'll tell you, Kiernan, it's been a challenge to make people realize that tanker accidents like the *Valdez* in Alaska have no more to do with oil platforms than steers do with steering wheels. I wish I had a dollar for every time I have to explain that in offshore drilling we don't use tankers, we pipe the oil from the platform to our onshore facilities."

"Not if Prop. Thirty-Seven passes, and you can't get the zoning changes, sewer permits and roads built to allow you to *have* onshore facilities."

He stiffened. "Hey, you sure you're not Leporek in sheep's clothing?" Glancing at her green wool suit, his eyes came to rest at the hem, which ended on her thigh. "Or should I say, fox's clothing?"

It was a tacky comment. What was it Hartoonian had said? A problem with the bottle. Didn't know when to keep his mouth shut, but he wasn't a thief.

Cummings finished his drink, held his glass up questioningly, and when she declined a refill, stood to make his own. With his back to her he said, "You're here about Robin. What have you unearthed about her death?"

No preamble, no words of regret, no movement to pour the Scotch or add fresh ice while he asked the question to which his nervousness was linked. Kiernan said, "We don't know that she's dead."

His hand stopped midair. It was a moment before he said, "Really? How could she have survived? It'd be a miracle." The words were enthusiastic but the voice was wary. That was rating as the normal reaction.

"You probably didn't realize this, but you were her most frequent passenger. Did you know her from Alaska?"

"Yeah." Now he eased several ice cubes into his glass. "Robin was a great captain. Once you went out with her, she had a lot of loyalty and she made a point of being accommodating."

"How so?"

"Not what you think!"

"I don't think anything, Mr. Cummings."

Cummings stared at his drink.

She let a moment pass before asking, "Did you arrange the fishing parties?"

He nodded and sat back down.

"Business parties?"

Again he nodded warily.

"You work for the Energy Producers' Group now, right?"

"I'm on loan," he muttered.

Three years. A long-term loan. "So the parties you brought on board were from more than one oil company?"

He jerked his head up. "What does that have to do with Robin's boat sinking? It's not as if we sunk it!"

Very jumpy, Kiernan thought. "No. But I thought you might have some clue about malfunctioning. You're an engineer, aren't you? The men you brought aboard were engineers."

"We're not all engineers. And even those of us who trained as engineers are likely to be pretty far removed from the slide rule. Besides, we were busy dealing with salmon or albacore or rock cod; we weren't down below fixing the engine. At two hundred bucks a day per guest, you don't spend your time covered in grease." He stared at his glass a moment, and when he put it down the lines of anger in his face had eased. "These trips are called tax trips. Perfectly legal. We bring guys from different companies together, let them get comfortable with each other so they can cooperate on projects. We could bring them in cold and hope they'd all think alike—that's the way it used to be done. But you can imagine that doesn't work most of the time. Everyone's used to being in charge. They don't want someone else telling them what to do. Or they're married to one way of doing things and they'd leave the oil under the surface before they'd consider another way of exploring. If you go into a project cold these guys are all sharp edges, all unknown quantities."

"And if they're indiscreet, it's not where anyone will overhear, right?" Anyone except Delaney with his wire. But Delaney had been investigating Robin, not the oil men.

He shrugged. "But if you got these same guys together on a volleyball court—"

"Or a fishing expedition?"

"Right. They're all buddies when they're pulling in thirty-pound steelheads."

"As long as they're *all* pulling them in?"

He raised his glass to her.

"So to ensure that you went with Robin?"

"Right."

He shifted in his chair. "Look, the election is less than a week away. I've got enough work to keep me up till two. Could you get to the point?"

"You knew Robin from Alaska. From the California Tavern?"

"Right."

"Did you ever run across a guy named Garrett Brant there? An artist."

"Artist? No. Closest I came to art or artists was the paintings in the conference rooms. But plenty of guys passed through the bar without shaking my hand." He glanced at his nearly empty glass but didn't freshen it.

Kiernan surveyed her remaining questions and went with the most pressing. "What about Robin's deckhand, Carlos Delaney? Was he with her in Alaska?"

"She didn't have deckhands in Alaska. She *was* a hand there."

"Was Delaney there?"

"Not as I remember."

"Up there you were in administration?"

"Probability Analysis, Marine Division Project Coordinator."

"That means chances of things going wrong?"

"That means running tests beforehand to make sure things *don't* go wrong."

Kiernan took a swallow of Scotch. "That's quite different from the media spokesman's job you have here."

"Look, I agreed to talk about Robin, I didn't—"

"A memo was stolen from your office up there. Then you were transferred down here. What happened?"

"I don't know where you heard—"

"A theft. You were transferred, so you were involved. But you weren't fired, just gotten out of the way, just warned. You—"

He slammed the glass on his knee. Ice cubes jumped. "Leporek! Of course, she's been feeding you these lies. A week before the election, and she's running scared."

Ignoring his outburst, Kiernan said, "If you'd been an innocent victim, no one would have bothered you, would they?"

Cummings's mouth tightened.

"Unless you had a reputation for indiscretion."

"I don't. Do you think the Energy Producers' Group would choose someone unreliable to represent the entire industry?"

If they didn't expect the job to become as important as it had; if they couldn't replace their spokesman without nudging the opposition to wonder why. "What was in that memo?"

"Out! Just get out of here. And you blab this slander to the press you'll see a lawsuit that will make your ass twirl."

"What, Dwyer? You ran tests to make sure things don't go wrong. Something did go wrong, right? What was it?"

"Nothing went wrong. Our tests are monitored. There's nothing that happened that I could have hidden."

Cummings was clearly so relieved to be able to give that answer that she believed him. And believed she was on the wrong track. "Still, that memo was enough to get you transferred. It was—"

He dropped the glass, grabbed her arm and yanked her to her feet, wrenching her around on the three-inch stiletto heels. She glanced down at his foot and drove her heel into it. He yelped.

"Don't try that again," she said as she walked to the door.

29

It was twenty to eight when Kiernan stopped at the top of Dixie Alley. She pulled her soggy jacket tighter around her and ran down the stairs, hoping to find Olsen seated at his dining-room table staring at the lights across the Bay in Oakland. She wanted to see him eating pizza, drinking a beer, looking so comfortable that it would take all her control not to kick the man.

She ran through the gate and up the stairs.

The apartment was still dark.

She knocked.

No answer.

Rain battered against the glass doors. Inside Olsen's, nothing had changed since yesterday. The flashlight-lit rooms still showed no signs of conflict. The coffee mug was still on the table, as if he'd stepped out for a minute instead of a day.

He had lied about hiring Delaney. What other fictions had he created, what errant paths had he suggested? She remembered their first meeting about the case. Olsen had been so earnest. She couldn't believe he was a good enough actor to stage a scene like that. And couldn't think of a reason why he should.

But if he hadn't hired the thugs and chosen to disappear—and those options didn't make sense—then there was no getting around the fact that Skip Olsen was missing against his will. Kidnapped in a city where he'd made enemies on the dock and maybe worse ones on the police force.

She climbed back up the staircase to the Jeep, picturing Olsen tied up, lying on his bad hip, his sciatic nerve shrieking down his leg.

The phone was ringing when Kiernan opened the motel door twenty minutes later.

"This is your office calling," Tchernak announced. "You know there's no point in leaving call-back messages if you don't answer your phones." After Cummings's down-home voice, Tchernak's deep tones sounded bearlike. She could hear Ezra's groan of canine pleasure in the background. Tchernak must be scratching behind his ears.

"*He* misses you. He spent all day moping in your office, your *former* kitchen. And you know he doesn't approve of that reconstruction."

"That modem and printer buy his dog food. Or they would if you hadn't spoiled him so he turns up his snout at kibble."

"Hey, hey. You wait!" Tchernak snapped. "Sorry, I was talking to *him*. But you probably figured that."

"It was one of the options." She laughed. "You did good, Tchernak. If you weren't destined to be a media star, I'd co-opt you for the world of crime."

"Always willing to help. Macho presence at your back."

Kiernan hesitated. Tchernak had been intrigued with the idea of investigating since the day he moved in. Her job had been a major selling point of his agreeing to be employed by her. No case had been concluded without his eager offer to stake out, to infiltrate, to intimidate with his looming presence. A houseman's place is in the home, she'd insisted: cleaning, cooking, shopping, dog walking! You don't spend all night cramped in the Triumph watching an entryway door that never opens, and come home and create a decent soufflé! She'd said it all before. Now she sighed and said, "Okay."

"Okay?" He was clearly amazed. "Does this mean you're hiring me on?"

"Tentatively. I'm going to need a bodyguard."

"You're in danger!"

Kiernan laughed at the outrage in his voice. "Tchernak, what kind of work do you think I do? There's always danger. But it's not me I need guarded. It's Olsen, *if* I can find him so you can guard him. See if you can get here first thing in the morning. Now let me speak to *him*."

The great slurp told her Ezra was on the phone.

It was 8:35 when she hung up. The motel room seemed emptier, shabbier. Like a cell, locked. "Damn," she muttered, as she realized how relieved she was that Tchernak was coming. "Damn, damn!" She missed him. She missed the easy comfort of his presence. And she resented his hold on her emotions. She wasn't likely to fall into the hole Maureen Brant had, but by wanting Tchernak here, she wasn't free either.

She tried to push thoughts of Ezra from her mind. She didn't want to think of Tchernak dropping *him* off at a cell. Tchernak always swore Ezra didn't mind the kennel, but Kiernan knew otherwise. When she got home Ezra would rush up, licking her cheeks and arms, wagging his tail, and leaping like a Chihuahua. But in those big brown eyes would be the unmistakable sign of hurt.

She dialed Olsen one last time. Again his machine answered. Slowly she put down the phone. She had done nothing but complain about him, but in an odd, baffling way she was fond of the guy. He reminded her of the old, overstuffed chair she'd moved from house to house. It ruined the look of her living room in La Jolla; she couldn't make a good case for keeping it, but she couldn't bring herself to haul it to the dump either. As for Olsen, she didn't feel quite the fondness for him as she did for the chair, but she didn't want to think of him lying helpless in pain somewhere either. He'd insisted on going to the Wharf yesterday. There'd been ample time for him to come home. Now she was going to have to spend the night tracking him down.

30

The area around Fisherman's Wharf was uncharacteristically deserted for quarter to ten at night. Cold and rain were never attractive qualities to tourists, and only the hardiest would still be considering the T-shirts or souvenir shops. With the rain and fog closing in, few regulars would head out into the Pacific tomorrow. It was the perfect place to hide a kidnap victim.

In the dim light, the wharf looked even shabbier than it had before dawn yesterday. Across the street the rain beat discarded bags and paper plates into gray slime. Behind it, the tacky shops seemed drabber than usual. Brine from the salt air had caked onto their plastic signs; it gave a scabrous look to the red and orange letters. The rain ran down the signs in rivulets, leaving a trail of dirt from the gutters above.

Kiernan pulled up the hood of her slicker and headed across the street to the wharf proper. The restaurants and huge storage building that enclosed the acre of docks loomed larger and the docks looked more out of place than ever: reality consumed by its own hype. To imagine the wharf as real meant keeping her head down, looking at the gray, seasoned planks, smelling the briny water, and listening to the soft whine of mooring lines pulling taut and the single sea lion baying in chorus with the foghorn.

The center dock was slippery. Most of the berths were dark. If the deckhands were on the boats, they were sleeping. But Ben Pedersen was awake and on board. Odd for ten at night. Through the misted-over window, Kiernan could see him sitting in his luncheonettelike cabin, writing on a yellow pad.

"Hello, Ben! Can I come on board?" Kiernan called through the steamy window. Pedersen looked more bearlike than she remembered—a wily bear, one who'd survived many winters and outwitted more than a few hunters.

Pedersen wiped clear a circle of glass. He squinted through it, his bearded face wary. "So what have you found out?" It was more of a challenge than an inquiry.

She climbed onto the boat. From the radio came the rumble of desultory conversation. The cabin was little warmer than the open deck behind it. Pedersen was seated on the bench farthest in, his back to the wheelhouse. He turned the yellow pad face-down, and without asking filled a second mug of coffee and slid it toward her. "So?" he insisted.

Taking off her slicker, she slipped onto the bench facing him, pleased to be closest to the door. "I need some help and some advice."

"Yeah?" he said, clearly making no commitment.

"Skip Olsen—plump, pallid guy with a limp—was on the dock asking question a few weeks ago. He talked to Robin until she wouldn't talk anymore. After she died, he was back asking about her. The last time he was here he got someone angry enough to smash his windshield. This time he didn't come home."

Pedersen leaned against the bench, staring down at his cup. The coffee sloshed back and forth against the sides, mimicking the rock of the boat. "You working with him?"

"He's working for me. Do you know him?"

It was a moment before Pedersen said, "I heard there was a gimp getting pushy. Word I got was your friend used to be a cop and he's still got a cop's sensibilities. Not everyone on the dock sees the cops as protectors of the peace."

Olsen's ability to annoy was impressive. "He's missing. I'm worried about him." When Pedersen didn't respond, she said,

"He said he was coming down here yesterday. What do you think happened to him?"

"Skip, that his name? I haven't heard anything." The lines of his face were pulled downward. And the expression in his eyes? Not just suspicion, but fear. Pedersen was lying, she was sure of it.

She took a swallow of coffee and said, "But what do you think? I don't want him lying tied up inside that storehouse over there for days."

Pedersen laughed. "No chance of that. The restaurants store their nonperishables in there, guys on the dock got gear in there. Guys are running in and out all the time." He shook his head. "Look, a while back I got the newest temperature indicator, good to a tenth of a degree; I didn't mention it to anyone—if it didn't work out I wanted to be able to return it without anyone ribbing me about 'electronic captains.' I stored it in that warehouse overnight, and before dawn half the guys were offering to help me install it *and* get a free look. That's how private it is. So don't imagine you could hide a man there."

The boat lurched to the right and back again. Kiernan grabbed for her cup and looked out behind her at the dark, deserted slips, across the wharf to the empty sidewalks. In the silence the foghorn seemed louder, the radio chatter sharper. "I'm relieved," she said. "Or at least I think I am. If he's not there where could he be?"

"Who'd he have the blow-up with?" His eyes took on that same wary look.

Who was it Pedersen suspected—and feared? She'd seen enough of him to know a direct question would be useless. Instead, she said, "No clue. Skip knew he'd been treading on someone's arches when he saw his shattered windshield. But isn't that the type of tale that would make the rounds here?"

"You'd think."

She waited, looking through the misted window at the shifting gray shapes outside.

Pedersen was running his fingers down his beard again.

Decision hair, she thought. "Like I said, Kiernan, I haven't heard anything. But maybe it's not as bad as you're imagining. Your line of work, it must lead you to suspect the worst."

"But if the worst is true, where would he be?"

Pedersen pointed down.

"If he's *alive*, where?"

"I can't help you with that. Good advice is: be careful. If an ex-cop can't protect himself, what chance do you think you have? His windshield got smashed; if I were you I'd keep my Jeep out of here."

She stood up and braced her feet against the sway. "Ben, how'd you know I had a Jeep?"

He smiled stiffly. "Saw you get out of it."

She looked across the docks to the street. "It's not visible from here."

"I'm not padlocked to the boat."

"You're also not wet. So how did you know?"

His thick hands tightened on his mug. He shrugged. "Okay, you got me. I made it my business. I asked around. I like to know who's on the docks." Smiling, he added, "Particularly if they're pretty ladies."

She smiled, one as forced as his. "Okay, just let me ask you one more thing. If I told you Carlos Delaney was a PI, what would you guess he was trying to uncover?"

Pedersen sat back. "Sonuvabitch! Delaney? He was nosing around here, too? Did he work for you, too? What are you, the biggest employer in town?"

"No." Unbidden she pictured Delaney on the slab. "If I'd known him before I saw what's left of his face, I'd be a whole lot more upset about his death."

The boat rocked. Kiernan looked outside, checking for a passing boat she missed, but no one on the wharf was leaving port this late on a cold, rainy night. She said, "Ben, now that you know about Delaney, think about Robin again. Did you notice any recent changes? Was she all of a sudden more nervous? More rushed?"

"Robin was rushed all the time. But, wait, I was talking to her a couple of days before she died. She was angry, scattered, complained about her deckhand, but"—he sighed and shook his head—"I just laughed it off. Bitching about her deckhands was Robin's way of blowing off steam. I used to think she always picked a donkey so she'd have an ass to kick."

"Were her complaints different this time?"

He didn't answer. Finally, he said, "I'll have to give that more thought."

"Would you be surprised if she knew about Delaney then?"

"No. I'd be surprised if a guy worked with Robin for a month and she *didn't* know." He slammed his foot to the deck. "Look, I don't know anything about it. I saw Delaney every day and didn't catch on to him." He turned momentarily and stared out at the empty docks. "Sorry. It's just that you're a little like Robin, and I still wake up nights thinking of her lying there on the bottom. But Kiernan, if I do get any good ideas, I'll let you know. You got a card?"

"At home. Here, I'll just write down Olsen's number. You can reach me through him."

"Or so you hope?"

She handed him the paper, put on her slicker and made her way across the rough gray surface of the boat.

"Be careful," Pedersen called as she stepped from the boat to the stairs. "Water's cold this time of year."

She pulled up her hood and headed along the slip. Rain was beating down on the pier and the hood protected only part of her face. Knowing it was ridiculous, she eyed each boat for signs of Olsen as she passed, stepped under the restaurant overhang at the inside end of the pier and looked suspiciously at the storage building. The block-long, gray, windowless structure might be Grand Central Station during the day, but at ten-thirty on a rainy night they could hide a train the length of the California Zephyr in there.

Despite Ben Pedersen's protest, it looked like a perfect place to stash Olsen.

31

The boat wasn't rocking, was it? Skip Olsen was too numb to tell. But it was cold, Jesus, cold as a witch's tit. He opened his eyes, but he couldn't see anything except blackness dotted with points of light.

His throat was wadded with dust, or sand, or . . . He couldn't swallow, couldn't yell up at the specks—stars?—for help.

Car tires squealed in the distance. A horn blared. Where the hell was he? Not inside a boat any longer, that was for sure.

He couldn't feel at all. He wasn't dead, was he?

No. He could still smell. They said that was the last sensation to go. The smell of pigeon shit, brine and rot clogged his nose. He was going to retch. But he couldn't move his throat. Christ, he was lying in it, in water up to his collarbone.

Icy rain was running down inside the collar he couldn't adjust, down into the freezing pool in which he lay.

His legs gave. He slumped farther. The water splashed on his face.

He was going to drown.

Skip Olsen was glad.

32

Kiernan began searching through the bars, dark taverns with neon Schlitz signs filling the small high windows. It was in the fourth one, the Half-Mast, that she found Zack, the deckhand. Unlike the wharf, the Half-Mast was mobbed. Every stool was taken, several with men and women sitting back to back, knees braced against those of their next-stool buddies or lovers. There was no music, only the murmur of talk ebbing and flowing in the smoky air.

Zack stood near the door, empty beer glass in hand. He hadn't looked good at dawn yesterday and a day and a half had not improved him. The salt-stained windbreaker that had seemed too thin for the morning chill hung damply over one shoulder. Despite the thick miasma of smoke filling the bar, Kiernan smelled grime and wet wool as she slid in next to him. "Seen an ex-cop with a limp on the dock today?"

He did a double take. "The breakfast lady. You come to buy me the kind of breakfast I like?"

"Depends on what you know."

"Buy me a beer."

She could have bargained. She handed him a five.

"You *really* want to know," he said, fingering the bill.

"Come on, Zack, yes or no. I'm looking for Olsen, the ex-cop. He's disappeared."

"As in kidnapped?"

"Maybe. Now either you have an idea where he might be, or you don't."

He stood unmoving, then held out the five. "No idea."

A terrible liar. And a frightened one. "Zack, how about a ride home? You could drown waiting for a bus."

Warily, he glanced out the door at the rain, then around the crowded room. No one reacted. Slipping on his thin jacket, he murmured, "You gotta stop for beer on the way."

By the time they got to the Jeep, Zack's windbreaker clung to his soaked shirt. Water rolled off the edges of his wool cap. He climbed into the Jeep and sat shivering but made no move to wrap his arms around his chest or clutch them to his sides. He seemed resigned to rain and cold. And likely, Kiernan thought, to an early death. While the engine was warming, she said, "Zack, you saw Olsen, didn't you?"

"No."

"Look, Zack, I need your help. You know the docks, and you know the people there. You were the one who spotted Delaney as different. You were right. He wasn't a deckhand at all. Probably doesn't surprise you," she said, watching his re-action from the corner of her eye. How long had he been drink-ing? Long enough for his eyes to be cloudy. Now he was smiling and nodding, dripping water from his drenched cap.

"I'm going to tell you an amazing thing I discovered, Zack. Maybe it won't amaze *you*." Even for bedside manner, this was overdoing it. She chanced a peek at him, but if the deckhand found her ingratiating manner suspicious, he gave no sign. "Car-los Delaney was a private investigator, checking up on Robin!"

Zack nodded vigorously.

She was about to add that Olsen was following in his tracks. But that would only scare Zack off. Instead, she asked, "Did Delaney ever talk about a place where a man could be held prisoner, maybe tied up and gagged, or even knocked out?" Ignoring Zack's slowly shaking head, she went on. "Someplace a guy could be stashed? Maybe in the warehouse?"

Zack shook his head more slowly, but Kiernan couldn't decide whether that movement came from lack of resolve or a lack of knowledge.

"Is there a man-sized box in there? Maybe a locker big enough to hold him?"

"Nope. The place is like a hangar; one big open space."

She was too suspicious to believe him. "What about around the dock?"

"Nope," he said, but the word seemed automatic.

"That empty restaurant? Any reason why someone couldn't be held in there?"

"The Crab Cage? No chance. Guard comes through every day." He leaned back against his seat. Beery, stubble-faced, in dank, shabby clothes the man still looked smug, as if he were playing twenty questions with a dim-witted friend.

She clenched her hands into fists. "Dammit, Zack, you know something went on at the dock. What happened yesterday?"

"Nothing but what goes on any Tuesday." Same told-you-so voice.

She yanked at his jacket and turned him to face her. "What . . . happened?"

"Hey, let go. I told you nothing happened *yesterday*."

"Okay, dammit, then when? Today?"

"Ah, today. Well, if you want to know about tonight, I'll tell you about the big blow-up. Lights went off all over the wharf. About eight o'clock. Off for half an hour. Chefs were flapping around like peacocks."

Releasing his jacket, she said, "Even without lights you couldn't carry a man who's tied up across the wharf and expect no one to notice." She glanced over at the wharf. The docks now were lit a blotchy yellow. Weak light streamed from all the shop and restaurant windows,—all except for the dark, closed Crab Cage Café with its ridiculous plywood "cage" on the roof.

"Zack, where else could you hide a man here?"

"Boats," he whispered.

"No. Not if your power outage plays a part in this. You don't need to knock out the lights on the entire wharf to haul a body into a boat. You just move the boat. Now, to haul a body

out of a boat and move it to somewhere else on the wharf . . .
But where?"

"Restaurants are too busy," Zack whispered impatiently.
"He's not here. Let's go."

"Dumpsters?"

"Here? They're full by noon. Come on, you promised me a
ride home."

"Roofs?"

"No!"

She could tell by the tension in his voice that she was on
to something.

"Which roof, Zack?"

He edged away. "That's crazy—"

Grabbing his wrist, she said, "Find me a ladder."

"Fifty bucks."

"Ladder first. Lead me to it." Rain slapped her face and
ran cold down her neck. "Come on, Zack, move!"

"Okay, okay," he said. Hurrying to the warehouse, he
opened the door. An aluminum ladder stood right inside. "You
take the end," she said. She picked up the front half and led the
way. Icy rain streaked down her face as she moved out of the lee
of the building. She turned back into it, watching till Zack
cleared the doorway, then turned forward again, adjusted the
ladder and veered toward the restaurants.

The back end of the ladder clanked to the ground. She
spun around in time to see Zack dash inside the warehouse and
slam the door.

She dropped the ladder and ran for the door. Locked.
There was no use going after him. Why had he run? And without
his money? Was the person who'd attacked Olsen still here? She
turned slowly, surveying the dock. Behind the curtain of rain the
pole lights were blurs of ivory, illuminating nothing beyond
themselves. Boats swayed against the slips, masts creaked.

She dragged the ladder nearer the buildings. It scraped and
clanked; she stopped, listened for rushing feet, but the boats
thumping against the slips and the MUNI bus changing gears

were all she heard. If she'd alerted Olsen's captors, they'd be on her before she knew it.

She had almost reached the dark windows of the Crab Cage Café when she spotted the alleyway beside it. Dark, secluded, the perfect spot to shift an unwilling climber or carry an awkward package to the roof unquestioned. Easy, especially in a convenient power failure arranged by someone who knew the docks. And this roof had the plus of a plywood box, the "crab cage." She pulled the ladder into the alley, propped it against the building and climbed up.

There was no place to hide anything. The only things on the roof were the silent exhaust fans from the restaurant and the thin metal pole that supported the fake cage.

She looked up at the four-foot-square box. It was a good ten feet above the roof. Even in the dark and the rain she could see how weatherworn and frail it was. Close up, the "cage" was a plywood crate with "bars" painted on it. The front side once had had a crab painted between the bars, but the design was barely visible now. She circled the box, hoping for an open side, finding none.

"Skip?"

No answer.

She ran back to the edge of the roof and slowly tugged up the heavy ladder. Then she dragged it across the roof and propped it against the crab cage.

The ladder reached to the bottom of the box with inches to spare.

The pounding rain shook the "cage." The ladder clattered against it. Her shoes were soaked through and her feet slipped with each step. Her hands were stiff with cold. She rammed the ladder hard into the wet tar and climbed slowly up, barely able to feel the rungs. Feet on the fourth rung from the top, hands on the shaky top of the ladder, her head was level with the bottom of the box. She tapped on the wood. "Skip?" No response. "Olsen, are you in there?"

There was a noise that could have been caused by the

wind, and could have been a foot weakly kicking against wood. Pressing her hands against the rough side of the cage, she climbed onto the next step. The ladder shimmied. She felt for the next step, and grabbed for the top edge of the box.

It was open to the sky.

At first she didn't see Olsen huddled in the near corner. He was out of the path of the rain, lying on his side in a puddle. His hands were behind his back, his feet together. She leaned closer and made out the tape. Water filled the box inches deep. Olsen's lank hair fell over closed eyes. "Skip!"

He groaned.

Well, at least he was conscious. He was lucky to be alive. Had the box been less decrepit, Kiernan thought, he might have drowned.

Careful not to jostle the ladder, she hoisted herself over the edge and into the box. "Skip, can you sit up?"

He gave a groan she took as yes.

Gently, she pulled him up. His face was gray, his eyes blank, his mouth covered with electrical tape. She ripped it off; he groaned again and spit out a wad of cloth. He coughed, gagged, coughed again, and held his mouth open to the rain. She pulled the tape from his wrists, then his ankles. At best his legs would be numb.

"Kiernan." His voice was so hoarse she could barely understand him.

"Good," she said, more relieved than she would have admitted. "I'm going down to get help."

"Kiernan!" His hand fluttered toward her, reaching.

"What?"

"No!"

"No? No what?"

"No help," he whispered.

The rain battered her face and shoulders. The whole box shook. She didn't want to think about how long the ancient wood flooring would survive, or how long the thin metal pole would support them. "Skip, you're too weak to stand and you're in a box ten feet above a restaurant roof! Are you planning to fly down?"

He coughed and swallowed hard. "No! You're going to call 911, aren't you?"

"Right."

"They'll laugh . . . in every stationhouse . . . in the city. No! . . . I'd rather turn . . . to bones . . . up here." He pulled a leg toward him, grimacing.

"What is this, the *Guinness Book of Records* Macho Idiot Award?"

"Call it pride," he said in a stronger voice. "No, call it business sense."

"Call it crazy."

He grabbed for the edge of the box and struggled to hoist himself up. Leaning against the corner, panting, he tried to say something else, but the words were too guttural to decipher.

Kiernan hesitated. He was in no condition to walk, much less climb over the edge of this flimsy box, find the ladder, navigate the rungs and climb down. Still, she knew in his position she would have done the same. As an investigator in a hostile city, he would never be able to survive the embarrassment of being dumped in a box above the tackiest restaurant on the wharf. A gust of wind shook the box. The whole contraption leaned ominously to the right. On the street below she could hear the groans of a bus braking. A million miles away.

Olsen pushed himself clumsily away from the support of the edge. "I may need help."

"May, indeed. Pigs may fly. Stay where you are." She kicked the side of the box. The boards gave easily. The ladder banged to the roof. "Damn!"

Olsen groaned.

"It's okay. I've done harder dismounts than this." She lowered herself over the edge and dropped to the roof.

Light blinded her. "Police!" a voice yelled. "Don't move or I'll blow your head off!"

33

Kiernan pulled up by Dixie Alley.

"Six A.M.," Olsen muttered. "Eight hours in goddamn Central District station. I thought I'd seen every let-'em-stew tactic in the cop shop. But these guys—"

"You'd still be there if anyone but Bill Quist were the captain. And if I hadn't done him a favor big enough to be remembered ten years later."

"What kind of favor?"

"Staying on the horn to every lab for every protocol in a case that wasn't important to anyone but him." She got out of the car, and opened his door, holding out an arm. "Take it!" she insisted when he tried to barge shakily past. He coughed. The coughs had progressed over the hours to long whooping gasps that left him gagging. "Either you do as I say, or I drop you at the emergency room!"

"No hospitals!" Grudgingly, he took her arm and hobbled to the stairs.

"You're sure you have no clue who deposited you in the crab box?"

"Jesus! You act like the idea never crossed my mind." He coughed. "I'll tell you one more time, probably a guy. Someone strong enough to poke me with a piece and conk me good." He grabbed the railing for support.

She waited till he was down the stairs and inside his apartment, seated on a dining-room chair, with a glass of orange juice in his hand, before giving in to her own urge and saying, "And so, Mr. Macho, you went off to the place you'd been warned away from and ended up just like any sensible person could have told you you would—" She sounded, she realized with a start, exactly like her own mother. Worry personified. Worry justified. Worry basking in its own existence. "Sorry," she mumbled. "I just wish you hadn't come up empty."

A grin crept across Olsen's ashen face. "I didn't say that."

"What did you get?"

"If I weren't so weak and dehydrated, I'd make you grovel." He took a long, slow swig at his juice.

"Skip!"

"Well, m'dear"—he coughed and swallowed hard against the orange juice. Tears squeezed from his eyes. His face reddened. "Delaney had a locker in the warehouse. That wasn't standard. Nothing is so organized as to be standard in that building." He coughed again. "So no one checked it out. *Until* yesterday. Yesterday, someone came and carted off the contents."

"Do we know what those contents were?" she asked, holding her breath.

"No."

"Oh."

"But we do know that the guy who took them was from the coroner's office."

"The coroner's office? How did they know about the locker?"

Olsen shook his head, sneezed, dragged out a disgusting handkerchief and stared at its wet wrinkles.

Kiernan grabbed the phone and dialed the coroner's office. The phone rang three times before she remembered it was six in the morning. She slammed down the receiver. She'd deal with Rosten later. Later, but today.

"You need a hot bath. Now!" she snapped at Olsen.

"You need to control your temper." He coughed. "I'm going to bed."

"Not before you drink something hot."

He leaned forward, pressed a hand on the table and started to lift himself up. "I'm going—"

She pushed him back in the chair. "I don't have much bedside manner even at the best of times. You've used up what little I had. The hell with how you feel. You can sit there and drink hot water and come up with a damned good explanation of why you hired Carlos Delaney, and why the hell you didn't tell me about it."

He coughed again, a long hacking roll that rattled his ribs and turned his face crimson. Sweat covered his face. The man was definitely sick. She said, "Delaney?"

He blew his nose.

"Olsen, you're going to end up with a lot worse than pneumonia if you don't answer my questions. I'm not in the habit of slapping men around, but pissed off as I am, I'd be real happy to start with you. You get it?"

Olsen stared at her only momentarily. "Well, hey, come on, we all know the reason you go private is there aren't any rules. You're a big girl—"

She smacked his face. His head snapped back. His eyes flew wide open; the white of the sclera showed around all edges of the cornea. Kiernan felt a rush of satisfaction that frightened her. It felt as good as kicking the television and seeing the picture clear up. Her palm was moist. Wet. She looked down at it. It was covered with snot.

She wiped off her hand. "Olsen, the truth. Now!"

"Okay, okay. I hired Devereaux, Delaney, to get close to Robin and get her to tell him about hitting Garrett."

"You picked a guy who could barely see in bright light and sent him out on the ocean?"

He honked into a tissue. "How was I to know the guy couldn't see? It's not like he put that at the top of his résumé. It was weeks before I realized he had a problem. He'd probably spent a lifetime learning to disguise it."

"Still, why him?"

"He was smart and available. I wanted someone I could count on to be around Robin and still keep his head."

"And what did he find out in these tête-à-têtes?"

"Not a thing."

"What'd he get from the wire?"

He started to cough but choked it down. "What wire?"

"Olsen, I can't tell you how sorry I am I didn't leave you up there in the crab cage. Or at least in jail. I tell you, every cop in town has got my sympathy dealing with you." What had ever made her feel a fondness for him? It must have been a well-hidden appeal.

Olsen let go a trail of coughs, whooping into the tissue until he was shaking. "I don't know anything," he gasped, "about any wire." He took a long, cautious breath.

"Olsen, the boat was wired for eavesdropping, from the cabin to the cockpit."

Olsen's eyes widened. He hacked, trying to clear his throat. 'I didn't"—he swallowed—"authorize any listening device."

"Why would Delaney install it without your okay? And without your paying for it?"

"He wouldn't. There wouldn't have been anything for him to hear. Robin wasn't likely to call someone on the ship-to-shore and tell them about running over Garrett Brant."

Kiernan nodded grudgingly. It made sense. Delaney would not have grandstanded by secretly installing the wire. But still, if he wasn't responsible who was? "Okay, Skip, what did Delaney find out during his weeks in your employ?"

Olsen opened his mouth to cough, but the only sound was a low gagging. He squeezed his eyes shut. His head and shoulders quivered. His voice almost a whisper, he said, "I didn't hear about him going down till the next day, on the news. That the coast guard had found him. I called them, said I was with the department. They told me about Devereaux's face and hands, the crabs gnawing away at them. Nothing but bone halfway to the elbows." He snorted. "I'd talked to Devereaux a couple times a week for six weeks. I *knew* the guy." He sniffed harder. "He called me the week before he drowned. He was sick of the job, ready to pack it in. He figured he wasn't going to get anything else, and he hated the boat and taking orders, and dealing with the glare out in the ocean nine hours a day. But"— he swallowed—"I leaned on him for one more week."

Kiernan walked to the stove, poured water in a pan and waited for it to heat. Delaney had died or been killed; Garrett Brant's was a death of a different kind. And Olsen was guilty, grieving, and just plain scared. She restrained the urge to look at him. She'd dealt with fear so often in gymnastics that it was part of the process, not a choking stop. But few people were that lucky. And certainly not Skip Olsen. For him that fear must have been as real as the gag and the bindings on his wrists last night. She poured the water over a slice of lemon and a generous spoonful of honey and handed him the cup. "Start with small sips. Let the hot water clear your throat."

While he drank she straightened his bed, then helped him into it. He sank back, looking as gray and lifeless as the pillowcase. "There's something else," he murmured, his words barely audible. "Something new I picked up down there at the wharf. It's floating around somewhere . . . I can't grab it." He shook his head slowly, then let his eyes close.

Against her inclinations, Kiernan said nothing. Given the state he was in, Olsen wasn't going to drag anything out of his memory. She wanted to find out what he knew about her assailants at Delaney's apartment, too. She hadn't told him about that bit of illegality. But something stopped her. If he wasn't responsible, he wouldn't know anything; if he was, he wouldn't tell.

She couldn't leave Olsen unguarded. She left the bedroom and went to lie down on the couch, telling herself she'd wake at eight-thirty.

The sides of the Crab Cage shook, the ladder was banging against them, a bigger ladder, with bars like the jail cell door. She could hear the sea lions in the water, growling their long, guttural demands. She hung onto the ladder, and braced her feet against the box, but the ladder banged louder. It pulled her over the side. It barked.

"Kiernan!"

She opened her eyes, looking at the strange room, realizing it was Olsen's.

"Kiernan, let me in!"

She staggered to the door. The rain had stopped; the sky was gray but bright. Brad Tchernak started in, but was shoved aside by a flying mass of gray-brown fur.

"Ezra!"

The dog leapt, paws landing on her shoulders, tongue lapping her face.

"Get down, you fool!" she muttered happily as she rubbed his ears and neck. Her command had no effect. The huge dog continued to lick her; she rubbed his wiry chest and murmured "Ezraaa." She hadn't realized how much she had missed him and Tchernak.

Sea lion–like snores shook the room.

"What's that racket?" Tchernak demanded, pushing aside Ezra and throwing his own arms around her.

"Olsen snoring," she said to his chest.

"Snoring? He could get work as a foghorn."

Kiernan opened the bedroom door and looked at the sleeping man. His body was rocking slightly with the thrust of the snores.

"Maybe his neighbors took up a collection and paid to have him kidnapped."

"Actually," Kiernan said, "someone really did do a number on him. The poor guy's sacroiliac was already so bad he couldn't walk without a limp. Now he'll be lucky if he can walk at all for a while, without a cane, anyway. Someone is real serious about stopping us."

Tchernak gave her shoulders a squeeze. "Well, Kiernan, Ez and I are on the job now. Christ, I thought you'd have to be dead to let me protect you."

Kiernan laughed, scratching Ezra's flank. "I would,

Tchernak. I can't tell you how pleased I am there was a good reason to call you. I could hardly charge Maureen Brant for bringing me a sexy man and the world's best dog. You do remember that it's Olsen you're here to guard. I don't want to leave him alone, and I can't stay put and hover over him. And considering that he spent a cold, rainy night out in the open, good, nourishing food will be just what he needs."

"Hey, I came here to detect!"

She flopped onto the leather couch. "Kiddo, this is a big part of the glamorous life of the investigator. But what about those backgrounds you requested from BakDat?"

"They screwed up. Lost everything." Tchernak kicked off his shoes and settled on the sofa arm, resting his feet on the cushion. "I had to argue with the guy on duty to convince him we'd even made the request."

"And did you convince him?" she asked, looking up at the six foot four, 240-pound form looming above her.

"Oh, yeah. He was falling over the phone apologizing by the time I hung up. Promised to run those free, and bump me to the top of the line with the next order."

"Okay. Have them run Robin Matucci again. See if anything new has come in. Get them to check the Uniform Commercial Code filings."

"What's that?"

"Sit down, novice investigator, and take out your pen. The Uniform Commercial Code filings are debts. The list is filed by the lenders to protect themselves. But what we can learn from it is whether or not Robin has taken out a sizable loan and put up collateral we didn't know about."

"Like if she planned to bankroll her disappearance?"

"Right. She doesn't seem like the type of woman who would wander off penniless."

Olsen groaned. She heard the word "bathroom."

"I believe your charge is calling you, Tchernak." She'd pay for this . . . but not till later.

She hurried into the bedroom, riffled through the printouts

in the desk, grabbed Robin Matucci's, and was just rounding the doorway when Tchernak emerged from the bathroom scowling.

"Can't we stick Olsen in the hospital?" he demanded.

"He's too sick."

A barrage of coughs shook the bathroom door.

Kiernan strode back to the sofa. Ezra clambered up beside her, filling the rest of the space.

Top of the list with BakDat turned out to mean an hour's wait. The Uniform Commercial Code check turned up nothing. If Robin bankrolled her escape, it was from funds she already had.

Kiernan wadded up the printout and threw it toward the fireplace. "Damn! Robin Matucci was a planner. I can't believe she'd disappear without some preparation."

"Or some you can trace, you mean?"

She sank back against the sofa. "Right. If I killed you and hightailed it out of La Jolla, I'd take every spare dollar and—"

Tchernak laughed. "You'd be a cinch to track."

"Oh yeah?" she demanded, offended.

"Sure. I'd just put an ad in the paper asking for anyone who'd seen a tiny woman with a huge dog. You wouldn't leave Ez behind."

She laughed. "Fortunately for me you'd be dead." She squeezed Ezra's head against her chest. He let out a yip. "Sorry, Ez."

"Too bad *Early Bird* sank, huh? Or I could put in my ad about redhead and boat. Sounds like Robin Matucci was as crazy about her boat as you are about Him." Tchernak shoved Ezra off the couch and sat down himself.

Kiernan jumped up, strode into the bedroom. Olsen was snoring. She shook him awake.

"Hey," he muttered groggily.

"Wake up. I need you to do some work."

"I'm sick."

"You're alive because I saved you. I need you to make a phone call."

Olsen coughed into his pillow. "Okay. Okay. What?"

"Do you have a connection at Motor Vehicles?"

He nodded.

"Have him run Robin Matucci."

"Don't you think I've done that?"

"How recently?"

"As soon as I hired Devereaux."

"Olsen, that was six weeks ago. Call again. Now."

Olsen pushed himself up. He grabbed a tissue and honked into it. "Okay, give me a few minutes. In private."

Shrugging, Kiernan walked back into the dining area. Tchernak was standing before the cabinets. All the doors were open. "There's no food here! Nothing fit for man nor beast. Certainly not a beast of *His* tastes. Where's the nearest butcher? Where's the vegetable market?"

"Tchernak, I'm on a case here. I can't sit around while you go shopping."

"You're going to be embarrassed to see headlines: NOVICE DETECTIVE STARVES."

"There's toast," she said, realizing as the words came out that half a loaf was an hors d'oeuvre for Tchernak.

Stretching up to his full height, he stared down at her, and said the irrefutable words: "Ezra is hungry."

She sighed. "No wonder Sherlock Holmes's only pet was his habit. Okay, go. But no butcher, baker and soufflé-maker. Only to the supermarket. One stop. Be back in half an hour, max."

"Boy," he grumbled, "you can certainly tell a woman who doesn't do her own cooking."

A quarter of an hour later, Olsen called her. When she opened the bedroom door, he was lying back against his pillow and smiling. "Robin Matucci sold her red Porsche for ten thousand dollars."

"She won't live in style on that for long, but she won't starve either."

Olsen waited a beat, then burst out with, "Don't you want to know who she sold it to?" Before she could ask, he said, "Carl Hartoonian."

When Tchernak returned, balancing four large grocery bags, she grabbed her jacket and ran out the door.

She made the trip to Marin County in record time, slowing to fifty-five only at the sight of a highway patrol car. The thought of Hartoonian, a baby holding a stick of dynamite, filled her with fear.

She pulled the Jeep up next to his Bronco and ran to the house.

Hartoonian was still in his bathrobe. His too-large eyes widened behind his thick glasses. "I'm busy."

"Carl, you are a nice guy, a good friend, and unwittingly, you've gotten involved. Carl, you're in a lot of trouble."

He took a step back.

Kiernan edged in around him. "Robin sold you her Porsche last month. Why?"

"How'd you know that?" One hand was still on the door, a mug dangled from the other.

"I'm an investigator, Carl. It's my trade to know these things." She forced a smile, not wanting to let her apprehension unnerve him. "But the fact is that you have a new Bronco; you've got a business with a lot of expensive equipment and one customer. How do you come to afford two vehicles? You didn't, did you? No money changed hands, did it?"

He was silent, but his shocked, fearful expression answered for him.

"She was planning her escape, wasn't she?"

His bony face paled. He clasped both hands around the mug as if for protection.

"She had to ditch the boat she loved, but she couldn't quite bring herself to leave her lovely red Porsche, right?" When he still didn't answer, she reached over and put a hand on his arm. "The police are going to be asking questions, you know that, don't you?"

"Oh, God," he muttered.

"Carl, you've got to trust someone. There's no one but me, is there?"

The gray light created pale blotches on the futon bed behind him. Hartoonian stared at the sharp hospital corners as if for reassurance. Then he sank into one of the basket chairs. Kiernan took the other, sitting on the edge. "Carl?"

"Okay. You were right, Robin was planning to leave. She said she was in a hole financially, she was afraid they'd take the car. I just let her transfer the Porsche as a favor."

She shook her head. "No, Carl, that story's not going to work. The police will ask just how closely you were involved in Robin's plans. They'll want to know where that car is."

The cup quivered in his hands.

Kiernan dragged her chair closer and rested her hand on his. Hartoonian was a scientist who dealt with figures, analyses, rules that define the game. But now he was in a game he didn't understand, that had rules he couldn't dream of. "Carl, Robin hit a man and left him for dead. Every bit of evidence suggests she killed her deckhand," she said, inflating the facts. "And you, her good friend, the friend she was in radio contact with, picked her up on the beach, didn't you? Carl, you could be charged as an accessory."

Hartoonian slumped back. "Robin's alive? I don't believe it. She would have called me."

"Carl, the truth!"

"Okay, I do know she's alive. But I don't have any idea where she is."

She took the cup from his hands and set it on the floor. "The police aren't going to believe that any more than I do. Suppose Robin is in your back room right this minute." She watched his face; his sunken eyes did not change expression. "If she didn't turn to you, then who would she have help her? Dwyer Cummings?"

He laughed weakly.

"He was her most faithful customer. She made a big effort to accommodate him."

"She thought he was a fool."

"Because he told her business secrets?"

He laughed again. "Not intentionally," he muttered, almost to himself.

"Not intentionally." She'd ponder that later. Now she chose her words carefully. "Carl, you picked Robin up after *Early Bird* sank." When he didn't protest, she said, "When did she call you?"

He picked up the mug and stared down into it. Kiernan found herself rooting for him, hoping he had been merely swept along by love, lust, yearning, whatever.

"She sounded like death," he said slowly. "She didn't call from the boat. She made it to a phone on shore."

"But you knew that she had been out in the storm." Again, she made it a statement.

He nodded. "She called a couple times, said it was bad, said she might need advice and that I should stay around. It was so bad out there, no advice was going to do her any good. When it's that bad, luck's all that counts."

"And then it must have been hours after that last call from the boat before she called again?"

"Forever. I was sure she'd drowned. God, I was so relieved to hear from her. I nearly got pulled over three times speeding down there. And when I saw her she was sitting against a dune with her survival suit draped over her legs, shaking all over. I was sure she had pneumonia."

"And you brought her back here?"

"Carried her in." Kiernan could picture him bent over Robin, holding out a mug of tea. She could imagine Robin's long red hair lying knotted, brine-coated on the pillow.

"Carl, where is she now?"

"I don't know. She was here for six days. I went to the bakery to get her a cranberry-cornmeal scone—she was crazy about them; when I got back she was gone." He glared at Kiernan. "And in case you ask, she hasn't called or anything since. Just left. Like checking out of a hotel."

Kiernan guessed. "And took the Porsche?"

"Right. Looks like you know her better than I did."

"Carl, we all make mistakes about lovers. The lucky ones don't marry them." He scowled; just the expression she would have had if someone had made that smarmy comment about her affair with Rosten.

She walked out, feeling at once excited and disappointed. Robin Matucci was alive! But she was no closer to finding her. Well before she took Delaney on his last trip, Robin had bankrolled her disappearance. Did she murder Delaney? Did she deliberately take him out in the Pacific to kill him?

Kiernan called the grocery in Big Sur and left a message for Maureen: Robin in good health, has driven off.

As soon as she put down the phone she regretted the tone of that message. Too uncertain. And, dammit, she wasn't uncertain. She was sure Robin killed Delaney, and just as sure now that the evidence was where she first suspected, on Delaney's body. Marc Rosten was not going to withhold it any longer.

34

It was 9:25 A.M. Kiernan circled through the morgue parking lot. Both the coroner's spot and the one labeled Rosten were empty.

The rain had stopped. Now the air merely hung thick and damp, clouding the windshield as she sat thinking. Could Rosten still live in the same Victorian flat he'd had as a medical student? Upstairs in his brother's building? The flat overlooked

Dolores Park, near the warm, sunny Mission District. Twelve years ago it had been a wonderful place. Now it would be a find. She stepped on the gas.

The south side of Dolores Park, 20th Street, was halfway between Bryant Street and Dixie Alley, where Olsen lived. She paused in front of the Victorian. Every parking space was filled. One thing that hadn't changed in twelve years. Even back then finding a parking spot across from Dolores Park would have been the equivalent of a spontaneous cure for leprosy. The block-long park was deep in shadows now, its hilly knolls rolling sharply together like an excess of breasts, with trees sprouting out of the cleavages. Kiernan shook her head. She'd forgotten how she and Rosten had laughed over that observation as they lay on a blanket in the park. Even then they'd admitted that was a sure sign of punchiness.

Shaking off the memory, she yanked the wheel hard to the right and pulled the Jeep into the driveway, blocking the sidewalk.

The Victorian had been repainted. Then it had been violet with brick red and navy trim. Now, in a more conservative decade, it was beige with eggshell and peach. She ran up the steps and checked under the name for the upper flat. "Rosten." She pushed the bell, and stood tapping her foot, again recalling that day when Rosten's brother appeared at his door. Momentarily she felt the hollowness that had numbed her when he'd said Rosten had left. But only momentarily. Now the memory stoked her anger. She clenched her fist to keep from jabbing the bell.

The building had been built nearly a hundred years ago to house offices. During some renovation the two front rooms, which faced the street and park, had been joined by the demolition of their common wall. Rosten's bed had stood in the turret corner, its own corners poking awkwardly into the round wall. A small tiled fireplace was almost forgotten on an interior wall. The proportions had been all wrong.

She strained for the sound of footsteps, realizing that she

was listening for Rosten's own quick-descending steps of twelve years ago.

Standing here on his porch. It was a moment she might have played over and over again in her mind, slotting in possible scenarios, dancing around the edges of how she'd feel. But she had never intended to be here again, and she had never permitted her speculations about Rosten's departure to reach this stage. She had buried him as if he'd been a body signed off after postmortem. "What if" was a game she had not allowed herself to play. She'd paid the price for that control, as had lovers who'd come after Rosten.

The door opened. Rosten stood there, his brown curly hair still wet from the shower, cord-clad legs apart. His expression of surprise hardened into something else. "You don't lack for chutzpah! You force your way into my office—"

"You left me no choice!"

He put a hand on the door. Before he could shut it, she pushed it back and stepped inside. "There's no avoiding me this time."

"I don't need to put up with this—"

"Yes, you do. We're talking murder here. Delaney was murdered. You blew the autopsy."

He blinked hard as if he'd been slapped. "There was nothing out of line with that postmort."

"Then why did you decide it was worthwhile to send someone to the wharf to check Delaney's locker? You didn't do that when you got the body."

"I didn't know there was a locker then."

"And since then, while Delaney lay in the crisper, someone just happened to drop by and mention it? Come on!"

Rosten took a step back, an uncommon move for him, she recalled. She could remember him saying, "Never give ground." "Who just happened to tell you about it?"

"That is protected information."

"Oh? Then I'm sure it's recorded in the Delaney file. When that becomes public information, as it will during the murder investigation . . ." His dark eyes narrowed but he didn't speak. She was surprised how vividly she remembered his moves. And this expression that meant he was bluffing. She took a long breath to calm herself. "Marc, you can tell me about it now, off the record, or you can wait and—"

"Watch you get revenge? A woman scorned?"

She smiled. "Right. Whatever your reasons, you were a shit. Twelve years I never thought about you, never let myself feel the fury. I've got a lot of control—"

He laughed. "I don't exactly recall—"

"All that anger's still waiting. It would be a pleasure to put it to a good cause like this. So you take your pick: Be straight with me now, or give me reason to have every reporter in town calling you. The question is: How did you find out about the locker and what was in it?"

Wind rustled the leaves of the plane trees out front. A motorcycle screeched around the corner onto 20th Street. Rosten leaned back against the wall, his forehead creased with lines that had been only vague shadows years before. There was no hint of those bursts of enthusiasm she had loved. And the soft, chocolate depths were gone from his eyes. Now they were merely opaque shields against the world.

"I got a helpful citizen call."

"From whom?"

Rosten shrugged. "Just a message. No name. I sent one of our investigators to see what was there."

"Didn't you wonder who would send you down there?"

"I deal in facts. I don't waste my time on questions I'm not likely to get answered." He crossed his arms and leaned back against the wall.

So stubborn, she thought with the frustration she'd felt years ago. *And so innocent*. "Look, Marc, there's something major— big money, big power, big fear: something—connected with this. My client has been threatened. Delaney was murdered, and the guy I'm working with, Olsen, was kidnapped. He'd be dead by now if I hadn't found him. Someone has a big stake in this game, and you are walking through the playing field blindfolded."

"Blindfolded. Shit, I'm not naïve. Maybe it was too rural around the coroner's office where you worked, but here we do get murders."

"You get murdered bodies. You don't deal directly with their killers. That's like confusing the restaurant with the slaughterhouse." She reached out to put a hand on his arm, but stopped herself. Marc Rosten wasn't Carl Hartoonian and that comforting gesture would not work with him. "Marc, I've been doing this kind of work for three years. When they're pressed, people forget the rules the rest of us play by. And if you're a decent person, it takes you a long time to realize that people can be as sleazy, as vicious, as casually dishonest as they are. I'd hate to think that you could grasp that in a few days." He frowned. He was coming to a decision he didn't want to face. She remembered that look from the Yallin case. She even remembered the case name! Patient with an inoperable tumor and two bad choices Rosten didn't want to offer. He'd had that look before he left, too.

"This is the most dangerous kind of investigation, Marc. There are a lot of people connected with the case. None of them seems vicious enough to commit murder. But people are dead, and someone, probably someone we trust, killed them." She started to say "your life is no more valuable to a killer than theirs," but caught herself. That wasn't the tack to take with Rosten. Playing her hunch, she said, "Someone is using you, Marc. And other people could die because of you."

Outside, the J-Church streetcar clattered along the track. She could almost hear it rattling the windows upstairs as it had done every ten minutes during the day, every fifteen at night. It made her shiver as she had back then, lying under the sheet listening to the metallic clatter, water running in the washbasin in the bathroom next door, waiting for Rosten to finish shaving a small circle around his mouth so it would be smooth and soft when he kissed.

She took a deep breath, pushing away the memories that crowded in. She called up the picture of Delaney lying on the slab, his occipital bone clearly visible through the raw edges of scalp, his fingers down to the carpals and metacarpals, the skin eaten away halfway to his elbows. It had the desired result. To Rosten, she said, "Shall we go upstairs and discuss this case?"

He didn't move. Neither did he stop her as she started up the long carpeted staircase. At the top, she turned sharply right and walked along the familiar white hallway. The decorative tin wainscoting was still there, its design muted by decades of paint.

She paused in the doorway to the big front room. No longer was it the bedroom/study of the old days, with the big bed in the round corner, Rosten's old pine desks, two of them lined next to each other under the side windows, and the mismatched collections of chairs strewn like half-read books around the room. They'd designated those chairs: the Chair of Pathology, the one with the weevils in the cushion batting; the Chair of Anatomy, with no cushion at all; the Chair of Radiology, stunning design, but one likely to collapse under weight, merely an image of a chair.

Now the round corner housed a circular couch and the rectangular section of the room a green leather sofa, an antique marble-topped chest, and large empty places that bespoke furniture removed and not replaced. The walls they had covered with anatomical sketches were now a mix of watercolors and oils, all in tones that highlighted the green of the sofa. It was, she thought, a room that would have pleased Dwyer Cummings. A room to which the Rosten she had known would have passed through without offering a glance.

"So," she said as he walked in, "what was in Delaney's locker?"

Rosten shook his head. "Nothing worth the expense of sending a man to the wharf. Sweats, rags, sweaters, extra pair of shoes. Just what you'd expect for a deckhand."

She dropped onto the sofa. "Start from the beginning. You got the body, did the postmort, and then what?"

He strode across the room and stopped in front of her. "Don't come in here and demand—"

"Marc, it's too late. You screwed up the autopsy." She couldn't restrain the rush of pleasure that it gave her to watch him cringe, the one man who had refused to support her in a similar situation. She said, "I know how that is. It'll catch up with you. Unless you face it now."

He didn't look convinced.

"Marc, I'm not out to get you." *Well, only incidentally, only briefly.* "I'm here to protect my client."

He sat in the far corner of the sofa, but he didn't look at her. A streetcar clattered by. Rosten turned toward the window.

"If you are still the man I knew, Marc, you are thorough, conscientious, responsible. Even in med school, when you were so exhausted you had to force yourself to eat before you fell into bed, you never called in sick and made someone else cover for you. You never shorted your patients when they needed answers. I don't believe you'd do a slipshod job on an autopsy. But I, of all people, know it's possible to misconstrue a finding, to miss a clue that someone else might have discovered. With all these people asking about Delaney, it's easy to see why you'd have second thoughts about the autopsy. What's worrying you about it?"

He swallowed hard. Suddenly he looked up. "Okay. There were two things, neither of which seemed at all unusual when I wrote the report, and which indeed may not be. The first was a subdural hemorrhage in left anterior, proximal temporalis muscle."

"The blow to the side of the head. What about contrecoup injury? Were the blood vessels on the right side of the brain broken?"

"There was no contrecoup. Do you think I'd miss something like that?"

"No. But didn't you expect there would be one? If that subdural hemorrhage had come from a blow Delaney got being bounced around in the boat there *should* have been a contrecoup. But there wasn't. Delaney wasn't moving; he was standing still, and something hit him. Somebody struck him hard enough to cause that hemorrhage." She caught herself before she blurted out: *Didn't you find that significant?* Obviously, it had slipped by him. "Maybe if we took another look at—"

"You'd love to get a real crack at Delaney's body, wouldn't you? Even after five days in the Pacific, it wouldn't bother you, would it? God, I never saw anyone so fascinated with decay. There were times when you just about made me sick."

"I did?" she asked, amazed. "You never said that then."

He laughed uncomfortably. "It would have sounded unmanly, or at least unsuitable for a medical student."

"And here you are acting coroner."

"Yeah," he said without enthusiasm.

She closed her eyes and let her breath out slowly. She could feel the frustration that numbed her body when she'd finished her residency at the San Francisco coroner's department and moved to a more rural county, knowing that, without the latest electron microscopes, the gas chromatograph to detect chemical elements in the blood, without access to the most sophisticated equipment, there would be conclusions she could never make, findings she would miss. "Once I would have sold two of my limbs for the chance to be coroner of the city of San Francisco. To have the equipment you do, the staff, the variety of cases. It would have been the next thing to being God."

He shook his head. "God of the dead. You see it all here, all when it's too late to do anything about it."

"You save others from the dangers. Your discoveries give other living people a chance. And sometimes, occasionally, you find the truth." It had been that—the illusion of truth revealed in the body—that had seduced her into forensic pathology, and eventually betrayed her.

Rosten laughed scornfully. "Most of the time you defend

the department budget, fight for staff, worry that someone forgot to disinfect a table and left bacteria or a virus that will kill them."

"Marc," she said, leaning forward, "these are all facts you knew before you decided to go into forensic pathology. These are very basic objections to the trade. I never had a second thought about forensic pathology, not until I quit. But you? What made you choose it?"

"You."

"Me? I never urged you into it. You wanted internal medicine. I never—"

"You remember the Salter case? Jesse Salter?"

"Salter? No."

"I'm not surprised. I probably never mentioned it aloud. I thought about it almost constantly for the three weeks before I left. But maybe I could never bring myself to admit my mistake."

She waited.

"They brought Jesse Salter into the ER at eleven in the morning. I had an hour to go on my shift. I'd been on thirty-five hours. Thirty-five busy hours. There'd been some kind of demonstration—antisomething, I can't remember what—and we had a couple of guys banged up pretty bad. A lot of internal injuries. At nine that morning I was seeing double. I lay down in the intern's room, just hoping I could sleep for a few hours. And then they brought Salter in at eleven. He was an old guy. Bleeding from the lining of the stomach, pancreatitis, esophageal varices from the back pressure of the blood his cirrhotic liver couldn't handle, kidneys all shot to hell. No family to make his decisions. No history other than what he could tell me. Dialysis? I knew it was too late. I should have taken my stand then. But I was so tired, and tired people are easy cowards. I chose the easy way out. I stuck a catheter into his heart and pumped him full of antibiotics, and plugged him into a respirator. I knew, dammit, that it wouldn't save him. And it didn't. He was conscious. For three weeks he suffered with every breath that damned machine forced into his lungs. At first I could hear him scream from the end of the corridor. Then at the end, I couldn't hear him even from the end of the bed, I could just see his chest move in a kind of dry heave." He looked over at her. "If I had made the right, the courageous decision, I would never have authorized those machines. He would have died that night, instead of living in agony for twenty more days. But I didn't, because I had allowed myself to get too exhausted to think."

He didn't say it, but the words hung between them: *Because I had spent too many hours, too many nights with you, here.*

What he did say was: "I wasn't responsible enough to be entrusted with living people."

Kiernan didn't move. He was still staring at her, and she stared back, unseeing now. Painful thoughts filled her mind: horror that he had wasted these years; distress at his dismissal of forensic pathology; anger, sorrow, amazement that after all these years he still blamed her. It was so appalling . . . And still it didn't quite fit the Rosten she had known. Had he changed so much, or had she not known him at all? "And so you just left?"

"I had a lead on the path residency. I didn't even know if I'd get it. It didn't matter. I just had to escape. It was all I could do to make it those three weeks till the end of the year."

She looked intently at him, seeing no traces of the passionate young man who had lived in this flat. Her voice was barely audible as she said, "You'd been planning to leave all along, and never once mentioned it! All that time I was sleeping with an imposter."

"I couldn't help it. I blamed us both. I blamed neither of us. I blamed the stupid system that kept me so exhausted that a private life could throw me over the edge." He turned and walked to the window and looked out into the night. "I was young, I had lots of energy, and enough natural smarts to make decisions with half a brain, or one that was only half awake. Or so I thought. I never misdiagnosed a patient. I never botched a medication. But, dammit, I was too fuzzy to deal with Salter." He swallowed hard. "You don't need to tell me I was arrogant.

Arrogance, the doctors' disease. If you had diagnosed me then, I wouldn't have believed you. And even if I'd suspected, I wouldn't have known how to deal with it. Arrogance was a big part of what got me where I was. After Salter, all I knew was that I had to get away from patients." He swallowed again, and wiped his eyes. "I've never admitted that, not to anyone."

Without turning around he said, "There's never been a day I haven't regretted my decision." Suddenly he laughed. "But my patients now aren't complaining. And, at least, it didn't change your plans."

Forcing herself to meet his eyes, she said, "It changed me." She could have told him of the years it had taken her to trust another man enough to spend more than a night with him. She said, "I'm sorry about Salter, and you, Marc. More sorry than I can say."

The J-Church car clanged by, iron scraping iron, bursts of sparks flying out into the damp gray sky.

Rosten ambled over to a ficus plant and began examining the leaves, tacitly asking for an end to the painful discussion. It suited her; she needed time to digest his explanation, and to deal with its effects. She said, "What was the other questionable finding in the Delaney autopsy, the one that made you wonder about the subdural hemorrhage?"

"Delaney? The skin by the head of the ulna was pretty well eaten away—"

"Halfway up the ulna."

"Wasn't enough left on either wrist for me to base a conclusion, but on the right, there was a linear scratch across the outside of the head of the ulna. But no mark by the styloid process of the radius."

"But the linear scratch on the outside of the wrist, do you think that could be from a wire? It's just where a ligature would be if his hands had been crossed and tied behind him at the wrist. Tied up with wire that cut through the flesh into bone."

Rosten nodded.

"What about the tendon of the supraspinatus muscle?" she

said with mounting excitement. The muscle that ran along the inside of the scapula and attached to the top of the arm. "With an internal rotator like that, if Delaney's hands were jerked behind him and tied, that forced external rotation could pull the tendon."

"A small tear, but it could have come from anything in a storm like that. Or, coupled with the scratch on the ulna . . ."

She sighed. She'd hoped for something conclusive. "Not something you'd take to court, right?"

"Yeah, but nothing you'd want to rebut in court, either."

"When *Early Bird* left the dock there were two people aboard, Matucci and Delaney. No matter what happened later, it was only Matucci who could have tied him up. Knocked him out, tied his wrists, and most likely pushed him overboard. Or maybe she cut him loose before she tossed him over." The information about the ulna was a gift, Rosten's way of saying *I'm sorry*. She stood up and smiled at him. "Thanks. I'll use your information carefully."

He shrugged. "Use it any way you want."

But his face seemed lighter, nearer to the Rosten she recalled. Impulsively she kissed him.

He nodded, turning away from her abruptly to one of the desks and picking up some papers.

35

"Did Maureen call?" Kiernan asked, leaning over the kitchen railing to take a cup of coffee from Tchernak. From the bedroom came congested snores. "I left a message for her two hours ago. I didn't say to call back, but that's never stopped her before."

"I thought she called you every time she got near a phone."

"The last time I heard from her, she was complaining about hearing noises outside. It could have just been nerves, but still . . . Tchernak, they're five miles from the road down there. I wish Big Sur weren't so far, that I could go—"

"Look, if you need someone to drive to Big Sur—"

"No!"

Tchernak sighed. "Well, if I had a wish, it'd be that Maureen traded places with *him*." He threw a disgusted glance in the direction of the bedroom.

Kiernan ignored it. She didn't ask about Olsen's condition. Tchernak had already given her a blow-by-blow description, which added up to bad cold, occasional fever, and major pain in the ass. "I've been here less than six hours and already I've thrown out enough tissues to qualify for Bay-fill. I've carried the guy to the john so often I ought to be a longshoreman." He glared down the length of his sharp, often-broken nose. "I even tracked down a grocery that delivered fresh, decent food—not that I got any help finding it from *him*, the local detective. Said he couldn't hold a thought. Unless that thought was wanting juice, wanting a drink, wanting Ezra to stop barking!"

"He complained about Ezra!" Kiernan asked pulling the wolfhound to her protectively. Ezra let out a low groan and rolled over to present his stomach for rubbing.

"The guy's a whiner, Kiernan. He'd complain about anything. He bitched about the crab box, he groused about the cops, he even said if you hadn't made so much noise kicking out the side of the box, the cops wouldn't have found him."

"All that and Ez, too?"

Tchernak was not amused. "That's not the worst of it."

"It has to be the worst. What could be worse than speaking ill of this best of all possible dogs? A dog who's bark is worthy of the San Diego Men's Chorus."

"I made the man chicken soup. Homemade. Cornfed chicken. Vegetables that came with the roots intact."

"That for a man who complained about Ezra?"

"Olsen turned up his stuffed-up nose at it. He'll only eat Lipton's!"

Kiernan threw her head back and guffawed. Ezra bayed. From the bedroom Olsen yelled, "Hey, what the hell"—and dissolved into a paroxysm of coughing.

"Congratulations, Tchernak," Kiernan after she'd got control of herself. "You are about to be inducted into a very exclusive club."

"What's involved in this induction?" he asked, his hazel eyes narrowing in mock suspicion.

"Nothing, you've already proved your worthiness." She lifted her glass. "To Bradley Walka Tchernak, second member of the No Bedside Manner Club."

Tchernak leaned forward and kissed her. "That is the initiation ritual, isn't it?"

The bedroom door burst open. "Jeez," Olsen growled. Dank brown hair clumped on his forehead, hanging halfway over his eyes. His face was a pale yellow, the fleshy cheeks drawn. He leaned heavily on the door frame, listing to his right as if to keep the weight off the left hip.

"Get back in bed," Kiernan ordered.

"I don't"—

"Do as I tell you or we leave you here on your own."

"You wouldn't."

"Try me. Look, Skip, it's only your miserable condition that's kept me from talking to you longer before. Now get back in bed and get ready to answer a few questions. And then, dammit, you can eat your dehydrated sodium-packed packaged chicken soup while Brad and I have the real stuff for lunch."

Olsen hesitated, then turned and slowly limped back to bed.

As Kiernan started to follow, Tchernak whispered, "You'll always be number one in the club!"

Olsen lay amidst a tangle of sweat-damp sheets and blankets. The pillow was clumped under one side of his head. It needed fluffing. Ignoring this, she said, "Okay. Answer some questions for me. You hired Delaney six weeks ago. How did you know about Robin then?"

"The car." Olsen shoved the pillow behind him. "I tracked down the red convertible," he said proudly.

And on the strength of that he put Delaney on the boat, and then Delaney was killed. Now it was clearer why he wasn't willing to take the chance of Kiernan turning down the case. By this point Olsen had nearly as much of himself invested as Maureen. Kiernan smiled grimly. Obsession was something she understood. "Tell me about the wire. Delaney didn't install that, did he? Robin put it in."

Olsen raised an eyebrow. "How'd you"—He tensed, grabbed for the sheet, and let out a sneeze of hurricane proportions.

Kiernan glanced away. "Hartoonian said Cummings had told her business secrets unintentionally. Quite a scam Robin had there, overhearing the business get-togethers Cummings set up. He gets guys from different oil companies together. They're all swapping ideas, admittedly carefully, but still one or two tidbits must have fallen every so often. Did she take out other oil company groups?"

"Specialized in them. She was the favored one with the oil guys." Olsen reached for a tissue and blew.

"So all Robin had to do was keep abreast of moves in the industry—no big deal when she heard men talking about it all day on her boat. She'd recognize the slip of the tongue that could mean money when passed on to the right party. When did Delaney realize Robin was on to him?"

Still holding the tissue in front of his nose, he mumbled, "Not what you're thinking."

"What am I thinking?"

"She didn't uncover him one day and kill him the next. Look, Delaney was the first operative I had to hire. I should have checked up on him more. But I got it on good authority he was honest. And it didn't seem like too tough a job. I thought he could handle it. I never would have . . ." A series of coughs shook him. He grabbed the sheet again, coughed into it. When he had got his breath back, he said, "Delaney screwed up looking for the wire. Two weeks before he died he told me he'd marked up the woodwork around the windows when he'd found the wires and he was afraid Robin would notice."

Kiernan didn't ask how Olsen had handled that. Judgment calls, they were part of the trade. She said, "We both know how fussy Robin was about that boat. Something like that she'd notice right off."

"But, Kiernan, he scuffed the woodwork two weeks before he died."

"Maybe she had to wait for bad enough weather to cover his drowning."

"In those two weeks we had enough small-craft warnings to sink a navy. Maybe it had something to do with her argument with Jessica."

"Argument with Jessica! Skip, is this another little fact you haven't bothered to tell me? How long have you known about this?"

"Hey, wait!" He held up a quivering hand. "This is the info I got on the dock day before yesterday. I paid a big price for this lead. It's not like I've been lying in the sun, you know. I've—"

"Skip, for Chrissakes, tell me about the argument!"

"I just did. That's all I know. What I got, from one of the deckhands, was that the two ladies were staring daggers at each other. There were words, but he was too far away to hear."

Kiernan sighed irritably.

Olsen waited a beat, then said, "This argument, Kiernan, it was two days before Matucci went under."

She would have expected to find a smug smile on his face, but he was still clutching the sheet in front of his mouth, uneasily, guiltily. Why? She leaned back against the wall and said, "What is it you can't talk about this time?"

"Nothing. They— Nothing."

"They? Who?"

Involuntarily Olsen glanced at his hip.

"The guys who kidnapped you. What did they want to know?"

"About Delaney," he muttered half into the sheet.

"So they knew he was an investigator."

"Yeah, they knew."

"What did you tell them?" Getting information out of Olsen was like pulling out pubic hairs, a painful proposition with ugly results.

"I told them nothing. I said Delaney hadn't reported his findings to me."

"Surely they didn't believe that."

Olsen snorted, then gagged in response to the snort. "No. That was when they said they were going to break my good hip. You know what that would do to me?"

Kiernan winced. "I can see why you'd talk."

"I didn't tell them everything," Olsen insisted indignantly. "I said it had taken Delaney a long time to learn the job and so he hadn't come up with anything except that Robin took out oil company guys."

"Surely they didn't accept that either. How long could it take a bright guy to learn to bait hooks and clean fish? So what did you give them?"

"Well, I had to tell them something, right?"

"If someone were going to break my one good hip, I'd talk."

Olsen was sweating. "I just told them that Delaney hadn't been able to report in ten days."

What was the man avoiding? What could he have told his captors that he was so afraid of admitting, to her. What would she— "Delaney's address, you gave them that, right?"

"Had to. They were going to break my hip." He slid lower under the covers.

He was still protecting himself; his whole posture screamed it. So what else had he told them? Delaney's address and . . . Blood heated her face; her hands clenched into fists. Very slowly she said, "You told them I would be breaking into Delaney's apartment, didn't you?"

Olsen coughed weakly.

"Skip, admit it!"

"Well, Kiernan," he spoke from a mouth half hidden by sheet. "What choice did I have? I didn't tell them *when* you'd be there."

"You didn't *know* that. And what difference did that make? They wouldn't expect me to break in in the middle of the day. So it meant that all they had to do was watch the place after dark—watch me go in, give me enough time to find what was important, and break in and take it from me!"

"Kiernan, I didn't know—"

"Forget it," she snapped.

"But—"

"I said forget it. You wanted to sleep. Sleep." She strode out of the room and slammed the door.

Tchernak was standing in the kitchen, half-sliced loaf of sourdough on a cutting board on the counter behind him, serrated knife clutched daggerlike in his hand. "So, I take it we're leaving?"

Kiernan shook her head.

Ezra hoisted himself up and walked over, shoving his head against her ribs.

"Look, I heard all that. The little whiner could have gotten you killed. Dumb enough you couldn't resist housebreaking . . ." He was waving the knife like a baton.

"Tchernak, I'm not about to give up the case. I'm too close. Jessica Leporek could clear up the whole thing. But," she said looking at the eager Tchernak, "we can't both leave here. We can't abandon Olsen, because we can't trust him."

36

Kiernan hurried into the "Yes on 37" office. The storefront was mobbed; phones rang cacophonously. Groups of volunteers huddled in every corner, clipboards in hand. At one side of the room a copy machine hummed and spat out papers. The whole place reeked of copier fumes and bad coffee. Kiernan smiled at the sandy-haired boy behind the desk and hurried through the cup-and-paper-strewn back room to Jessica's office.

Jessica Leporek's appearance gave new meaning to the phrase "three days before the election." Her red hair was scraped back in a rubber band; it appeared to have been finger-combed. If she'd started the day with makeup, she'd rubbed it off. She was brushing papers from the top of a pile with her right hand, clutching the phone with her left. "Don't tell me offshore drilling will reduce the need for tankers! Do you think the oil companies are going to allot every drop they drill out there to gas stations along the coast? Of course not. They're going to transport that oil. How are they going to move it? Tankers, right? The cities of Santa Monica and Los Angeles won't allow pipelines through their waters. Any platforms there have to load tankers. Up here we've already got more than a thousand tankers a year coming through the Golden Gate. Just one of average size carries sixty percent more oil than the Exxon *Valdez* spilled. That's over seventeen million gallons a ship. Do you know what the clean-up capability for this area is? I'll tell you. Eight hundred forty thousand gallons. You got those figures? Good, well, print that!" She put down the receiver, clearly restraining the urge to slam it. Glancing up at Kiernan, she squinted. "You're the detective, right? Look, I answered your questions, gave you time I couldn't afford. You want to ask me more, you'll have to wait till after the election. Then I'll have forever. If I live so long."

Kiernan moved a pile of papers, sat on the corner of Leporek's desk and said, "I'll be brief. Robin—"

"I told you I'm sorry if the woman is dead, but—"

"You're not, of course. But that's beside the point. The point is you had an argument with her two days before she disappeared. It's not your fault, doubtless it wasn't your intention, but whatever you said to Robin pushed her over the edge."

Jessica laughed. "Robin Matucci is not the type of woman to be pushed over the edge. And certainly not by mere words."

"What did you tell her?"

"Nothing that would cause her to take her boat out in a deadly storm." She turned her attention back to the most precarious pile, batting ineffectually at the edges.

"*What did you tell her?*"

"Look, I don't need to talk to you."

Kiernan lowered her voice. "Jessica, I'm going to reveal to you something I've discovered in my investigation. Robin Matucci is definitely alive."

Jessica stopped abruptly. "Are you sure?"

"What did you and Robin argue about? The memo that was stolen from Dwyer Cummings?"

She turned back to the pile, tapping the edges frenetically.

"Jessica, I'm good at my job. I found out about Robin. I'll discover the rest, but you can save me a lot of time. I'd appreciate that."

Jessica's hands slowed, then stopped. "Okay, okay. Here is the whole, full, entire story. Three years ago at the gallery opening Garrett Brant told me he had a memo that would skewer the oil industry. He said he'd give it to me."

"How did he get this memo? And why was he so willing to part with it?"

"I didn't ask. I figured I'd get the memo first and ask questions after I had it in my hand. He'd promised it to a woman charter captain—"

"Robin. Why would he give it to her?"

"Money. I got the impression she offered him plenty. But between then and the time he talked to me, he found out he was a finalist for the Arts of the Land prize. Even if he didn't win—he expected he would, Garrett wasn't modest about his work—even as a runner-up, he knew he'd get enough press and shows and sales so that he wouldn't need the money, wouldn't need to sell his principles. He really did care about the environment; his canvases show that. And"—Jessica laughed—"he'd been working as a janitor for the oil companies for months. He loved the idea of getting back at them. So he was willing to give the memo to me."

"But he didn't."

"He said he needed to tell his boat captain first. That was a principle, too. He was going to see her the next day." She turned and looked directly at Kiernan. "The next day he was hit by a car. He never got his memory back. I never got the memo."

"And that's why you kept after Robin Matucci, because you figured she might have it?" Kiernan began to feel the excitement she always found when the pieces came together.

"Right. She denied even seeing Garrett. There was no proof."

"What exactly was in the memo?"

With an irritated sigh, Jessica slammed back against the

chair. "I told you: I don't know. If I knew—if it's as important as I think it is—I've have it in every ad in the campaign."

"Surely you asked Garrett."

"Of course I asked. But Garrett was a tease and he loved having a secret."

"Still he had to have told you some fact. You wouldn't have coveted this memo for years because an artist you just met thought it was important."

Jessica grabbed a pencil in her fist. "Garrett worked maintenance for the oil companies. He knew some of the scuttlebutt." She stabbed the eraser into the desk. "Look, I told you, the election is three days away. If I had even a clue about what was in that memo, I'd leak it to the press and pray something turned up."

"Do you think Robin had the memo?"

From the front room came a wave of unintelligible words, as if every phone canvasser had hit the apex of his pitch simultaneously. Taking the pencil in both hands, Jessica said, "No, I'm sure she didn't. She was too accommodating to me. If she'd had the memo, she would have used it. She wouldn't have put up with me. But she was playing the same game I was, hoping to find out something, to get an edge, to get it."

"So if Robin didn't have it, then it's still with Garrett Brant."

"Wherever he is."

"Haven't you been in contact with him since his accident?"

She shook her head. "It's not for lack of trying. I tracked him down to San Francisco General just as they were about to transfer him to a rehab hospital. They wouldn't say which one, or even if it was in the city. It took me two weeks to ferret out where he was, and when I went there they wouldn't let me in. The closest I could get was the nurses' desk. Garrett's wife was running interference. How did I find him? she asked. What did I want? He'd lost his memory, she told me. Even when I explained that he'd offered me the memo, and how important it was, she didn't believe me. She didn't care about the coastline;

she didn't care about the memo. All she could think about was that he had promised to drive from wherever it was they lived—she wasn't about to tell me where that was—to San Francisco to see me. As if it were for some kind of assignation."

"Her husband had been virtually killed, her life was on hold, she probably wasn't as tactful as she might have been another time."

"You think that didn't occur to me? I'm not that insensitive," Jessica said, pressing her thumbs into the pencil.

"And the memo never surfaced?"

"Not unless Maureen sold it to someone with an oil company and they burned it."

"Jessica," Kiernan said slowly, "the day of Garrett Brant's accident, he drove into the city to meet Robin. It was Robin Matucci who hit him. Hit-and-run."

The pencil dropped and rolled under the edges of a pile of papers. "I can't believe it. I mean, I can; it's logical. Robin Matucci is as ambitious a woman as I've met. But still it's incomprehensible that a woman I know would do that."

Kiernan held up a palm. "But now that you know that, do you still think she didn't get the memo from him?"

A green-clad form rushed past the door in the next room. Metal clattered and the smell of bitter coffee cut the stale air. Jessica said, "She didn't get it. Look, the last time I saw her, she'd had enough of me. That was when we had the argument. If she hadn't thought before then that I'd something she wanted, she'd have given me the boot."

Kiernan slid off the desk. "One more thing. My original question. What was it you and Robin argued about two days before she sunk?"

"Nothing to do with this."

"Just tell me, and I'll leave."

She started to hunt around for the pencil, but gave up. She looked at Kiernan, then shrugged. "It came out of nowhere. I just asked her deckhand out for a drink. It was a long shot. I thought maybe he'd have some idea, maybe he'd heard something that didn't seem important to him, but would be a lead to the memo. I didn't know Garrett had it then, you see. Robin heard me ask Delaney. She sent him off for something and then she lit into me like a high school girl who's worried about her boyfriend. Maybe she was involved in a great romance. Who knows? But you don't sink your boat because a woman asks your guy out."

But you do to keep an investigator like Delaney from cozying up to a rival, pooling her info with his, and realizing that the hit-and-run was not an accident between strangers but an event that occurred on the day the victim refused to give her the vital memo. The statute of limitations might have run out for the hit-and-run, but it was still in effect for attempted murder.

37

Kiernan had just started the engine when the phone rang. "Kiernan, it's Maureen. God, I'm glad to get you." She was panting. "Garrett's acting terribly nervous. He was bad yesterday, but today he's scaring me. Kiernan, something's going on. I'm really worried."

Kiernan shifted into first but kept the clutch in. Both her feet were tense on the pedals. "What do you think it is?"

"I don't know. Somebody outside the studio, maybe? I just don't know. Kiernan, I'm scared."

"Do you want me to come down there?"

"Well, I hate to have you come all this way, but . . ." Maureen's voice sounded hopeful.

"Don't worry, it's part of my job. I'll see you in three and a half or four hours."

"Oh, Jeez, thanks. God, I feel relieved. Oh, Kiernan?"

"Yes."

"Could you stop here at the store on your way? The delivery truck broke down today and the stuff I need isn't in. I've been so upset I've barely got any food in the house. I'll pay for it, Jannie will have the bag ready. All you need to do is stick it in your Jeep."

Kiernan sighed. Grocery delivery was *not* in the job specs. "Well, if you're not worried about being alone that much longer."

"We should be okay till dark. I've got a gun." She paused. "And Kiernan, thanks."

She called Olsen's and left a message for Tchernak. Then she drove under the freeway—one of the sections that the last earthquake hadn't damaged—to the on ramp and headed south to Route 280 along the San Andreas Reservoir, on the edge of the Fault. Driving on the hillside of death had usually added a pleasant soupçon of danger to taking this road. But now the thought of Maureen and Garrett alone in their cabin provided ample tension.

At San Jose she turned west on Route 17 through the redwoods and pines to Santa Cruz, south to Monterey and stopped there for a sandwich and a Coke to fend off the exhaustion from having been up most of the night.

By the time she reached Big Sur, the ocean was pushing a wall of fog toward the cliffs. The few times Kiernan could take her eyes off the narrow, winding road long enough to look beyond its edge, she could see the breakers two hundred feet straight down. In another hour or so, all she'd be able to see would be heavy gray cloud. An hour after that, the ocean would thrust the fog up over the roadway, masking the hairpin curves. By nightfall, the visibility would be down to ten feet. But the drop off the edge would still be two hundred.

It was after five by the time she reached the grocery near

Big Sur. Other than three teenage boys and a silver Alfa Romeo Spider, the parking lot was empty. And the store was closed. A note on the door said: *Back in fifteen minutes.* Fifteen minutes could mean half an hour. Groceries could wait. Better Maureen and Garrett eat beans and stay alive.

She turned inland and followed the narrow road. Knives of sunlight cut between the redwood branches, momentarily blinding her. In the distance she could hear the grind and sigh of an engine. She was glad it was behind her; this was not a road on which to pass another car. The pavement ended; she braced herself, bouncing along in rhythm with the Jeep. In twenty minutes she pulled up behind Maureen's car, and glanced at the seven redwoods topping the bluff. They seemed to be teasing her city eyes, daring her to look high enough to see to the tops of their centuries-old trunks.

Kiernan started up the stone path, past the abandoned swimming pool. Four days ago she had sensed an air of fey neglect about it, the leaf-filled pool of an artist whose reality was in his imagination. But now the broken cement slabs on the bottom seemed to thrust up their jagged edges in defiance. She quickened her pace till she was running, and pounded on the faded red door.

There was no corresponding clatter of feet rushing across the hardwood floor inside. Just the afternoon breeze hissing between the branches of the redwoods making the fallen cones and leaves rustle against the cement, and the low rumble of a car on the road.

"Maureen! It's Kiernan! Open the door!"

No response. She should have come earlier. She shouldn't have left them alone . . . She ran around the side of the house, leaped over a clump of dead rosebushes. The door to Garrett's studio was just shutting. "Maureen! Garrett! It's Kiernan!" she yelled, remembering as she did so that her name would mean nothing to Garrett Brant.

The door opened a crack, Maureen peered out, her pale

face flushed. "Kiernan!" she said in surprise. "Oh, I'm so relieved it's you."

"Who did you think it was?" Garrett's voice asked from inside the studio. His tone held no urgency, merely a hint of amusement, as if his wife had heard the mailbox clatter when she had expected the milkman. The blandness of his tone highlighted the tension in his wife's voice. "Who is Karen?"

"Kiernan, Garrett. She came a few days ago. Maybe you didn't see her."

"Well, I guess not." In that same vague way, he said, "Are you going to let her in?"

"Oh." Maureen pulled the door back.

The studio was the same as it had been four days ago. Dark walls, open beams, the big window overlooking the redwoods. The photo of the Alaskan mud flats curled away from the wall. On the easel the painting that had been just lines when she first saw it now held a peninsula of browns and blacks and greens in the lower right corner. The rest was still white, with only a line or two sketched in to suggest the shoreline or the deceptively clear sky. Would Garrett have it finished in a week or two? And the day after would a fresh canvas be up there and this one secreted in a closet?

Shaking off that thought, she said to Maureen, "Are you all right?"

Maureen nodded. "I think so. I mean *we* are. It's my car that's got the problem now. It won't start. Probably the battery."

"You should have told me," Garrett said, grabbing a denim jacket. "I'll go and have a look at it." He hesitated at the door as if half-expecting something he couldn't name, a validation of his action, perhaps a contradiction. Then he rushed out.

"You don't worry about him going that far?" Kiernan asked.

"Not much. He'll never lift the hood. He won't remember why he went, not that long. If he'd taken a tool, he'd be able to reason out where he was headed . . ." She dropped into a canvas chair. "It's too late in the day for him to wander off. He'll see the shadows and know it's almost dinnertime. Did you bring the groceries?"

"I stopped but the store was closed. Surely, you can—"

"Closed? You got out and checked the door?"

She put a hand on Maureen's arm. "Trust me. I'm an investigator; I can tell when a grocery store isn't open."

Maureen shrugged. "Sorry, I guess the tension's getting to me. We're hardly going to starve."

Looking down at Maureen's lank blond hair, those stooped shoulders, the taut face that made her seem ten years older than her husband, she was surprised. She would have expected Maureen to look even more haggard than she had before the tension of the last four days. But the gray was gone from her skin, replaced by the ruddy flush of nervousness. Sitting on the other canvas chair, she said, "What do you do when the car won't start?"

"It doesn't happen so often that I have a routine for it, thank God. If I had to I could walk to the store. It's only five miles. But," she said, catching Kiernan's eye, "I didn't want to be gone that long right now. Maybe you could call triple A when you leave."

"I can call them now."

"No!" She jerked forward as if to get up. With a sigh, she leaned back and said, "There's no rush. Besides, I don't want strange men coming out here. Not with Garrett as jumpy as he's been."

Sitting in the chair opposite her, Kiernan said, "Frankly, Maureen, you seem a lot edgier than he does."

Maureen shrugged. "Chronic."

"What's gotten to him?"

"I don't know." She was rubbing her hand again. The raw spot Kiernan had noticed Monday was larger, redder, painful to see. "I left Garrett in his studio working when I went to do the shopping yesterday. When I got back he was very jittery. Today I·started out, then came back—I'd forgotten to bring cash. When I got here he was worse. Garrett runs a constant very low-grade anxiety, as if he were playing in a game and hasn't been told one of the rules. But he's never noticeably agitated unless something attacks right then, like I did the first time you were here."

"But as soon as you distracted him he forgot what you'd said. Did he forget it entirely?"

"It's hard to say." Maureen's voice sounded more normal. "Maybe some part of his brain keeps some things he no longer has the means to pull back up. For all practical purposes his memory is gone, and so the emotion is gone. No highs, no lows—" she stopped abruptly. "My theory is that the neuronal pathways in his brain that transmitted the impulses for excitement are atrophying day by day." Maureen's voice was shaking. "Eventually he'll do no more than exist, like a paper doll."

Kiernan could hear her own sharp intake of breath. She shut her eyes against the horror of that empty existence, and the greater horror of watching one you love decay slowly. "So what was different yesterday and today, Maureen?"

"I can't find out. I asked Garrett what had happened, but of course he could only tell me about the previous minute or so."

"Did Garrett acknowledge that he was upset?"

"No. Here's the interesting part. He denied it. He had an expression I hadn't seen in years: he looked guilty, wary somehow. And at the same time he had a little grin, like if he played things right, he'd win. It took me a couple of hours to recall what it meant." She looked directly at Kiernan. "Garrett was hiding something."

"Do you have any idea what?"

She shook her head stiffly, jerkily. "No. He keeps checking his plaid jacket." She glanced at the brown wool jacket hanging on a hook. "He looks in the inside pocket, like he just remembered something should be there."

Kiernan reached for the jacket. The rough wool felt rugged. Thin lines of brick red and a brown so dark it was almost black sparked the plaid. It was a jacket that would suit Garrett's blond hair and blue eyes. And the texture would underline his years in a rough climate. She pictured him standing at a gallery opening in that jacket, wineglass in hand leaning against the mantel, knowing just how good he looked, smiling as he talked to someone like Jessica Leporek. To Maureen she said, "What did he keep in that pocket?"

"Nothing particular. It's a city jacket, too nice for down here."

Kiernan put the jacket back on the hook. "Did Garrett wear it the day of the accident?"

"He took it. He didn't have it on. It was in the back of the car. What he was wearing was the hooded sweatshirt he liked to drive in."

"But now something has unnerved him and he connects it with that jacket," Kiernan said, trying to control her excitement. "This new stimulus would have to have touched some memory of an incident that occurred before the accident for him to react to it. Is that right? Who did you know before the accident who knows where you are now?"

"No one"—Maureen shook her head— "I told you how insistent Garrett was. It was like he expected to be robbed. Or worse."

"But—"

The door opened and Garrett wandered in. He glanced from Maureen to Kiernan. "What an odd place for you ladies to have a chat, here in my studio," he said. Then, extending a hand to Kiernan, he said, "I'm Garrett Brant. Now where is it we've met before?"

Forcing a smile, forcing down her frustration at the interruption, Kiernan took his hand. "Good to meet you."

Garrett unfolded another director's chair. Maureen wandered to the front window and stood looking out, her back to Garrett. He smiled at Kiernan. "I hope you didn't come far. This place is a whole lot less accessible than my house in Alaska."

Kiernan glanced toward the jacket. But it would be too abrupt to ask about that. Better to ease in. "I wanted to ask you about Alaska. Garrett, do you remember the California Tavern?"

He smiled and flopped into the chair, one leg sprawled over the wooden armrest. For the first time she had a sense of the real person behind that pale façade of skin and yellow hair. "You been there? The old C. T? Great place. Only spot in Alaska where you could get a glass of white zinfandel." He threw back his head and laughed. The motion brought color to his face. His hair, which had looked merely unkempt, now gave him the intriguingly unruly look of one too involved to worry about trifles. Sailor's hair, artist-at-the-end-of-the-day hair. This had to be the Garrett Brant Maureen had married. The man who had worn the brown plaid jacket. "Only place where you could drink zin and not be mocked to death."

"They say every Californian in the area goes there at some time."

"Diego, the guy who owns it—Diego's not his real name, I'm sure, I think it comes from San Diego, and obviously, that's not his name. But no one asks—anyway, Diego runs videos of the beach in Santa Barbara, the sun setting behind the San Francisco skyline, the sailboats tooling across San Diego harbor. Those are the biggies. He's got a great one of the cliffs here at Big Sur. But he's got home videos of, oh, it must be half the towns in California. He brags that no Californian leaves without seeing someplace he's lived."

"So you met a lot of people there?"

"Oh, yeah."

"Do you remember a guy named Carl Hartoonian?"

"Hartoonian?"

"Average height, short brown hair that lies flat on his head, bony face, black-rimmed glasses. He reads atmospheric printouts to predict where the fish will be."

"Oh, Harpoon," he said, grinning. "Sure I know Harpoon. The guy's crazy about all his machines. I mean the guy can be a real drag if you get stuck alone with him. He talks about computers the way a normal guy discusses"—he shot a glance at Maureen—"sex."

Kiernan wondered just how he would have phrased the comment in her absence. "So you must have known Robin Matucci, too."

His animation disappeared. "No."

"Tall woman with long red hair. She was working as a deckhand," Kiernan prompted.

"No. That doesn't ring a bell. But there were plenty of people I didn't know. They came and went. No one was there every night. It was easy to miss people." He smiled uneasily.

No wonder Maureen knew when Garrett was hiding something, Kiernan thought. He was one of the most transparent liars she had ever seen. Was deception one of the skills that had faded with his memory? She stood up and fingered Garrett's plaid jacket. "You sure you don't remember Robin?"

"No!" He grabbed the jacket. "Look, I don't want to be rude, but I'm going to be gone tomorrow and I need to get some things in order before I leave."

"Thanks for your help." She stepped outside. A damp breeze chilled her neck. Near the trees beyond the house a wild rabbit stood quivering, instinctively avoiding eye contact with her, the threat.

It was a moment before Maureen followed. "I need to talk to him alone," Kiernan said.

"But—"

"No buts. Too much is riding on this. I'll see you after. In the meantime you might be thinking about what to do with your car."

Without waiting for a reply, Kiernan walked back into the studio. Garrett was standing by the window, staring out at the redwoods. The sunlight between the branches had grown paler. Without it to brighten the dark walls, the whole room seemed more like a forgotten garage than an artist's studio. She put a hand on Garrett's shoulder.

He turned, smiled and took her hand in his. "Hello, there. Now where is it we know each other from?" The stubborn set of his jaw had relaxed. In this smile there was no residue of his earlier uneasiness.

"We met in Alaska," she said. "The California Tavern, remember? I'm a friend of Robin's."

He shot a glance behind him so quickly that it seemed less a decision than a muscular reaction.

Kiernan sat in the director's chair next to the jacket. "Robin said to look you up."

His eyes widened slightly.

Kiernan hesitated. The tack wasn't quite right. Don't lead with Robin, ease in. She said, "Remember those nights in the California Tavern? What time was it you used to get there?"

He smiled now and settled into the chair opposite her. A lock of blond hair dangled over his forehead. "Late, at least late for most people. I was on maintenance crew then. The California was just across the street from the AlaskOil building. I'll tell you on those January nights it was all I could do to get across that street without freezing my balls off."

"Yeah, but it was worth it, wasn't it?"

Hitching one ankle on the other knee, he smiled. "Yeah. The C. T.'s a little cutesy, but then so what, right?"

"And the videos were such a kick. Do you remember the one about San Francisco?"

"Oh yeah. I must have seen it a dozen times. You know Diego," he said, catching her eye and smiling, "every time a new customer comes in, he asks where he's from—"

"And whips out the video."

"Yeah, San Diego, Eureka, Monte Rio. Monte Rio was the best, with the old tin hangar for a movie theater like it was still summer nineteen fifty and everyone had vacation houses by the river, and hope. The others were fine for what they were, but Monte Rio, once you saw that tape you knew the town, the people's communal soul." Impulsively, he reached for her hand, and she felt his skin quivering with the excitement of his vision.

He was so alive, so seductive in that focused passion, she hated to break the spell. "Remember Robin Matucci, the red-haired deckhand?"

His animation vanished. Dropping Kiernan's hand, he shot a glance around the room.

Kiernan forced a smile, and made herself lean back, let a moment pass, and waited till his expression more nearly mirrored her own. "Who was it Robin came with? You remember, don't you?"

"Sure. It was the oil guys. The engineers sometimes, but mostly the corporate types."

"Just like Robin, huh? Never did let any grass grow under her feet, did she?"

"Sharp cookie. One helluva a looker. Nice, too."

"Of course you knew her pretty well, didn't you?"

His open-palmed motion said yes and no. His expression suggested more, but more *what* Kiernan couldn't decide. "Robin knew everyone."

Kiernan screwed up her face as if searching her memory. "But the guy she was with most of the time? You remember . . . Who was he?"

Garrett shook his head. His face was losing its color. Was this what happened to him before a thought faded out?

Struggling to keep the smile on her face, the atmosphere of camaraderie she'd created, Kiernan said, "Robin told me about the memo you've got for her. The one you 'liberated' from Dwyer Cummings's office." She was holding her breath, waiting for him to validate her assumption. "You're not going to take it to the city when you see her, are you?"

Garrett's blond eyebrows drew down over his eyes. He looked assessingly at Kiernan. Then a sly grin flashed and was gone.

"Clever of you to spot it in Cummings's office," she said.

"Was it just sitting there in his Out box, or maybe in the trash? One of the perks of maintenance crew?"

He didn't comment, but his face colored and the corners of his mouth twitched.

"Garrett, Robin told me that that memo would make a real difference in whether the Energy Producers' Group could get an okay for offshore drilling here."

The intensity of his gaze faded. Had she led him too far from fact with her speculations?

But there was no turning back—she was sure she was right. "You've decided to give the memo to the environmentalists, haven't you? You've decided to do the right thing?"

A watery smile crossed his face.

"But, Garrett, I don't understand how the memo you took from Dwyer Cummings's office in Anchorage will effect things here in California."

He leaned forward and let his fingers brush her hand. "I guess I can tell *you*."

"Of course, you can, Gar."

"Well, the oil companies aren't quite as entrenched here in the lower forty-eight as they are up there. Half the people in Anchorage work for oil companies. Big money doesn't change hands without it coming from or going to them, or to some subsidiary, some builder building for them, some restaurateur leasing a place so he can get their trade. They've got Alaska by the balls. But here it's not too late. They can't buy California."

"Dwyer Cummings was in Probability Analysis. What was he analyzing in that memo?"

Garrett squeezed her hand. "Well, now this memo wouldn't be of much use to anyone if I spilled the beans first, would it? Wait a couple days and you'll see it in the papers."

In a teasing tone that mimicked his, Kiernan said, "Oh, Garrett, you can give me a little hint."

Smiling, he fingered the cuff of her sleeve. Kiernan wondered how often he'd played out this type of game. "Well," he said, slowly, "okay. Blow-out protectors."

"What did it say about them?"

"No, no. You said a hint, and that's it."

"Garrett, let me see the memo. This memo is going to affect the history of the state. It's an historic document."

"No, no."

"Just a peek?" God, she hated wheedling.

Outside, behind him, a branch broke. He whipped around, looking out the window. Kiernan rushed toward it and looked as far to the right as she could, then to the left. No one was visible now. She thought she'd seen a tuft of brown, possibly an animal. Possibly not.

Garrett followed her to the window and stared out.

From behind him, she said, "The memo you took from Dwyer Cummings's office, Garrett, where is it?"

He stiffened, then turned "Memo? What kind of memo?"

He was lying. Obviously lying. His expression shifted from apprehension to confusion. "Who are you?"

She let out a great sigh of sheer frustration. "I'm a friend of Maureen's. I'll go get her." She stepped outside, shut the door and stood in the dark, thinking of Maureen living with Garrett, one frustrating, disappointing day leading nowhere but to the next.

But the memo wasn't what motivated Maureen. Neither was finding out whether Delaney had been murdered. These weren't the reasons for this investigation at all.

Kiernan strode across the yard and pushed open the door to the main house.

38

Maureen was standing by the kitchen door, her face still flushed, her hands clasped tightly together. "I just hate leaving Garrett alone. He's so helpless. It's like leaving a child."

"Leaving him alone with me? Were you afraid he'd tell me something that wasn't in your plan?" Kiernan slammed the door. She moved into the dining room and stood by the window, from which she could see the studio in the failing light of evening. "Garrett knew Robin Matucci in Alaska. He had no problem telling me that once you were out of the room."

Maureen stared at the window. The dusky light carved angry furrows in her forehead and hollows in her cheeks.

"That's what was bugging you, wasn't it, Maureen? Whether Garrett was having an affair with Robin? Whether he drove to San Francisco to see her? Whether he was screwing around behind your back and now, because of that, you're stuck with him the way he is. Right?"

Maureen slammed her fist on the table. "Well, goddamn it, wouldn't you want to know? I'm here twenty-four hours a day, alone, with a man who gets more and more distant all the time. I loved him. I put up with his being away for months, with picturing him in a bar in whatever city he happened to be in, chatting up a new woman each time. Garrett Brant, the friendly artist. I knew he wasn't taking all of them to bed, but I suspected there were a few he did sleep with. I accepted that. I figured at least he'd be careful." She glared out the window. "But god-damn it to hell, after he'd been gone for nearly six months, if he came home and then took off the first week he was here to go and screw some lady in the city, then he can damn well spend the rest of his days in an asylum."

"That's what this whole investigation is about, isn't it? You don't care if Robin Matucci killed her deckhand or even if she hit Garrett. You hired me to find out if Garrett was sleeping with her."

"Wouldn't you?" Maureen demanded.

Kiernan took a deep breath. Bracing both hands on the edge of the table, she said, "You didn't tell me about Delaney, a man who was killed investigating for you. And you didn't even level with me about the goal of this search."

"But Kiernan, you wouldn't have taken the case if you'd known the truth," Maureen pleaded.

Kiernan shook her head in disgust. "The truth is not one of several options."

"But—"

"There's nothing you could say now that I would believe. And there are plenty of other investigators who can look into your questions about Garrett."

Maureen shrugged. "Why should I hire someone else?"

"Because I doubt Garrett was having an affair with Robin Matucci. He knew her in Alaska. But nothing he said indicated he was physically involved with her."

Maureen sank back against the window ledge.

Kiernan waited for some sign of relief. But none came. Behind Maureen, outside in the studio, the light came on. Garrett ambled past the window, a shadowy form making his way to nothing.

Her own anger dissipated. To Maureen, she said, "I'm sorry. That wasn't the answer you wanted, was it? You needed a good reason to leave Garrett, a reason good enough to allow you to face his friends and family, a reason that would permit you to live with yourself."

Maureen gritted her teeth and squeezed her eyes closed, but it was no use. Tears ran down her cheeks. In the dusky light she looked small and abandoned. Kiernan put an arm around her shoulder. She said nothing. There was nothing to say.

She wouldn't have been surprised if Maureen insisted the investigation continue so she could have the satisfaction of seeing Robin as imprisoned as she was. But Maureen seemed beaten. She pulled back, glancing nervously at the windows. Kiernan said, "When I was in the studio with Garrett he was distracted by some movement outside. I got a glimpse of something brown, I think, but I'm not certain."

Maureen shrugged again. "It could have been a deer, or some smaller animal. We get them all the time."

"You're not worried about someone prowling around outside?" Kiernan said, aware of the edge to her voice. "Or was that part of the fiction?"

"Let's just say it was an embellishment. I'll bring Garrett in here when you leave. We'll be okay." She wiped the back of her hand hard across her eyes, as if to punish them for their betrayal. To Kiernan she said, "Do you want a cup of coffee or anything before you leave? Use the bathroom? It's a long drive back to . . . well, wherever you're going."

"No, I'm fine. I'll send you a report and have my office write you to settle accounts."

"Thanks. I appreciate all you've done. I appreciate your coming today. When I called you and the call kept fading I wasn't sure you'd really heard me."

"The call didn't fade."

Maureen laughed thinly. "It must have been me fading, then. Whatever. Thanks." She held out her hand.

Kiernan shook it and started across the living room toward the door. But even as she walked she knew she wouldn't leave right then. It galled her to have made the point about betrayal so firmly, so damned well, and then to have to undercut it. But as things stood, the investigation had more of a hold on her than on Maureen. She turned around. "Maureen, what about Dwyer Cummings's memo? Does Garrett still have it?"

"Memo?"

"Hasn't he mentioned it to you?"

"No. Look, it's getting dark. You'd better go."

Just like Jessica Leporek had said, Maureen had no interest in the memo. "The memo he was going to give Jessica. He was going to the city to tell Robin he wouldn't sell her the memo."

"Not to set up a show, but to sell this memo?" Her voice was almost a whisper as she said, "He lied to me."

"Why would he have lied about that? Or is dishonesty just the coin of the realm here?"

Maureen shrank back against the window. It was a moment before she said, "I guess I can't put up much of an argument against that. You're right, we've always had a pretty high level of falseness. We were apart so much that it was no problem to keep back what we wanted, to show what we chose; we only had to do it for a few weeks at a time. It was just easier that way: a little play-acting when he was there, and when he left I still had my picture of the 'real' Garrett undisturbed." She laughed bitterly, "I guess that's what trained me for living like this." She walked to the front door. "It's getting late, and with the fog like this, driving is going to be slow."

"I'll be okay. But I need a few answers before I can close this case in my mind." Kiernan stopped by the couch. It seemed ages since she'd stood here watching Garrett Brant stare in horror at the three pictures of the mud flats. "You remember Jessica Leporek telling you how important the memo Garrett took from the oil companies was. Garrett was going to the city to break his agreement to sell it to Robin. Why do you think Garrett lied to you about that?"

"He would have been ashamed of ever making the deal, and I would have been disgusted with him. We may not always be honest, but we do have some principles."

She turned to face Maureen. "But if Garrett didn't sell the memo to Robin—"

"My God, that's why she stopped after she hit him, isn't it? She stopped to search for the memo? She stood over his body, and went through his pockets looking for it. Isn't that right?"

"Probably. But the point is that she didn't find it. If Garrett had taken it with him, she would have found it. She didn't. So, we can surmise that it's still here."

"Surmise, yes, but—"

"And, Maureen, anyone else who knows about it can surmise the same thing." Kiernan watched as her words sunk in, and Maureen's whole body quivered. "I can stay—"

"No!" she snapped. She shut her eyes as if to calm herself. When she walked to the door she was shaking. "No, I'm used to it here. We'll be okay."

"Maureen, don't take the threat of intruders too lightly. I could hear a car coming along the road after me when I drove in."

"Other people live along here. I—" Her voice cracked. She swallowed. *"We will be all right."* She reached for the doorknob.

Kiernan braced her arm against the door. "You said you have a gun?"

She nodded. "Garrett's got a big old revolver. He has to hold it with two hands now, but he can still shoot. And I have a rifle."

"Have you shot it?"

Again, she nodded. "Target. A lot. One of the things I can do here. I'm good, very good for a woman with hands and arms this small."

"Okay, but you realize that as long as you have this memo in your possession, as long as anyone *thinks* you do, you and Garrett are in danger."

"That's why Garrett was so insistent that no one know where we were." She was shaking harder. "Even though he only expected to have his memo a week or so."

"Maureen, where would he put it?"

"I have no idea. And there's no point in asking him. He lives in the day before the accident, not the day of it. If he put it somewhere before he left, now he'd have no clue as to where." She twisted the doorknob and this time Kiernan let her open it.

"Maureen, don't be too cavalier. Take precautions. Get Garrett in here. Bolt the doors."

Maureen put a hand on Kiernan's arm. It was ice cold. Her voice was almost inaudible as she said, "Now go."

Feeling uneasy, angry, and very frustrated, Kiernan walked through the fog to the Jeep.

39

Maureen Brant stared out the front window into the fog, listening to the Jeep driving away. She knew she should have. . . . Dammit, she should have planned better.

She forced her fingers to relax on the rifle barrel. She'd be okay. She was prepared, rifle loaded, the old Ruger revolver ready in Garrett's studio. She wouldn't be taken by surprise. Anyone would be a fool to come before it was completely dark. She smiled. Outsiders didn't realize how acute your hearing becomes when you've got nothing to do day after day but listen for the meter reader or some tourist with a four-wheel drive and the urge to explore. Sound carries in darkness. No city person wants to walk miles in the strange woods at night. No, tonight, she would hear the engine die. Then she'd wait, ready.

She propped the rifle against the fireplace and walked across the living room, pausing to straighten a pile of magazines that was barely out of kilter. She glanced through the window at the studio. She had been cavalier. Why hadn't she asked about the car following Kiernan? Did it pass the house?

Her heart beat in rapid little flutters, but her mind was slow, unfocused. To come to each decision, she had to think through the steps three times, silently, slowly pronouncing the words that described each step so she would remember them long enough to move on to the next.

But that couldn't be helped. She thought about Garrett out in the studio. He had the revolver there. And as edgy as he was, he would shoot. There was nothing she could do now but prop the rifle next to the sofa and wait.

Fog hung from the branches of redwoods and pines and cypress trees like decade-old cobwebs holding Kiernan back. It clung doggedly to the Jeep's windshield, and gave way only momentarily before the wiper blades. She squinted into the dark; she just wanted to get out of here, away from Maureen, and Garrett, and the bottomless pit of lies, and, she had to admit it, humiliation. She felt for Maureen, but God, she hated being taken in.

The fog moistened the redwood. The smell of them was so strong it was almost bitter, and the deep brown dirt of the road wafted up in musty waves. A steep curve came out of nowhere; she jammed on the brakes and the wheels skidded momentarily on the wet ground. The road dipped down into a valley. She wanted to call Tchernak, to hear Ezra's low whine. She started to reach for the phone. No, the road was too bad. And this stretch was too low, too surrounded, she'd probably be out of range till she reached the coast road.

Out of range? She had worried about it, but the cellular phone had operated fine, even outside the Brants' house. She hadn't had one problem with it the whole trip.

So what had Maureen been talking about when she said she was afraid Kiernan wouldn't come, that the call had faded? *Her* phone hadn't faded.

She turned right on the twisting two-lane road. The fog was thicker, backed up against the wall of trees. The Jeep's headlights bounced off it. Though she would never have admitted it, not to anyone, Kiernan was relieved to be driving north, on the *inside* lane of Highway 1, where she might graze the rocks but wouldn't bounce off the edge into that thick white abyss, ten feet down—or two hundred.

Maureen hadn't even called her today, she'd called Olsen. So who had she been talking to? Whose phone had faded?

Irritably she followed the taillights of the car ahead, unable to pass in the fog. When she came abreast of Barrow's Grocery she hurried inside the store, bought a Coke, used the bathroom. Then, unwilling to leave the relative normality of the store, she dialed Olsen's number and stood watching two teenaged boys by the magazine rack.

Tchernak answered on the first ring.

"Hi. It's Kiernan. Everything okay there?"

"No, it certainly is not." His tone was piqued, not worried.

Before he could launch into a full complaint, she said, "No signs of anyone threatening Olsen?"

"Look, I have to get out of here. I'm—"

"Dangers other than you?"

"He'll live, unless he coughs his brains out. But I may not."

The teenagers slapped their magazines back in the rack and headed for the door. Kiernan turned toward the wall. Lowering her voice, she said, "Well, you'll only have to hold out a few more hours. I'm off the case."

"You've closed it?"

"Not really. Once Maureen found out that Garrett hadn't been two-timing her, she couldn't wait to get rid of me. Just about pushed me out the door."

"A little indecisive? First she's dying for you to get there, then she wants you to leave."

"Yeah. If this is an example of her inconsistency it's a good thing she's living with Garrett. Only someone with no memory would put up with it."

"Kiernan"—she could hear Tchernak drinking something —"you don't sound like someone who's done with a case. This is not the voice of a woman who's closed the file."

Kiernan sighed. She heard the grocery door open behind

her. She glanced around in time to see a couple head for the cooler. Shivering in white shorts and sweaters, they had the look of tourists surprised by the fog. "The truth is I hated to leave Maureen in the state she is. And, well, the woman's lied to me so much, I'm not sure what she's told me now is the whole truth. With her, I feel as if I'm walking on quicksand, or on Garrett's Alaskan mud flats. The whole thing bugs me." She leaned against the wall.

"Don't you want to speak to *Him?*"

Kiernan hesitated, then said, "Tchernak, I'm in a public grocery."

"Well, I'll have *Him* call you on the car phone. If you don't get out there fast enough I'll have *Him* leave a lovely message for you."

"Enough, Tchernak. I'll see you soon."

She hung up and strode out and was almost to the Jeep when she saw three teenaged boys leaning against the silver Alfa Romeo, the same boys who had been there when she had stopped earlier. Still thinking of the car phone, she walked over. "You guys see a red Porsche here late this afternoon? Driver was a woman with red hair?"

"Yeah, great car. I mean, this lady, she must really take care of it. You know her?"

"She left going south, didn't she?"

"Yeah, but why—"

Kiernan ran to the Jeep and headed back to the Brants'.

40

So dark and white. White cuts through the night. Men die in this kind of white, in the snow, the ice storms, when it's fifty below and even the haze freezes. I have to get out of here, down to the lower forty-eight, home to San Francisco. Standing inches from his studio window Garrett Brant stared at the thick fog that draped the outside. *Chugash Mountains in the distance. Could see them if it weren't for the haze. Damn haze, and cold, and slaving over oil men's garbage.* His eyes closed and he could see the polished wood desk, the brass-on-mahogany name sign: Dwyer Cummings; the risk analysis charts stacked on the left, the "to be signed" pile on the right. Garrett smiled as he pictured the memo there "Subj.: Blow-Out Preventers." His smile stretched wide across his tan face and without realizing it his hand reached out toward the remembered pile to pocket the memo. "Gotcha, bastard!"

He was still smiling as he opened his eyes and recognized his own studio, his brown plaid jacket, and remembered he was going to the city the next day.

Maureen Brant cocked her head. That noise in the distance, was it an engine? She looked out the front window into the milky dark. *Nothing to see. Of course. There wouldn't be. Not yet.*

Without releasing her gaze, she felt the rifle barrel, moving her fingers slowly, silently. Listening. What made that kind of sound? Straining engine, pulling a car out of one of the deep holes in the road? Engine shutting off? But no, the noise was gone from her mind now. She smiled to herself. Gone from her mind, just like things passed through Garrett's, leaving no trail.

She shook her head sharply. *I'm losing it. Not enough sleep. Can't lose it now. Not now, when everything is at stake.* Her second finger struck the rifle barrel. She wrapped her hand around the metal. Pressing her ear to the window, she listened for the rustle of underbrush.

The salty smell of the ocean mixed with the scent of junipers and redwoods as Kiernan drove south on Highway 1, peering into the fog for the road to the Brants'. The fog chilled her arms and legs, but sweat glued her shirt to her back. She clutched the wheel tighter and tensed her ankle to keep from pressing down on the gas as she thought of Robin Matucci waiting at the grocery this afternoon, waiting to follow her. "God, I hate to be used!"

Maureen stood by the window, her body so tense it felt like metal, old rusted iron ready to flake at the touch. How could she expect to hear the rustle of feet, carefully placed feet, when her heart was thudding so loud?

Garrett heard the studio door open. "Mau—" He turned around. "Oh? Robin. What are you doing here?" He stared at her in the open doorway. She didn't look good, not like she had at the California Tavern. He didn't remember lines like that in her face. She had always been smiling. She wasn't now. Her red hair was dripping from the fog, and the weight of the water had pulled those lovely swaying waves almost straight. And those brown slacks she was wearing were too short. Odd. He'd never seen Robin Matucci when she wasn't dressed just right. If he weren't seeing it himself, he couldn't imagine her wearing a baggy white sweater like that. And her makeup . . . "Aren't you feeling well, Robin?"

"Garrett, I want the memo."

He smiled. "No 'Hello, how are you?' After all the way

you've come? You didn't have to come here, you know. I would have been at Baker Beach tomorrow, like I said."

Her eyes opened wide, like in slow motion, he thought. He watched, taken aback, as she just stood there and stared at him. She was a mover, always rushing here, jumping up to run over there; if she couldn't leave, she'd be tapping her finger. He had a couple of sketches of her he'd done from memory; he'd wanted to capture that sense of motion.

She swallowed and moved toward him. "Garrett, the memo. Give it to me."

He'd forgotten how tall she was. Not quite his height, but strong, too. All that work hauling in lines, being a deckhand.

"Garrett, I don't have all day. Where is it?"

Now she looked more like her old self, as her eyes darted around the room, at the coat rack, the chairs. She didn't even stop to notice his painting. He shouldn't care about that, he told himself; most of it was still white; it wasn't ready to be seen yet. But nonetheless it left him feeling exposed. He wanted to close the door, but he didn't move.

He watched her look at the window behind him, and at the desk. Her eyes paused for the first time. She was staring at the handgun.

Garrett swallowed. He'd known it wasn't going to be easy to deal with her. She wouldn't like hearing that he had decided not to sell her the memo. He had qualms about that meeting alone, tomorrow, in the fog at Baker Beach. But this, here . . . He forced himself not to look at the Ruger lying there out of reach. He said, "Robin, I'm sorry you've come all this way for nothing. I'm a finalist for an award. So I don't need to sell the memo now."

"Garrett, we've been through all that. You told me all that on Baker Beach. For an hour!" The lines in her forehead deepened, then they eased as she smiled. That little tilt to the head. He'd tried to capture that. To capture the charm and the steel beneath. Red and gray. "Garrett, you gave me your word. I like to think of you as an ethical man."

"I am. I'm giving the memo to a woman who's working to save the shoreline."

She moved in closer. Was she going to waft a hand across his shoulder, give him a playful kiss like he'd seen her do in the C.T.? A little encouragement? "Garrett, I need the memo. It's very important to me."

"I'm sorry. I've made my decision."

She turned and picked up the gun.

Robin pointed the revolver. She'd heard, from that pain-in-the-ass environmentalist woman, that Garrett had some kind of brain damage. He looked all right. His hand was shaking and he seemed like he was in no hurry. But he looked a helluva lot better than she did! When she'd hit him, on the Great Highway, she should have crushed him into the sand, never let him recover and threaten her this way. As hard as she had worked. All those nights she'd slept on the boat, downed enough coffee to keep the entire fishing fleet awake, all so she could listen and relisten to those tapes of Dwyer Cummings and his buddies down in *Early Bird*'s salon drinking her liquor, describing her breasts, her butt, speculating on what kind of lay she'd be, and maybe once in twenty trips letting drop something like the specs on land they'd need for onshore support buildings when the offshore platforms were operational, or some other bit of information she could sell. She'd done well with what she'd gleaned. But nowhere near what she could get for that memo. She was no dreamer, like her father was. She'd used what she had and put out of her mind what didn't work. She'd given up thinking about the memo until that environmental pest had started coming around. And then that damned Delaney! Momentarily she shut her eyes against the picture of *Early Bird*, shattered, by the explosion.

And all those years Garrett Brant was sitting on his ass out here in the woods, planning to give the memo to Jessica Leporek!

She could still see Delaney's forehead wrinkling in shock

when she aimed the chop at his neck. He hadn't seen it coming, not until the last instant, then the bastard had ducked and she'd hit him too high. By then he was drunk. After the first swallow she hadn't even needed to threaten him. She'd thrown the gun overboard halfway to the Farallons. She could still see Delaney falling, stunned from the blow, not out cold as she'd planned. She could feel the shock giving way to action as it always had for her. She could feel the muscles in her arms tightening as she'd grabbed the rope and bound his wrists and ankles. The storm had picked up then, bounced him around. He'd never gotten to his feet again. It had taken hours to get out past the Farallons, fighting the thirty-foot waves, waiting for the moment when she could leave the wheel long enough to cut him loose. Not too soon and have him get to his feet and be banging around in the cockpit, or trying to get at her in the wheelhouse. But she couldn't let him be washed overboard still bound. If anyone found his body . . . That fear was a long shot. The whole god-damn Pacific floor for the man to settle on and he had to float up on the Farallons. It was her worst nightmare come true. Bastard! If he hadn't floated up and been found, she could have come back to the wharf in two weeks, collected the insurance and gone on with her life. Goddamn bastard. Now she had nothing. She needed that memo.

"Garrett"—her voice was guttural—"I'm not fooling around with you. I've already killed one man."

His smooth brow wrinkled lightly.

"Goddamn it, do you realize what I'm saying? Give me the memo now or I will shoot. You *and* your wife."

Kiernan turned off Highway 1. Was that the Brants' road? It didn't look quite the same. But everything looked different in the white-out fog. She eyed the odometer. The pavement ended in about a mile. That would be the clue. If *all* the roads off the highway weren't paved for an equal distance!

The pavement ended. She checked the odometer. One mile down, four to go. The Jeep bucked into a hole. There was no way to avoid them now. She pulled to the edge of the track, and kept going, watching the odometer, clutching the wheel, the Jeep slamming into holes and rocks and the bank of the road when curves came too fast. A mile to go. A half.

Maureen's car was still parked under the redwoods. Kiernan pulled up. Grabbing the flashlight, she raced up the bluff, head down, straining to see as far as her stride, flashing the light back and forth to spot the abandoned swimming pool before she tripped over the edge and cracked her head on the cement.

The house was dark. Kiernan knocked. "It's Kiernan!" No one answered.

She didn't bother to knock again. Wound tight as Maureen was, she'd have heard the first time.

She made her way around the side of the house, stumbling over roots that hadn't merited a thought in daylight.

A blur of light shone from Garrett's window. She ran forward, across the bramble of grass, and peered in. The room looked empty.

She opened the door and saw the body.

It was a woman's.

41

The smell of death—urine, excrement, blood, and ripped tissue—filled Garrett Brant's studio. Automatically, Kiernan breathed through her mouth. The studio was empty but for the body on the floor. Robin Matucci's body.

Kiernan shut the studio door and wedged one of the chairs

against the handle. It wouldn't keep out Robin's murderer, but it would make any entry noisy.

Matucci lay facedown, her long red hair fallen over one shoulder, knees slightly flexed. Her feet faced the door, her body away from it, as if she had tripped in the doorway and hit the floor. But her right arm was flung over her head, her left out to the side, suggesting she'd twisted around on the way down. She faced to the left, toward Garrett's half-finished canvas. One shot had entered through the bridge of her nose, rupturing the tissue and sending blood spurting out of her left eye socket.

Keeping clear of the windows, Kiernan bent down and rolled the body over, flinching instinctively, knowing how the local coroner would feel about her moving it.

She closed her eyes momentarily, shutting out the death of a woman she almost knew. The body was still warm, but already the cell walls were breaking down, allowing the bacteria to roam the corpse. This woman had killed a man and wrecked two lives; a decomposing pile of flesh was all it had come to.

A closer look revealed that lividity had already taken its toll—blood was settling in deep red bruises on the right side of Robin's face. But the damage from the bullet was greater on the left. It had entered at an angle, she speculated. Three wounds to the chest, one near the sternum. Here the pattern with the face was repeated: lividity on the right shoulder, but tissue damage on the left. She lifted the shoulder to make sure. Yes, the wounds in the back were larger—exit marks. And they were more lateral—nearer the shoulder. The other shots had also entered at an angle and spun her around, or entered that way because she herself was turning.

Carefully, Kiernan backed away from the window and straightened up. The easel had been knocked over. A coffee cup lay smashed on the floor, both the director's chairs were overturned. She looked at the wall opposite the door, expecting to find blood splatters and noted a wide red band feathering out to where the easel had stood. She picked up the canvas of the Alaskan mud flats and leaned it against the wall. The blood on the painting was thicker, the band narrower, indicating that the canvas had been closer to the body. The dark red splotches seemed eerily at home on the brown of the mud. Most of the canvas had remained white. But now, on the left side, it was decorated with a dark-gray flash mark, a V lying on its side like a deadly wind blowing toward the mud flats.

"Kiernan."

She spun around. It was Maureen's voice, slightly muffled. Coming through the intercom. She could hear Maureen's panic.

"Kiernan, are you okay?" Her phrases were coming in anxious gasps. "Be careful. Don't try to operate the intercom. The controls work from this side." Her breath hit the speaker. "Garrett and I are in the house. We're okay. Can you get over here? Be careful. I know the killer's out there. I'll watch for you and wait at the back door."

Kiernan tapped her finger on the doorknob. Should she believe Maureen? Why trust a woman who'd lied throughout the case? Slowly, she opened the door, glanced in both directions even though the fog obscured all but the ground in front of her. Then she ran full out across the slick grass toward the house.

The lights were off. The kitchen was dark. She caught the scent of Maureen's shampoo before she made out her taut face, then the rifle she was holding. "Where's Garrett?"

"Asleep."

"He went to bed?"

"Of course. He saw Robin get shot. He came close to getting shot himself. He was jittery afterward, but as soon as that faded it all became just another moment to him."

Squinting into the gloom, Kiernan stared at Maureen in disgust. "Maureen, you lured Robin here. Did you kill her?" she added, knowing that Maureen had not.

She heard the other woman's quick intake of breath, saw her shrink back against the kitchen counter.

"No."

"But you called her, didn't you? You'd gotten the number of her car phone from Olsen. Delaney would have found *that*."

When Maureen didn't answer, Kiernan said, "There's no other way Robin could have found Garrett. You called me with your fake emergency, then you called her and told her I'd be at Barrow's late this afternoon. That was the call that faded, not your call to me, right?"

"If I could call Robin, why wouldn't I just give her directions here?" She shifted the rifle, one hand on the barrel, the other near the firing pin.

"Because she'd have arrived whenever she felt like it. This afternoon, two in the morning, maybe not until tomorrow. The advantage of surprise would have been all hers. No, Maureen. You called me; you figured out just when I'd get here. You let Robin follow me. And once I was here you chased me off as soon as you could. Then you just waited for Robin to show up."

"I didn't kill her!" She held out the rifle. "Smell it."

Kiernan leaned against the doorway. From where she stood she could see the kitchen, dining room, and living room. The rooms were in shadow, but her eyes had adjusted enough for her to be able to make out the tables, chairs, and sofa. She wouldn't miss a person moving through. "Okay, Maureen, if you didn't kill her, what happened? Tell me."

She clutched the rifle. "I heard her drive up, about half an hour after you left. I was right by the front window. She was pretty noisy when she went around back—must have rustled every leaf, bumped into every branch that would snap. I was at the back window when she reached the house. I could have shot her. I had the rifle. I'm a good shot. But I let her go into the studio. I had to . . ."

"You had to see . . ."

She nodded.

"They argued. No, *she* argued. Garrett just looked confused. The fog blurred everything, but I could tell from the way he was standing that he didn't really understand what was going on. I kept watching that lighted square, waiting for the right moment to stalk out there and . . . and . . . I was watching, waiting. I was *there* at the window when someone shot her." She shifted the rifle. "You have to believe me."

"Someone?"

"I *heard* the shot."

Kiernan sighed, then pulled Maureen away from the window and into the dining room. "Tell me *exactly* what you saw out there."

Maureen was holding the rifle across her body like a shield. Her voice was tight as she said, "She was yelling at Garrett. I was looking out this window at the studio window. He was standing in front of it. The door opened. I caught that out of the corner of my eye. By the time I glanced over, whoever it was had gone in. It's all so vague. I couldn't say who it was." She stared at Kiernan. There was desperation in her face. "I've tried to see it again in my mind, but it's no use. I heard the shots, three or four of them. Robin spun around. Then she fell. When she hit Garrett's canvas, it went flying. I ran to the intercom. It's on the living-room wall, so I couldn't see the studio from there. I screamed through it, 'Get away! Get away from him. He's harmless. He'll never remember!' Or something like that. I was so worried about Garrett. I was terrified he'd been killed, I didn't care *who* had killed Robin. I ran for the back door, yanked it open. By then, the person had gone." Maureen grabbed Kiernan's arm. "My screams, they saved him, didn't they? He would have been shot just like Robin, wouldn't he?" Her hand was sweaty, her breathing rough and choked. "I didn't kill her. I swear I didn't."

"Okay." Kiernan put a hand over Maureen's. Maureen's breathing slowed. Her grip eased.

Kiernan grabbed the rifle from her hand.

Maureen cringed against the wall. "Kiernan! I thought you believed me!"

"You *didn't* run up to the studio door and shoot her. No one killed her from the doorway. Robin was shot by someone standing next to the canvas."

"How do you know that?"

"Because, Maureen, there was powder residue on the painting. Dark-gray powder that ballooned out of the cylinder of that revolver as the bullet passed down it. The Ruger is a big gun, an old gun. There's a good deal of space between the cylinder and the barrel, and in the few seconds the barrel is blocked by the bullet, there's no other place for the gases to go but out through the spaces around the cylinder. They blew past the left hand that was steadying the gun and outlined the V between Garrett's thumb and forefinger."

Maureen took a deep breath. Her voice shook. "The V between *somebody's* thumb and forefinger. You can't prove it was Garrett's."

"The residues of barium and antimony will be on his hands and the cuff of his shirt. And Maureen, the cylinder of a revolver spins fast when you shoot. Garrett was using his left hand to steady it. He's got metal burns on his left hand, doesn't he?"

Maureen gasped. She leaned back against the wall. Then, she reached over and flicked on the light. Her face was pale and damp, her blond hair matted. She took a breath and her face hardened. "He was defending himself. It was self-defense. The sheriff won't charge him. Even if he were normal, they wouldn't charge him." There was a thread of hysteria in her voice. "That woman came into his studio. She had his gun. He had to grab it from her."

"How?"

Maureen hesitated.

"Searching for another lie?" Kiernan demanded. "It was the intercom, wasn't it? You called, it distracted her just long enough?"

Maureen nodded. "I did save him. It didn't occur to me till then that Garrett might be killed."

Kiernan walked over and leaned against the couch. "No, Maureen, that's one lie I'm not going to buy. You knew he could be killed. It was a chance you decided to take. You set up that investigation to bring Robin here where you could kill her with impunity. You put the revolver out in Garrett's studio."

"He had to protect himself!"

"From what? He wasn't in danger. As far as Robin knew, he could lead her to the memo. She wasn't going to kill the only person who could get her what she wanted. Right?"

When Maureen didn't respond, Kiernan went on, "You left the revolver in the studio to up the ante. You knew Garrett wouldn't talk about the memo. You'd asked him often enough yourself. You knew he'd drive her into a rage. They'd argue, and one of them would grab the gun and shoot. And your plan worked perfectly. Garrett shot Robin. But it could easily have happened the other way around. He could have threatened her with the gun. They could have fought. She could have shot him in fury or in fear. Then what would you have done, Maureen? Would you have picked up your rifle and killed *her* in self-defense?"

A draft carried the smell of long-cold ash across the room. Maureen walked to the other end of the sofa and sat on the arm. "It's justice." She smiled.

Kiernan laughed. "I kept hearing how obsessed Robin was. I began to worry that I was too much like her. But it wasn't me, Maureen, it was you. You haven't just killed Robin, you've become her."

42

It was dawn before the sheriff was ready to take Garrett and Maureen into town. Garrett's neurologist would meet them there.

Kiernan wandered through the dark, paneled rooms. She had spoken to Maureen only long enough to convince her that the sheriff would want Dwyer Cummings's memo. After an hour's search, Maureen had pulled it from a terra-cotta vase and handed it to Kiernan. Then she'd walked into the bedroom, crouched on the bed with her knees pulled to her chest, and watched Garrett sleep.

Kiernan unfolded the sheet of AlaskOil stationery.

Re: Blow-Out Preventers
Platform Nina

The blow-out preventers (BOPs) for Platform Nina are due for delivery next month. At that time, we will be ready for production from the oil reservoir 2000 ft. below the surface as originally designed. Note the cost of the BOPs for the 15 wells was 2.6MM$.

When we deplete the 2000 ft. reservoir, we plan to deepen the wells and produce from the 10,000 ft. reservoir discovered last month. The BOPs to be delivered will not give 100% assurance that we can prevent a blow-out and subsequent chance of a severe oil spill when we produce from the deeper reservoir.

The cost to retrofit our BOPs for higher pressure will cost an estimated 3MM$. In addition, retrofitting will delay production by at least 30 days. Production revenues from Platform Nina are expected to be at least 0.6MM$s/day (180MM$s/month).

Our present financial state does not allow us to incur such costs. Therefore, we will not be retrofitting the BOPs.

Dwyer Cummings

Amazed, Kiernan sat back on the couch and took a deep breath. Then she ran out to the Jeep. The sky was still dark, the scent of the redwoods so strong and clear that it stopped her in her tracks. She was about to call Jessica Leporek. But that would be Tchernak's reward. He could astound Leporek with the tale of how her yearned-for memo had been sitting in a dusty vase on the top shelf of a cupboard for three years without Maureen even knowing it was there. It was only when Kiernan had brought up the subject that Maureen had searched the spots in which Garrett might have hidden it.

She settled in the Jeep and copied the memo.

Tchernak arrived just before sunset. Not giving him a chance to get out of his wolfhound-sized rented car, Kiernan climbed in, handed him the copy of the memo, and watched the broad grin spread across his endearingly ugly face. "Jesus Fucking H. Christ! They would have taken the chance of a major oil spill because they were too cheap to shut down for a month and install the proper equipment. Prop. Thirty-Seven is a shoo-in!" He was yelling. Ezra was licking Kiernan's face.

"So," he said, "what now? Do we have to go back to San Francisco?"

"No."

Tchernak smiled. "What about Olsen? Aren't we leaving him open to the threats of his enemies? I mean, after they snatched him off the wharf—"

"That wasn't the cops. It was the same guys who followed me to Delaney's. Ex-dockhands Robin had paid off. Cops wouldn't have left visible bruises on Olsen's body. They wouldn't have known where to cut the wharf lights. And they wouldn't have taken the chance of being caught on the Crab Cage roof with a kidnap victim. That's careless stuff, just the type of thing Robin's deckhands would do."

"What about your parking tickets? Deckhands didn't do that."

Kiernan laughed. "Marc Rosten? I was right about him, that he'd get me for invading his office. I'm only thankful I got off as cheaply as that. In medical school, practical jokes had been a whole lot more pointed." Rather than feeling annoyed at the ticket episode, she found it comforting to discover that traces of the young, passionate Marc Rosten had survived despite a job he regretted. Neither he nor she had the job they'd dreamed of. The evolution had been good for her; maybe it was more suitable for him than he was willing to admit.

"Where is this Platform Nina?"

"Up in Alaska. But that doesn't matter. Policy is policy. And once the California voters see this memo, they won't allow these guys to get anywhere near our state."

Kiernan leaned back against the car door. "Can you imagine what the oil companies would pay for this? No wonder Robin Matucci was so hot for it."

Tchernak laughed. "God, I can hardly wait to see Jessica's face. Piles of paper will go flying around her office. She'll be talking ten miles a minute, racing out to Baker Beach and having the biggest press conference of her life." Tchernak's mouth was actually quivering. He dove across the seat and hugged Kiernan. "She'll stand there on the beach and sift the sand through her fingers and know that that sand will never be covered with oil."

Kiernan tugged on Tchernak's beard to pull him closer, gave him a blowsy kiss, and said, "I just hope this memo won't make you such big stuff in the environmental world that you'll never make me another mahimahi-and-arugula salad."

Ezra shoved his way into the front seat and pointedly

nudged the car door. Kiernan opened it and followed the big dog onto the grass. The early morning sun was streaking through the redwoods. Tchernak walked up the bluff and stood, his arms braced against a redwood bole, stretching his thigh muscles. Then he sprawled under a tree and tossed a stick for Ezra who, for once, disdained it. The wolfhound circled behind Kiernan, pushed between her and Tchernak, and flopped down, flinging one enormous paw across her knee.

The red front door of the house opened, and the sheriff's deputies escorted Maureen and Garrett outside. In the clear light, Maureen looked exhausted. Garrett, however, appeared rested, neat in a fresh plaid shirt and chinos. His stride was long and steady, that of a man on a normal, everyday errand. The deputies merely looked tired.

Garrett veered toward the pool. He walked to the edge and looked down at the broken pieces of cement. Was he seeing the pool as it had been when he was a child, or was he looking at the empty, useless space that would grow more dangerous, more irretrievable with each new season?

Maureen followed and paused beside him on the edge, then stiffened and moved a few feet away.

One of the deputies called Garrett. Garrett started toward him. Kiernan was still looking at the abandoned pool, but she could hear Garrett's voice.

"Now where is it we know each other from?"

ABOUT THE AUTHOR

SUSAN DUNLAP has been called the "leading proponent of gutsy, nontraditional women who nimbly tread in he-man territory." She is the author of eleven novels, including *A Dinner to Die For* and *A Diamond in the Buff* in her series featuring homicide detective Jill Smith, and *The Last Annual Slugfest* in the VeJay Haskell series. She lives near San Francisco with her husband, and is currently president of Sisters in Crime.